Sarah Price's delightful adaptation (Jane Austen fans and lovers of Ami: *Chances*, a clever retelling with an Amish setting, captured me from the first page to the last.

—JENNIFER BECKSTRAND
AUTHOR, *HUCKLEBERRY HILL*

All the appeal of a classic love story, caught between perception and truth, affection and duty, choice and expectation, doubt and faith, regret and hope.

—OLIVIA NEWPORT
AUTHOR, *WONDERFUL LONESOME* AND
MEEK AND MILD

Sarah Price has managed to, once again, seamlessly combine a heartfelt Amish romance with a timeless classic. The story of Jane Austen's *Persuasion* comes alive in a unique way in *Second Chances*. It is a beautiful story with vibrant characters who will remain in my heart for quite a while.

—BRITTANY McEUEN
BRITT READS FICTION BLOG

In *Second Chances* masterful storyteller Sarah Price pens a delightful retelling of Jane Austen's classic, *Persuasion*, harmoniously intermingled with the Amish! Readers everywhere will fall in love with the frustrating Anna, who in her inability to say no to others brings much heartache upon herself. An eloquently written tale of family, forgiveness, second chances, and lessons learned, this is one that will long be remembered, even after the last sighworthy page is turned!

—DIANA FLOWERS
SENIOR REVIEWER, *OVERCOMING WITH GOD* BLOG

Second Chances is another winner in Sarah Price's Amish Classics series, where she puts her own twist on a classic story and brings it to new life in an unexpected setting. Readers will enjoy following the journey of Anna, a young Amish woman struggling against the persuasion of her family and friends as she tries to find her second chance at love.

—PAM BURKE
BLOGGER, *SOUTHERN GAL LOVES TO READ*

A moving love story once told by Jane Austin and now by master storyteller Sarah Price. One in old time England, and the other in the American Amish Community, the same and yet very different telling of the same story. I loved it!

—MAUREEN TIMERMAN
BLOGGER, *MUSINGS BY MAUREEN*

Timeless as the classic itself, Sarah Price's retelling of *Persuasion* by Jane Austen will have your heart skipping beats and leave you completely captivated until the very last page, wishing the story would go on and on. In true Price fashion she shows us how God's mercy works in our lives, even when wrong choices stray our paths. Both captivating and beautiful, this book will make you want to crawl within these pages and follow each character through their journey of "second chances."

—SUE LAITINEN
DESTINATION AMISH

Sarah Price crafts a story of heartbreak, self-examination, and love restored in this Jane Austen adaptation. Her writing style rivals the classics while her characters come to life and make their way into her readers' hearts. *Second Chances* will appeal to lovers of Amish Christian romance as well as lovers of Jane Austen and Christian romance.

—Lisa Bull
Blogger, Mommalisaof2 and Walking Bare
Souled in the SONshine

Sarah Price has once again written a book with a meaningful message. The theme of forgiveness and the ability to overcome, with God's direction, is evident throughout the intricate plot. Again, Sarah has used her unique talent to develop characters that are realistic and somewhat quirky individuals who appeal to the reader's emotions and sense of humor. Indeed, they become part of you. As you get lost in the plot, everyday life will be forgotten, and you will find yourself transported to this small Amish community. *Second Chances* is yet another Sarah Price book that will live on in your thoughts long after you finish reading!

—Karla Hanns
Welland, Ontario
Canada

SECOND CHANCES

AN AMISH RETELLING OF JANE AUSTEN'S *PERSUASION*

THE
AMISH CLASSICS
SERIES

SARAH PRICE

REALMS

Most Charisma House Book Group products are available at special quantity discounts for bulk purchase for sales promotions, premiums, fund-raising, and educational needs. For details, write Charisma House Book Group, 600 Rinehart Road, Lake Mary, Florida 32746, or telephone (407) 333-0600.

SECOND CHANCES by Sarah Price
Published by Realms
Charisma Media/Charisma House Book Group
600 Rinehart Road
Lake Mary, Florida 32746
www.charismahouse.com

Cover design by Justin Evans

Visit the author's website at www.sarahpriceauthor.com.

Library of Congress Cataloging-in-Publication Data

Price, Sarah, 1969-
　　Second chances / Sarah Price. -- First edition.
　　　　pages ; cm. -- (Amish classics)
　　ISBN 978-1-62998-239-7 (trade paper) -- ISBN 978-1-62998-240-3 (e-book)
　1.　Amish--Fiction. 2.　Lancaster County (Pa.)--Fiction. 3.　Austen, Jane, 1775-1817--Parodies, imitations, etc.　I. Title.
　PS3616.R5275S43 2015
　813'.6--dc23
　　　　　　　　　　　　　　　2015006718

First edition

15 16 17 18 19 — 987654321
Printed in the United States of America

There are times in our lives when we come to a crossroad and need to make a decision. Sometimes we make the right choice. Sometimes we don't. This book is dedicated to those people who made a decision that they later regretted but maintained their faith in God's plans for their future, regardless of the outcome.

❧ A Note About Vocabulary ❧

THE AMISH SPEAK Pennsylvania Dutch (also called Amish German or Amish Dutch). This is a verbal language with variations in spelling among communities throughout the United States. In some regions a grandfather is *grossdaadi*, while in other regions he is known as *grossdawdi*.

In addition, there are words such as *mayhaps*, or the use of the word *then* at the end of sentences and, my favorite, *for sure and certain*, which are not necessarily from the Pennsylvania Dutch language/dialect but are unique to the Amish.

The use of these words comes from my own experience living among the Amish in Lancaster County, Pennsylvania.

❧ *Acknowledgments* ❧

IT TAKES A village to raise a child, and it takes a team to write a book. God has blessed me with an amazing team. My family and friends help me with brainstorming ideas, proofreading, and watching me pace the floor as I think out loud. My Charisma family provides unlimited support to me—this time tolerating several delays due to medical reasons, a laptop incident involving coffee (that shall never be discussed again, for I am still in mourning), and multiple rounds of editing.

Thank you to my husband, Marc Schumacher, my parents, Stan and Ellie Nice, my children, Alex and Cat, my Charisma team, Adrienne and Lori, and my dear cheerleading team, Lisa, Michelle, Judy, Iris, Gina, and Marisol.

Yes, God has blessed me in many ways, but this amazing team surrounding me with love and support is one of His greatest gifts of all.

HUGS!
SARAH PRICE

❧ *Preface* ❧

THE IDEA FOR this book was a long time coming. I started to read quite early in life, and my taste for books transcended the typical chunky books that preschoolers are made to read. I confess that my first love was Laura Ingalls Wilder's books, which I devoured practically on a daily basis. To say I was a bookworm would be putting it mildly. Children would take bets on whether or not I could finish a book a day, a challenge I won easily most days.

So my transition to classic literature came at an early age, with my favorites being Jane Austen, Charlotte Brontë, Emily Brontë, Charles Dickens, Thomas Hardy, and (a personal favorite) Victor Hugo. Christmas was fairly predictable in my house. Just one leather-bound book always made it the "bestest Christmas ever."

In writing Amish Christian romances, something that I have been doing for twenty-five years, I have always tried to explore new angles to the stories. I base most of my stories on my own experiences, having lived on Amish farms and in Amish homes over the years. I have come to know these amazingly strong and devout people in a way that I am constantly pinching myself as to why I have been able to do so. I must confess that, on more than one occasion, I have heard the same from them: "We aren't quite sure what it is, Sarah, but…there's something deeply special about you."

Besides adoring my Amish friends and "family," I also adore my readers. Many of you know that I spend countless hours using social media to individually connect with as many readers as I can. I found some of my "bestest friends" online, and despite living in Virginia or Hawaii or Nebraska or Australia, they are as dear to me as the ones that live two miles down the road.

Well, something clicked when I combined my love of literature with my adoration of my readers and respect of the Amish. It is my hope that by creating this literary triad, my readers will experience the Amish in a new way. They will experience authentic Amish culture and religion based on my experiences of having lived among them and my exposure to the masterpieces of literary greats from years past.

It's amazing to think that a love of God and passion for reading can be combined in such a manner to touch so many people. I hope that you too are touched, and I truly welcome your e-mails, letters, and postings.

BLESSINGS,
SARAH PRICE
sarah@sarahpriceauthor.com
www.sarahpriceauthor.com
www.facebook.com/fansofsarahprice
Twitter/Pinterest/Instagram: @SarahPriceAuthr

❧ *Prologue* ❧

S HE STOOD AT the window, her arms wrapped around her chest as if trying to keep warm even though the autumn weather was perfect. The trees at the backside of her father's small farm were colorful and bright with yellows, oranges, and reds. As beautiful as the scenery was, she couldn't enjoy it. Not today.

"Anna?"

She turned around and looked at her younger sister, Mary, but did not respond.

"Why haven't you changed?" Mary asked, her voice sharp and disapproving. She paused to look in the small mirror hanging on the wall by the staircase. She tucked a strand of her brown hair under her white prayer *kapp* and retied the long strings hanging under her chin. "Aren't you going to the youth singing?"

Anna shook her head, hoping that she didn't look as forlorn as she felt. She still wore her dark blue dress from the worship service, although she had removed her white apron and cape when they had returned home earlier that afternoon. "*Nee*, Mary," Anna replied.

Ignoring the expression on Mary's face, one that clearly displayed her lack of approval with Anna's decision, she turned back to the window and stared outside. "Suit your-self, then," Mary said, a tone of criticism in her voice, before she headed out the door. "I'm not about to sit home and let all of the young bachelors pass by *me*!"

Wincing at her sister's words, Anna wished that she could tell Mary how hurtful her comment truly was. The only problem was that only one person knew the truth about what Anna was about to do: Lydia Rothberger. A longtime friend of their now deceased mother, Anne Eicher, Lydia had taken charge of providing maternal advice and personal counsel to all three Eicher daughters, even though neither of her two sisters seemed too inter-ested in either advice or counsel from anyone. Elizabeth was quiet and spent most of her days at home caring for her father instead of courting young men or socializing, while Mary was quite self-absorbed and vocal with her opinions.

So, when Anna had a decision to make, one that she thought Lydia would gladly approve, she had been sur-prised to learn that she was wrong. According to Lydia and her father there was only one answer to give Freman Whittmore, and the sooner Anna told him, the better.

Earlier that day, immediately following the worship ser-vice and during the organized chaos of setting up for the fellowship meal, Anna had managed to find a moment to speak with Freman in the mudroom. Her heart had felt heavy as she stood on her tiptoes to whisper in his ear, "I have to speak with you today. Alone."

The look in his eyes further tore at her heart. She knew what he thought and she wished he was right. "Shall I fetch you early for the singing?" he asked.

She replied by simply shaking her head.

"Is everything all right, my sweet Anna?"

His term of endearment caught her off guard. Usually he only called her that when he drove her home from the youth singings, away from any prying ears that might overhear him. Courtship was a private matter, after all, and while some Amish youths didn't seem to care if others knew about their relationships, Freman was definitely more conservative when it came to such matters. It was one of the things that Anna loved about him.

"I'll see you tonight," she managed to say before one of the older women came into the room to retrieve something. With a forced smile, Anna had hurried away, her eyes downcast and her heart breaking into what felt like a hundred little pieces.

Now she stood at the window, waiting for the sound of his buggy. He always parked on the street, just beyond her father's mailbox. He had been doing that for weeks, and thanks to his discretion, no one except Lydia knew that they were courting.

Ten minutes passed before she heard the familiar sound of horse hooves in the distance. She looked in the direction of the approaching buggy to make certain it wasn't the neighbors heading for the youth singing. It wasn't.

Grateful that Elizabeth and her father were out visiting so that no one would ask where she was going, Anna grabbed her black shawl from a hook near the door and hurried outside to meet up with Freman. She clutched it around her chest as she walked as fast as she could up the driveway. There was a chill in the air, the wind starting to pick up as the sun started to descend in the sky. Soon it would be dusk, and once the sun set, the night temperature would drop even further.

He stood by the side of the buggy, the door already open as he waited for her. Without a word, he reached for her hand and helped her step into the buggy. When he followed, it jiggled under his weight, and she steadied herself as she sat on the small seat.

"It's getting cold," he said and reached behind the seat for a blanket. With great tenderness, he covered her lap and smiled at her. "Better?"

She nodded.

"Now, tell me," he said as he depressed the foot brake and gave the reins a slight slap upon the horse's backside. The buggy lurched forward and headed down the road. "What has you looking so perplexed, my sweet Anna?"

Words escaped her, and she remained mute at his side.

Slowly, his expression changed. She wondered if he suspected what she was going to say. If he did, surely he knew how heavy her heart felt.

"Anna?"

Taking a deep breath, she shut her eyes, saying a quick prayer to God for the strength to speak what weighed so heavily on her mind. There was no easy way to tell him, so she chose to be candid instead of softening her words. "Freman, I cannot marry you in November."

She waited for his response.

For a moment, he remained silent.

She felt tears welling up in her eyes and blinked rapidly to stop them from falling. She couldn't imagine his devastation at the news. After so many long buggy rides home from the youth singings on Sunday evenings, their compatibility more than apparent to both of them, it had been only natural that they would marry. She *wanted* to marry him. But when she informed Lydia and asked how best to tell her *daed*, she quickly learned that her admiration for Freman was not shared by others. How could she defy the advice of her mother's best friend or the wishes of her own father?

He focused on the reins of the horse and seemed to contemplate her proclamation. "I see," he finally said. "I know you think you must wait until you turn eighteen, Anna. So, if we must wait until spring…" He let the sentence linger between them.

"Freman, spring isn't the answer."

"I know it's unusual, but more young couples are doing that these days," he responded.

When he glanced at her, she looked away. "It's not that I cannot marry you in the spring," she whispered. "It's that I cannot marry you ever."

She saw his hands tighten on the reins, the only indication that he had heard her words. The horse sensed the tension and slowed its pace. A car approached from the other direction and slowed down as it passed them. When the noise of the engine faded, he finally asked the one question she had not wanted to answer. "Why?"

How could she explain it to him? For three nights, she had barely slept as she lay awake in her bed, staring at the ceiling as she tried to think of the words that might possibly explain her reasons.

"It's…it's my family," she admitted. "Lydia said *Daed* would not approve of our marriage."

The muscles tightened along his jawline. "Not approve of our marriage," he repeated. She knew that he wasn't asking for clarification. Instead, he was speaking out loud as if in disbelief of her words. "That doesn't make sense, Anna."

"You aren't established yet," she said softly.

"But I will be established, Anna. You know that."

And she did know that. He was hard-working. Success would come his way; of that, she had no doubt. He was also a good man, the first one to offer assistance to those in need. Still, she had hoped that he would simply accept that explanation and not inquire further into the reasons behind her decision.

"There is something else, Anna," he said, and when he looked at her, she lowered her eyes and stared at her feet on the floorboard of the buggy. "What is the real objection to our marriage?"

She couldn't lift her eyes to look at him, but she knew that he needed to know the truth. "It's...it's your background, Freman."

At this, he laughed haughtily. "My background?"

"Lydia says *Daed* won't approve because you intend to pursue carpentry."

Another mirthless laugh. "And he thinks that is not a viable profession?" He paused for a moment. The silence in the buggy was broken only by the gentle rhythm of the horse's hooves on the road and the gentle hum of the buggy wheels. She knew that he was thinking, and considering how smart he was, he was connecting the pieces to the puzzle. "Is this because my family needed help from the *g'may*?"

She didn't dare respond.

"That was years ago!"

How could she explain that her father, William Eicher, would never allow one of his daughters to marry into the Whittmores, a family that had been debt-ridden and sought financial assistance from their church district, not just once but twice? While such shameful antipathy coming from a conservative Amish man defied logic, Anna also knew that it was the truth, as her father had often spoken disparagingly of the Whittmores and seemed somewhat cold in his interactions with Freman. Lydia prevailed upon Anna to see that, whether or not she agreed with her father, she would have to make a choice: either Freman's love or her father's approval. Despite her own feelings toward Freman, Anna was persuaded that Lydia and her father knew best and, as such, had decided accordingly.

Clearly, her silence explained everything. Still unable to look at him, she knew that he would not try to argue his case any further. He was a man of strong resolve; it was one of the things that she had grown to love about him. Neither aggressive nor arrogant in his views, he would accept her decision without further discussion. After all, what more could he argue?

At the next crossroads he guided the horse so that the buggy turned around and headed back in the direction from which they had just come. They rode back in silence toward the Eichers' home. There was nothing left to be said. When she stepped down from the buggy at the same place where he had, just minutes before, retrieved her, he bade her good-bye instead of good night. As he drove away, she watched until the buggy disappeared in the distance, wondering how she would be able to live without him in the bleak months and years ahead. It was not going to be easy, she pondered, realizing she may have lost the only man that made her feel that special way.

❧ *Chapter One* ❧

ANNA EICHER SAT in the old rocking chair by the wood-burning stove, quietly quilting as she listened to her father and her two sisters converse with Lydia Rothberger, the elderly woman from the *g'may* who had taken on the role of dispensing maternal wisdom ever since their mother passed away ten years ago. Lydia's presence in the kitchen was always welcome, even if she charged the air with a tight energy of propriety and despite the fact that she had changed Anna's life irrevocably with her advice eight years ago—tearing Anna away from the only man she had ever loved in the process. With each stitch that Anna pulled through the fabric, her dark eyes glanced up just for a moment. No one noticed. They were too engrossed in their discussion, the three other women focusing all of their attention on her father.

"What will people think if we ask for aid? They will talk for weeks! *Mayhaps* months!" William said, his hands raised just slightly in the air.

Anna's heart sank, the irony of the moment not lost on her: the very same fault that her father had used to discredit the Whittmore family so many years ago had now become his own fate. The deep wrinkles and dark circles

under his eyes spoke of sleepless nights and hard decisions. His long white beard, untrimmed and wiry, hung
from his wide jaw and covered the first two buttons on
his dark blue shirt. Anna noticed that it was dirty and
she reminded herself to ensure it was laundered before
he wore it again. He looked first at Elizabeth and then
at Lydia. "You know those people who love the Amish
grapevine. Gossiping and speculating, all of them." He
said the last part with a dismissive wave of his hand.

Anna bit her lower lip, too aware that the biggest con-
tributor to that gossip-filled grapevine was her own father.
With a silent resolve, Anna tried to concentrate on her
work, knowing that the tiny stitches in the baby blanket
she was quilting for her younger sister Mary was the only
input she would most likely make today. No one cared
what *she* thought about the possibility of her father losing
their small family farm, anyway. The affront did not
bother her. Indeed, she was just as happy to stay out of
the heated discussion.

Elizabeth shook her head, equally as distraught. "There
must be another way; perhaps to hire young men to farm
the fields."

That suggestion invigorated William. A new look of
optimism lifted the cloud of despair that had rested upon
his face. With great hope in his eyes, he pointed at his
oldest daughter while he glanced over at Lydia for her
response. "*Ja*! That's a right *gut* idea! Hire men to work
the farm!"

"William," Lydia said, leaning forward and gently
touching his knee. The gesture was one of familiarity
without intimacy.

Over ten years had passed since Anna's mother, Anne, passed away. When Anne married William Eicher at an early November wedding, Lydia Rothberger stood by Anne's side as her attendant. The two women had grown up together in Sugarcreek, Ohio. Furthermore, they had sat in the one-room schoolhouse, progressing through eight years of schooling. At sixteen, they went to their first youth singing, standing awkwardly at the back of the barn. It was only natural that, as best friends from childhood, the two young women remained just as close when Anne and her new husband moved to the small town of Charm, just ten miles away.

Since long before Anna's birth, Lydia Rothberger had been a constant presence in the Eicher family in births, baptisms, and deaths. Her own husband, Edward, had died only one year after their marriage, a union that resulted in no children but left Lydia with a small dry goods store in the outskirts of Charm, only a mile or so from the Eichers' home. Over the years, she had continued to operate it, and despite the initial speculation from the community and her deceased husband's family, she had managed to become an impressive business owner in her own right.

After Anne passed away, Lydia stepped in to provide a maternal presence to her best friend's three daughters, especially to Anna, the middle daughter who was named after her mother. Even at the young age of fourteen, Anna resembled her mother, after whom she had been named, in temperament as well as presence. Quiet and giving, she wanted nothing more than to please the people she loved. For the past ten years, while it was most often Anna who sought out Lydia for advice, Lydia's sensibility guided the daughters and, on occasion, their father.

Today was one of those days.

"It's time to consider alternatives. You simply cannot maintain it, William, and you have spent your savings. There is no money left to hire young men." She hesitated, glancing at Anna with a sympathetic look in her eyes. "Barely enough to even make it through the winter, I fear. You might consider selling the *haus*. Since it's paid off, you could invest the proceeds from the sale and live off the interest for a while. You'd fetch a good enough sum for that."

He stood up and began pacing the room, twisting his hands in front of him. "This *haus* has been in the family for generations!" His feet shuffled across the perfectly waxed and shiny linoleum floor, Anna having worked hard to ensure that it was never dull or filmy. "Selling it is not an option, Lydia!"

"I'm afraid your options are few, William," Lydia said with a sigh.

But Anna's father appeared determined. With a fierce look of unshakable insistence, he stopped pacing and turned toward Lydia. "There are always options! What about taking out a mortgage?"

Anna glanced up in time to see Lydia shake her head. "I don't see that as being very wise. You still must pay it back. Besides, with no real income, I'm not even certain you could get one, William."

Exhaling sharply, William continued pacing. "I could sell that Florida property." He lifted his eyebrow as if this was the solution. "I haven't been down there in years anyway."

Even Anna knew that this was another futile idea. The small house in Pinecraft, Florida, had been left to her parents in the will of her maternal grandmother. Only twice had the family traveled to the house, and as far as Anna was concerned, that was twice too often. The place was no more than a two-bedroom trailer house situated on a very small lot in a community of elderly Amish and Mennonites. With only one flower bed for gardening, Anna felt far too confined there. She much preferred the open fields, rolling hills, and winding roads of Holmes County, Ohio, that was for sure and certain.

"Now, William," Lydia replied gently. "You know that place is barely worth five percent of this property. That wouldn't do you much good."

"Such a sorry state of affairs!" he declared before adding, "If Anne were here..." under his breath.

At that statement, Anna shifted her eyes back to the baby quilt. She knew that the absence of her mother continued to haunt her father. After all, it was her mother, Anne, who had managed the finances and kept William on a strict budget. William had simply adored his petite wife and yielded to all of her advice. Once she died, he seemed incapable of budgeting his money. Lydia had tried to help him, as had Anna, but when it came to money he refused to listen to either one of them.

"You need to observe the practicality of moving to a smaller house, William," Lydia offered, clearly not offended by his comment that insinuated his deceased wife might have offered a better solution than Lydia. In truth, if Anna had not passed away, she would not have let her husband become such a spendthrift.

Anna looked up in time to see her father stop short and turn to face the three women. "Sell the house and move to a smaller one?" He shook his head and continued pacing. "People will say I cannot provide for my family! Humiliating!" With stooped shoulders and glazed eyes, he paused to consider this thought. "*Nee*! Disastrous!"

"Scandalous, indeed!" Elizabeth added, always the one to follow her father's concern over what others might think of their good family name.

Anna studied her older sister. Ever since their mother died, Elizabeth had assumed the position of the female head of house, helping their father make decisions. But it was Lydia who provided a maternal presence, at least to Anna. On most occasions, Elizabeth deferred to Lydia. However, if Lydia was not around, there was simply no reasoning with her father and elder sister: they seemed to agree on anything and everything as long as it maintained their image within the community. And that left out Anna.

As for Mary...

Anna looked at her other *schwester*, the prettiest of the three and, being married to Cris Musser, Mary was the only one who wore a white prayer *kapp* at worship service. Her waist, while not quite as thick as Elizabeth's, still showed the extra weight that went with bearing children, although Anna wondered if she might be expecting another baby already.

Unlike Elizabeth, who worried about the family reputation, Mary tended to fret over having to support her destitute father and two unmarried sisters. Being the only married member of the family, and with a husband's family that lived quite nicely, Mary frequently expressed her anxiety of shouldering such a burden. "If you sold your house, where would you live?"

Once again, Anna lifted her head and stared first at her father and then at Elizabeth. Neither one spoke. She knew what they were thinking, so with a soft smile, Anna spoke for them. "We could stay with you, Mary."

This idea flustered Mary. The color rose to her cheeks and she responded with a quick excuse. "You know that our *haus* is already too small! Salome Musser refuses to give up the larger one!" She pursed her lips and sighed. "Imagine that! Putting us into the *grossdawdihaus* with two small *kinner!*" She clicked her tongue three times as she shook her head, clearly disapproving of her mother-in-law's decision. "Her own son, me, and two grandchildren! Living in such cramped quarters! Why, it's a wonder the bishop doesn't interfere with Salome for being so selfish!"

No one responded to her complaints. Nor did anyone point out that she still had a spare bedroom, given that the two young boys shared one. However, the Eicher family all knew what was required when Mary went on a self-indulgent rampage: a proper moment's hesitation, as if permitting a respectful silence to acknowledge Mary's complaint, before continuing to address the real situation at hand—finances.

At last, Elizabeth broke the compulsory silence. With her hands folded together and resting so primly on her lap, she appeared almost like an austere schoolteacher reprimanding rambunctious young children. Only she wasn't: she was scolding her father. "I dare say that selling the house would raise eyebrows, *Daed.*" She paused, hesitating as if mulling over her own words. "But there must be something we can do. Why, the Hostetlers kept their family place even after all of those medical bills required not one but two rounds of aid from the *g'may!*" She turned her head, her sharp eyes staring at Lydia with a look of disdain. "Certainly we are better off than that!"

The challenge was set. Anne could only hold her breath and wait to hear what came next. When she glanced at her father, she saw the glimmer of hope that shone from his eyes and her heart ached for her father. But he was oblivious to his middle daughter's thoughts. Instead, for the second time that evening, William pointed at Elizabeth as if her comment might solve his problems. "*Ja*, that's the truth!" A glow of eagerness returned to his face. "No one can doubt that we have done much better than that Henry Hostetler!"

Lydia shook her head. "I've gone over your numbers, William. You have simply spent far more than you have earned...or saved. The maintenance on this property plus the taxes on the land are only part of the problem. You also spent almost ten thousand dollars on that new buggy last spring."

"And the horse," Anna whispered.

Lydia nodded at the reminder and clicked her tongue disapprovingly. "And the horse. A Dutch Harness horse? That was a very expensive horse, William."

At this comment, regarding the horse, Mary chimed in. "And you already have that Standardbred!" She laughed—a short little burst of air—and looked at Lydia as if expecting her to join her. "And then you purchased that fancy harness from Benny Zook. Custom made, if I do recall what you told people after worship service."

"Fancy harness?" He bristled at the words spoken by Mary. "I see nothing wrong with purchasing a good quality harness for a horse that is sound and capable."

"Sound and capable, yes. But that horse was as green as they come, William," Lydia reminded him, with just enough gentleness in her voice so that he did not become more irritated. "Need I remind you that you had to pay John and Martin Wagler to break it?"

"I'd be happy to talk to Cris about buying your new buggy," Mary cheerfully offered, as a way of moving the conversation along, ignoring the glare that Elizabeth sent in her direction. She smiled as if this alone would solve her father's money problem. "Our own buggy is so old anyway. I'm sure Cris would agree, although your buggy *is* used now, so it wouldn't fetch the same price, I reckon."

This suggestion did not sit well with William. "I just purchased that buggy! It has the new battery that recharges! I shall not part with it!"

Mary pursed her lips and looked away.

"Perhaps I should just sell a few acres."

"I'm afraid it's not as simple as that," Lydia said, a gentleness to her voice that did little to lighten the news. "Even selling those unused acres that you never farm wouldn't help, William. And, frankly, it would make the property less valuable in the long run."

It wasn't a big property, just ten acres. Many years ago, it had been much larger, but as customary among Amish families, parcels were divided and given to sons throughout the generations. Anna loved to walk through the tall grasses in the back acres, sometimes finding a broken piece of metal from an older plow or harvester in her path, especially after a sweet spring rain. She knew that her grandfather, *Grossdawdi* Eicher, had lived on the property, helping his own *daed* farm those acres a couple of generations ago. When he married and acquired the small farmette, he chose not to farm the land but worked in minerals, instead. He bought them in bulk from suppliers around the country and sold them mostly to communities of Amish in Ohio, Pennsylvania, and Indiana. After all, dairy cows and horses needed minerals to stay healthy.

With only two children who survived into adulthood, *Grossdawdi* Eicher didn't have to worry about decisions regarding inheritance. His son, David, eight years older than William, had married and moved to the southern part of Holmes County. With his wife, he raised their five daughters and one son. Now that David was older and bound to a wheelchair, he lived on the same farm with that son and two grandsons, the oldest of whom ran the large farm.

As for William, he followed in his father's footsteps. When *Grossdawdi* Eicher passed away, William had inherited the farmette, the perfect size for raising his own small family.

Minerals had been a valuable career path for William, given that there was limited competition. The rewards for his efforts were great from a financial perspective. The only problem was that he had sold the business three years ago, retiring when he hit sixty-one and his vision worsened. Too many years refusing to wear glasses when the sun went down had quickened his visual impairment. Without a steady income, his unwillingness to decrease spending had begun to seriously deplete his nest egg. And though not spoken aloud, everyone knew that William could not accept assistance from the *g'may* without revealing that pattern of profligate spending that was so contrary to the Amish doctrine.

Now, he sat in his chair, trying to digest Lydia's words while rubbing his hands as if attempting to ward off a deep pain. A flare-up. Again. Without being asked, Anna set down her quilting and quietly stole across the room to retrieve a small plastic container from the propane-powered refrigerator. She unscrewed the lid of the jar as she approached her father. Kneeling by his side, she dipped her finger in the jar and began to rub the wax-like ointment onto his hands, the scent of lavender slowly filling the room.

Only Lydia appeared to notice.

The older woman smiled as she observed Anna's attentiveness to her aging father's arthritis. It always seemed to flare whenever he became upset. Over the years, however, he stopped seeing doctors, claiming their *Englische* medicine was too suspicious and full of ingredients he couldn't pronounce.

Abruptly, William withdrew his hand from Anna's, motioning for her to leave his side. It was not an overtly rude motion, or at least Anna didn't take it that way. No, she merely picked up the lid to the jar and got to her feet, quietly returning the ointment to the refrigerator while he talked.

"I just don't understand how this happened." It sounded as if he had finally embraced the inevitable: the house and its land must be sold. As the realization sunk in that this was the only course of action that would provide any financial assistance, he frowned, the deep wrinkles by his eyes mirrored by the ones engraved in his forehead. Lines of age meant years of wisdom, Anna thought as she sat back on the sofa and watched him. Or, in his case, years of foolish spending. "So many years! So much work! Where has all of the money gone?" This last question, directed at Lydia, was spoken in a tone that bespoke genuine worry and fear.

"*Daed*," Anna chimed in, her soft voice barely audible. "No one will think any less of you for selling the *haus*. There are worse things, I suppose."

"What could possibly be worse?" His voice cracked as he addressed Anna. Her sensible nature often conflicted with his vanity, a character trait so contrary to the Amish life that Anna often wondered how he had not once been reprimanded by the bishop. Now, and not for the first time, he stared at her, an expression of incredulity on his face, as if the words she had spoken were that of a child and not an intelligent woman. "It isn't *your* reputation at stake, need I remind you?"

"William!" Lydia gestured toward the reclining chair. "Please sit. You're working yourself into a tizzy."

Silently Anna watched as her father did as Lydia instructed. *Bless her heart*, she thought. Dear Lydia with her calming influence over stressful situations in the Eicher house. Without Lydia, Anna knew that there were times that even Elizabeth would not be able to handle her father's anxieties. Clearly this was one of those.

William took a short breath and lifted his chin. "*Ja vell*, I won't be letting that Willis get his hands on it, that's for sure and certain!"

"*Daed*!" The anger in her father's expression caught Anna off-guard. As soon as the word slipped from her lips, she covered her mouth. She hadn't meant to reprimand him; however, his display of anger, especially so pointedly at one particular individual—and family at that!—upset her. She was thankful that no one else paid attention to her outburst.

William turned toward Anna. Lifting his hand in the air, he pointed toward the heavens. "God is my witness, I don't care whether or not he's my nephew's son! The injustice he did to this family!" His anger dissipated just enough so that, when he looked at Elizabeth, there was less fire in his eyes. "*Ach*, the humiliation! It's unthinkable that his banns were read after he came calling on you!" He reached out to pat her hand, a gesture of comfort to his oldest daughter. "Why, the entire church district whispered for months, and not even John David would invite me to play checkers that winter!"

Anna looked away, the color flooding to her cheeks, but not before she saw Elizabeth's jaw muscles tighten.

Despite her own discomfort with her father's rebuke, Anna felt even more shame as she remembered her sister's stoic response when it was announced after worship service that Willis Eicher and Barbie King were to marry. At that time, seven years ago, there were plenty of unmarried young women in the *g'may*, five of whom sat between Anna and Elizabeth on the hard pine bench, since the single women always entered the room in chronological order. Even though she hadn't been able to comfort her sister, Anna felt the sting of the announcement. Elizabeth, on the other hand, never once mentioned his name nor the four times that he had come calling at their house.

The intention had been clear and, frankly, presumed by all.

Instead Willis Eicher chose to marry a woman from a faraway church district. That decision always brought out the fire in William's eyes, for the woman was the only daughter of that *g'may*'s bishop. Besides the whispers about Willis snubbing Elizabeth, there had also been scuttlebutt over the motives behind his surprisingly sudden decision: the King family owned a rather large farm in another church district in a neighboring county.

Anna had never truly decided which one of them had felt more disgraced: *Daed* or Elizabeth. Even today, she couldn't decide. The one thing she did know was that the wounds remained fresh for them both and reminded her far too much of the pain that she too had once caused.

Her thoughts were interrupted when Lydia reached out and, with a calm hand, touched William's sleeve. "William, that's pride speaking."

He ruffled at her words and shifted his weight in his chair.

"Besides, maybe you won't have to sell the *haus*. Not yet, anyway." Her eyes brightened from behind her glasses. "I have another possible, perfectly reasonable solution!"

"The only perfectly reasonable solution," he grumbled, "is staying in my own *haus*."

Elizabeth leaned back in her chair and rested her head against the cushion. "I just hate the thought of all those people talking about us."

"Speculating...," he added.

"I knew we shouldn't have donated so much money last year!" Elizabeth clicked her tongue disapprovingly. "You know that the amount we donated was shared to others by Bishop Troyer's *fraa*! Everyone knows and now speculates about our situation!"

"Scandalous!" William cried.

Anna felt as if the two of them were playing volleyball.

The kitchen clock chimed six times. Lydia glanced at it, for she needed to leave in less than thirty minutes. Certainly she had her own work to do, Anna thought. Already, Lydia had spent almost an hour with William and his daughters reviewing the situation, a situation about which he merely grumbled and complained with no inclination to act upon a viable solution.

"If you should like to hear my solution?" Lydia interrupted. She spoke louder than usual, but still with a degree of patience. Once William and Elizabeth settled down, she took a deep breath and began speaking. "It's simple, really. You have that small *haus* in Florida. Move there for a while. Winter and spring are lovely down there. It's less expensive to live there. *Mayhaps* you'll find Florida to your liking. If you don't, you can always return to a smaller place. Either way, you can sell this farm without anyone raising an eyebrow."

Anna looked up again from her quilt. "Why, that's the perfect solution!"

Lydia nodded and added, "Especially after last winter being so difficult and causing the flare-up with your arthritis. Certainly no one will question why you have left." Pausing, she let that suggestion register with William.

"If we move that far away, I'd still have to sell my horse and buggy," William grumbled.

Anna glanced up at him sharply. This was the first indication that her father might—just might—be willing to listen to reason.

Lydia nodded gravely to acknowledge William's loss before pressing her point home. "In the meantime, you should rent out this property. The income from the rental will help pay your way until you sell it."

A silence fell over the room. Anna waited, her breath caught in her chest. Elizabeth almost broke into a rare smile while Mary developed a typical scowl, the two very different reactions almost amusing to Anna except she knew the serious reasons behind them.

Finally, Elizabeth nodded her head in approval, her agitation from moments prior quickly vanishing. "That's an agreeable solution!" She met her father's worried gaze. He often sought her validation on important decisions, and even those that did not qualify as very significant. She was, after all, the maternal head of the house, at least since their mother departed from her earthly life to begin her heavenly one. "Especially with the cold season soon upon us. I'm rather partial to that idea."

But the idea of William and his two unmarried daughters leaving Charm was not received as well by everyone.

"Florida?" Mary scoffed at the idea as if someone had just given her a glass of spoiled milk. "Oh bother! Who will help me with the *kinner*?" With a helpless expression on her face, she looked first to her father and then to Lydia. "You know I haven't been feeling quite well! The headaches and fatigue! And those two *kinner* are so active. Cris's family provides no help at all. Why! They return the boys to me in worse shape than when they left, what with all the cookies and sweets they give them!" Disgusted, she returned her attention to her father. "If you move to Florida, you simply must leave Anna behind. It's not as if anyone would miss her..."

The comment, while seemingly harsh, didn't faze anyone in the room. With the exception of Lydia, Anna knew that it was an accurate statement and not necessarily spoken with malice. Her quiet nature often caused people, especially her family, to overlook her at larger gatherings. And to be needed by someone, *anyone*, was better than to be needed by none.

"And when we return? Then what?"

Mary sighed. "If Salome Musser would let us move into the big *haus*, we might have room." She picked at a white thread on the blue sleeve of her dress. "*Mayhaps* this might be the catalyst for her to finally do the right thing, *nee*? Who ever heard of such selfishness? And with only Leah and Hannah living there." She looked up, suddenly aware that everyone watched her, stunned by her sharp words. "*Ja vell*, it's true! Her son did buy the farm, after all."

Another glance at the clock and Lydia suddenly stood up. "Think about it, William."

For a moment, Anna's heart broke. Her father looked around the room, his eyes taking in the freshly painted walls (for he always hired three young men to repaint them in the springtime), wood-stained trim work (something that Anna worked tirelessly to clean each week), and perfectly waxed linoleum floor (another task that fell upon Anna). Cleanliness was, after all, next to godliness.

"To have another person sit in my kitchen?" Emotion welled up in his throat. "Tend my Lizzie's gardens? Who could I possibly entrust with such a valuable piece of my life?"

Gathering her black sweater, Lydia ignored his reservations. She spared a genuine smile in Anna's direction before picking up her basket. "I heard that George

Coblentz is returning to the area. His older sister is ailing and they may need a place to stay."

"They?" William's mouth fell open. "You mean he has young *kinner*?" He shook his hand in front of his chest as if warding off something bad. "*Nee*! I won't have undisciplined young ones tearing through this *haus*! They'll trample the rose bushes, for sure and certain!"

Laughing, Lydia placed her hand on his shoulder, the closest gesture of intimacy she ever shared with him. It was a simple touch that spoke of a deep friendship and even deeper tolerance on her part. "Oh, William! You fret over the most mundane things! Besides, it's just George and his *fraa*, Sara. Their children are all grown up now."

Anna picked up her quilting, readying herself to continue working on the blanket since Lydia was leaving.

"Coblentz?" William tugged at his beard, a sign that Anna knew too well: he was searching his memory. He remembered everyone that he met, a social practice he had perfected over the years. "I don't know anyone named Coblentz."

Lydia slipped her arms into her sweater and quickly extracted the strings to her prayer *kapp*. Her hand on the doorknob, she turned to wave one last time to the three young women before responding to his statement. "Of course you do," she said, opening the door. "George's *fraa* grew up here, just north of Berlin. Don't you remember Sara? Sara Whittmore?"

Anna's fingers froze over the material, the needle only partially pushed through the fabric. She dared not raise her eyes. To do so, she feared, would allow Lydia, of all people, to read her thoughts. The casual nature in which Lydia said the name startled Anna almost as much as hearing it. Was it possible that Lydia had forgotten her advice to Anna to forget marrying Freman since her father would not accept a Whittmore into the family? Even after she broke off the engagement, very little was said of Freman's abrupt disappearance. Indeed, no one in their house had spoken of the Whittmore family for years. That, however, had not hindered Anna from thinking of the Whittmores, one in particular, each and every day for the last eight years—a fact that she now knew was unknown to everyone, even Lydia!

"They are the most delightful people, and you know what they say about a woman without *kinner*," she said, her voice light and breezy. "They take the best care of the *haus* and gardens!" One last wave and Lydia disappeared out the door. Behind her, she left four people in deep thought: three who wondered about this George Coblentz and how the *g'may* would react to the news of the Eicher departure and a fourth who stared at her lap, her eyes glazed over and her fingers unable to extract the needle.

Whittmore. The name was far too familiar to Anna. While the voices of her family faded into the background, some long-repressed memories awakened. She lifted her eyes and looked around the room, her eyes seeing the very objects that so alarmed her father just moments before. Rather than fearing the hands that might touch them in just a few short weeks, her heart pounded at the very thought of the Whittmores staying in their house.

She sighed, lifting her eyes to the ceiling as she fought the intense pounding of her heart. *Oh*, she wondered, a deep and hollow feeling forming inside of her chest, *was it possible that, once again, he might actually walk these floors?* The very thought led her to distraction and made her so uncomfortable that she had no choice but to claim a head-ache and soon after Lydia's departure, retire to the safety and isolation of her room. The only problem was that she was not alone, for the memory of Sara's brother, Freman Whittmore, accompanied her.

❧ *Chapter Two* ❧

BEFORE A WEEK had passed, the arrangements had
been made. George Coblentz was eager to return
and assist his sister's family during her illness.
Therefore, changes came quickly for the Eicher family.
Rooms were packed away, memories boxed up, and
clothes transferred from pegs and hangers to suitcases. It
amazed Anna how, despite so many years living in the
house, there was little to show for their existence beyond
a few boxes left in the attic.

Of course, she thought as she dressed for the day, they
had yet to tidy up the main room in the house: the kitchen.
Already she could hear Lydia moving about downstairs,
bustling to clean up breakfast dishes, a meal that Anna
had voluntarily slept through so that she could avoid the
daily complaints and rants from her father regarding the
injustice of having to leave the house for so many months.

Even though the leaves on the trees were still green and
the noon sun still warm, William had scheduled his trip
down south. To Anna's concern, Elizabeth convinced her
friend, Martha Canton, recently widowed at the young
age of thirty-two, to journey with them. When she joined
Lydia and her sisters downstairs, she was gratified to find

that Lydia shared her concern and was discussing it with Elizabeth.

"*Mayhaps* people might talk," Lydia suggested to Elizabeth as she wrapped their mother's fine china with newspaper and packaged it into a cardboard box. While the Coblentzes would live in the house and William had agreed for it to be furnished, there were some valuables that he insisted be packed away. The three women were packaging up and cleaning the kitchen, William too concerned that leaving the house anything less than pristine might be cause for gossip. "It's not sensible for such a newly widowed woman to travel such a distance."

From the look on her face, Elizabeth did not agree. "Why ever not?"

"I think Lydia means," Anna said softly, "that it's not sensible for Martha to travel with *Daed*, *ja*?"

Lydia lifted an eyebrow as she placed a piece of wrapped china into the box. She remained silent and said nothing in response to Anna's comment.

Elizabeth, however, clicked her tongue disapprovingly. Always the one that focused on maintaining appearances, despite the Amish culture's emphasis on being plain, Elizabeth took great satisfaction that her reputation remained untarnished and above reproach. The idea that anyone might question her judgment (for certainly it would reflect on *her* in the long run) horrified Elizabeth. After taking a few seconds to compose herself, she frowned as she sharply chastised her sister. "Don't be *verrickt*, Anna!"

Lowering her eyes, Anna flushed under the disparaging scoff from Elizabeth. While she knew that she should be used to such reprimands and usually remained unaffected by them, this one stung more than usual.

"Anna's not crazy," Lydia replied, her voice calm and level as she jumped to Anna's defense. "Martha has been widowed for nine months now, Elizabeth. You know how that Amish grapevine works. Tongues are bound to wag."

Anna admired the older woman's ability to always sound calm and collected. Dealing with her sisters and her father could rattle even the most stoic of people, she thought.

"She is traveling with me," Elizabeth said forcefully. "Accompanying me. Not *Daed*. Why would anyone give that matter a second thought?"

Lydia was quick to respond. "Your *daed* is hardly immune to the thought of remarriage."

At this comment, Elizabeth scoffed. "If he hasn't married yet," she said, "why would he now? Besides, Martha is a right *gut* friend to me, but certainly can be of no interest to *Daed*! While she has a righteous heart and good intentions, she knows no scripture and is far too used to working outdoors. Her skin is dark like leather and she lost her bottom front teeth when the mule knocked her into the fence post!"

Anna stopped wiping down the cabinet next to the sink and laughed, a soft sound that hinted, just slightly, at repayment for the previous reproach by Elizabeth. "I should think the former two characteristics could far outweigh the latter! Who knows but she might learn how to please *Daed*."

"Oh, Anna!" Unlike Lydia, the unspoken matriarch of the family ever since their mother had died, Elizabeth was not one who easily hid her displeasure or her inability to accept criticism. "You know what I mean! Besides, their age difference alone is far too great! He could practically be her father!" Shaking her head, Elizabeth scoffed once again at such a proposal. "Ridiculous, Anna. I simply will not entertain another word of this conversation!"

Anna returned her attention to the counter, too aware that Elizabeth would not easily relinquish her place as one of the two women of influence in her father's life. She had acquired the role by regrettable chance, yet she was determined to maintain it by resolute choice. As far as Elizabeth was concerned, no one in the community would dare question her reputation, and therefore, Martha's presence was purely just companionship and shame on anyone who might think otherwise. In Elizabeth's eyes, her own spotless reputation would eliminate anyone's need to gossip or speculate about the situation.

And Anna had learned long ago that what Elizabeth wanted from her father, she usually received.

By mid-September, with George and Sara Coblentz expected to arrive any day, William and Elizabeth departed with Martha accompanying them. Their personal belongings packaged in boxes and stored in the attic, William and his oldest daughter clambered into the hired van for the long journey down to Florida. There hadn't been much fanfare in the community about their departure. Despite her father's worries, Anna knew that it wasn't uncommon for older Amish couples to spend colder seasons in the Amish and Mennonite community of Pinecraft, Florida. As for the renting of the house, William's explanation was accepted by all, even if he did tend to speak far too often (and too long) about his reasons for leaving.

Anna, however, stayed behind. She stood in the darkness of the early morning hours, a black shawl wrapped tightly around her shoulders as she watched the van pull out of their driveway, the red taillights casting a soft glow in the darkness. She noticed that neither her father nor her sister looked back to grace her with a final wave before disappearing down the road. Instead, Anna was left standing in the empty driveway, shivering in the cold and knowing that she wouldn't see them for almost a year. For her, their absence would be felt; for them, her absence would be nothing but an afterthought.

Minutes after the van disappeared, Anna continued standing there, alone and cold, thinking only of her own mixed feelings. While she agreed that the move was the best solution for her father's dilemma, she found herself fighting the urge to resent the state of affairs that he had created for the family. If only he had been more thrifty, they could have stayed in their own home. Instead of packing away their mother's china, Elizabeth and Anna would have spent the past week canning food for use over the winter months. Now the pantry shelves remained empty, waiting for Sara Coblentz to fill them.

Shivering in the cold, Anna headed back into the house. Since the decision had been made to rent the house, she had given thought about God and His plans for the Eicher family. Certainly there were reasons for everything, and she knew better than to ask the simple question "why?" Asking wouldn't change the fact that her father, eldest sister, and her sister's widowed friend were to stay, temporarily, in Pinecraft, Florida, while the remaining two daughters would stay in Sugarcreek, Ohio. Besides the Florida house being too small for more people, Anna much preferred to stay behind, even if it meant moving to Mary's.

After all, her sister needed Anna's help.

"I simply cannot do without Anna," Mary had insisted, all but stomping her bare feet in the dust of the worn path by the porch when the plans for William's departure had been discussed and solidified. "You both know I have those headaches, especially when the trees begin to change. Tree mold. And I'm so tired of late!"

As usual, she had won her argument. *A squeaky wheel always gets oiled*, Anna thought when Mary became, once again, victorious in her request...*nee*, demand!...for Anna to remain behind in order to help her with the *kinner*. In truth, she didn't mind. She loved her nephews, little Cris Junior and Walter. While loud and rambunctious, they showered her with attention and affection that warmed her heart. She didn't even mind bathing them each evening before tucking them into their shared bed.

Two days after William and Elizabeth departed, Anna made the sixteen-mile journey from Charm to Sugarcreek. Now she stood at the counter of Mary's kitchen kneading bread while her sister sat at the kitchen table, half-heartedly darning one of her husband's socks. From her sister's repeated sighing and fidgeting, Anna knew that something was on her mind. Time alone would provide insight into the cause.

Outside the window that faced the road, just a mere twenty yards from the house, a horse and buggy passed. Anna glanced out the open window, squinting to see if she recognized the driver. An older man lifted his hand and waved to her and she responded in kind, even though she wasn't certain who it was.

As soon as the rhythmical sound of the horse's hooves faded into the distance, Mary began her routine of sighing until, unable to remain silent anymore, she began.

"I'm rather embarrassed for Salome Musser," Mary said, yanking at the string as she pulled it through the loops of the sock. She had pushed a worn tennis ball to the heel in order to close the hole, but her stitches were too tight and the thread broke. "Oh, bother!" Tossing both the sock and the needle onto the table, she sighed and rubbed at her temples.

"Another headache, Mary?"

With a dismissive wave, Mary didn't answer the question. "Why, they should've invited you over for a meal, or if that is too much trouble, a visit after supper, then!"

"It's fine, Mary. Truly it is." And she meant it. She knew how busy people were during this season. After all, it was time to cut down the garden, prepare the final canned goods for winter, and make preparations for the upcoming autumn baptism and communion services. Anna loved this time of year, knowing that, shortly after those two important gatherings, wedding banns would begin to be announced after Sunday worship. And, from the way that the Amish grapevine talked, it promised to be a very busy wedding season.

Mary, however, seemed intent on lamenting the affront. "Are they expecting us to walk over there? That just seems quite prideful, I must say!"

"I see them at worship, Mary," Anna said, maintaining her typical cheerful nature. Plopping the kneaded dough into a lightly floured bowl, she covered it with a cloth. It would take some time to rise. In the meantime, she could join her sister at the table. "It's not as though we are strangers." As she sat, she reached out to gently claim the abandoned sock, knowing full well that it would never get darned if she didn't do so.

That wasn't good enough for Mary.

"They know I haven't been feeling well," she said. "You would think that Leah or Hannah would come check on me, even if their *maem* won't!"

Not prone to speaking ill of anyone, Anna concentrated on mending the sock and kept her silence on that statement.

For a few moments, the only sound in the room was the gentle ticking of the clock on the wall, a gift from Cris when he became engaged to Mary. Their courtship had been brief and tarnished only by the knowledge that the clock was intended for another, a fact that Anna never once discussed with Mary. While the entire family knew of Cris's initial interest in Anna, Mary hadn't seemed to care. She was the first of the sisters to secure a husband, and that joy far outweighed her awareness of being the groom's second choice. After all, Mary once whispered to Elizabeth when she thought Anna was in the other room, Cris Musser had the best reputation (and largest farm) in Sugarcreek, Ohio. "I reckon it doesn't matter which Eicher *dochder* secures such a marriage!"

Anna had pretended not to overhear, masking her disappointment in her sister's statement by retreating outside to weed the flower garden in front of the porch. Long ago, she had learned to quietly retreat from the private affronts to others that were so often verbalized within the four walls of the Eicher home. Tending the garden had become one of the simple ways for Anna to quietly remove herself from unpleasant confrontations. If only her sisters knew that Mary's indifference to *being* a second choice contrasted greatly with Anna's decision to not *marry* her second choice. Only her sense of respect for Cris and propriety for herself kept her from disclosing the truth.

Truth be told, the marriage of her younger sister to her former suitor, no matter how briefly he had called upon her or offered her rides home from youth singings, brought joy to Anna's heart. She never once looked upon their union with anything less than satisfaction for both her sister and for Cris Musser. While Anna knew her future happiness disappeared when she broke off her engagement to Freman, she never would want to wish her sad fate on another. Cris was, after all, a good (if a little unexciting) man with a godly reputation. She took pleasure in his ability to harbor no ill-will toward her for rebuffing his attempts at courtship. And, as she quickly learned, he certainly demonstrated an endless amount of patience when dealing with his young and sometimes overbearing wife.

"Where are those *kinner* anyway?" Mary said sharply, standing up to walk to the back window and peer outside. The main house, the older farmstead, sat a bit farther back from the road. One day, Mary and Cris would move into it to raise their family. However, Cris's mother did not seem in a great hurry to vacate it for the smaller house, the one occupied by her only surviving son and his family, a dwelling that sat closer to the road.

Finishing her mending, Anna lifted the needle and thread to her mouth and snipped it free with her teeth. Satisfied, she folded the sock and set it on the table. "They're visiting with their *grossmammi*, probably having a *wunderbarr* time!"

"And being fed endless numbers of sugar cookies, no doubt!" Instead of returning to the table, Mary sank down onto the sofa, stretching out with her hand upon her forehead. "I can hear the noise now. Running and romping through the kitchen, all worked up before supper."

Anna laughed, mostly because she knew that Mary spoke the truth.

"She does it on purpose, you know!" Lifting her head, Mary stared at her sister with a serious look. "Gives them lemonade and cookies before sending them back to me, making them sugar high, knowing how afflicted I am with headaches!"

"Oh, Mary..."

Sinking back into the pillow on the sofa, Mary sighed, ignoring the objection, no matter how soft, from her sister. "Then they'll come back here and run around, making all sorts of noise. This *haus* is too small for all these people!" Rubbing her fingers along her temples, Mary made a soft noise, like a wounded animal in the underbrush. "If only Hannah would marry that Caleb Wagler! Salome would have no choice but to move out at last!"

Shaking her head, Anna frowned. "It's their home, Mary. One day it will be yours, *ja*, but for now, it is theirs. What does it matter if the boys run about in the evening? They'll fall asleep soon enough."

At this comment, Mary dismissed her with a wave of her hand. "What would you know, anyway?" A single laugh escaped her lips. "I suppose you would have been just as content here as anywhere. Although I don't see where you had many options: Pinecraft or here, *ja*? It's a wonder that you are not more appreciative of that!"

The reminder, regardless of whether or not it was spoken with the intention of stinging, cut through Anna, especially since she had been so emotionally jarred by the recent reflections on Freman. After all, for eight long years, she had purposefully, and unsuccessfully, tried to suppress her feelings for him. Hurt filled her heart at Mary's not-so-gentle words, a bitter reminder that not only had Anna lost Freman to the whims of her father and Lydia, but she had also turned down any other subsequent suitors, including the timid attentions of her now brother-in-law, Cris.

Taking a deep breath, Anna tried to focus on her breathing. Inhale, exhale. She felt a new sense of calm wash over her. The tremors in her heart slowly ceased and she felt herself relax.

A cool September breeze blew through the window. Shutting her eyes, Anna inhaled the fresh air, her eyes shut and a hint of a smile on her lips. Autumn was her favorite season and she was particularly pleased that she did not have to travel to Pinecraft with her father and Elizabeth. She'd have missed the beautiful colors of the trees changing on the rolling hills and along the back roads. While she had not been one to travel very far or too often, she had never seen a place as spiritually beautiful as the landscape of her community in Charm, Ohio.

"Let's go for a walk," she announced, standing up abruptly. "It'll do you good, Mary, and we can stop to visit the Mussers on our way back." The senior Mussers, Salome and Raymond, resided on the same property as Cris and Mary. As was common among the Amish, particularly those who were fortunate enough to still have large farms, multiple dwellings housed generations of the family, passing down from the parents to a married child as the years went on. At the Musser farm Cris's parents still resided in the main house that was set farther back on the property while Cris and his small family resided in a cramped dwelling that faced the road, a bone of continual contention with Mary.

"*Nee, schwester.*"

Good-naturedly, Anna went to the sofa and pulled gently at Mary's hands, forcing her sister to get to her feet. "*Kum*, Mary! Such a beautiful day, *ja*? Let's enjoy the weather while we can."

With great reluctance, Mary got to her feet and let Anna lead her to the door. She did, however, do so with a few more complaints, all of which fell on deaf ears.

They walked down the winding road lined with alternating white picket and wire fences, a subtle way to define property lines in a friendly manner. In the distance, a small herd of Guernsey cows lingered in the dirt paddock outside of a red barn with white roof and silo. As the two women approached it, a man wearing black trousers, a dirty white shirt, and a battered straw hat leaned out a window of the barn and waved. Anna waved back while Mary ducked her head.

"Mary!" she scolded.

Her sister fussed and turned on her heel, heading back toward her home. "Oh, Anna," she said sharply. "You know how private I am!"

Without a word, Anna fell into step with Mary, knowing full well that it wasn't privacy that her sister sought. The man distributed fertilizer and, as such, the farm had a reputation of smelling less than pleasant. In fact, despite the man's good nature, he hadn't married until he was almost in his forties, an age that caused many wagging tongues in the *g'may*.

By the time they arrived at the elder Mussers' home, Cris was already starting the late afternoon chores. When he saw them, he lifted his hand and waved, a smile of appreciation as well as happiness on his face. Anna was only too glad to return the gesture while Mary was more than happy to disregard her husband's salutations.

"Oh, Anna!" Salome Musser smiled when they walked into the room. "How dear you are to visit us!" Her two unmarried daughters, Leah and Hannah, sat in the kitchen nearby, working.

The two young boys were playing with an alphabet puzzle on the floor, barely looking up when their mother entered the room. Anna noticed their distance, both physical and emotional, from Mary and quickly positioned herself in between her nephews and her sister in the hopes of quelling any bad feelings.

"Mary insisted!" Anna said, smiling at the older woman as she stepped forward to shake her hand in greeting. "It is Mary you should praise!"

Looking unconvinced, Salome looked over the rim of her glasses at her only daughter-in-law and pursed her lips. "Indeed, I'm sure."

"*Aendi!*" her five-year-old nephew, Cris Junior, cried out when he saw Anna. Both boys looked alike, with straight brown hair and dark brown eyes that sparkled with mischief and curiosity. For as much as they did not respond to Mary's lack of affection, they doted on Anna's abundance of it. "*Das is een* zebra!" he said as he pointed to the puzzle piece shaped like a Z.

"It *is* a zebra! How clever you are!"

The boy beamed and nudged his younger brother who, just shy of three years of age, fell over at the slight. Immediately, they began to tussle, wrestling on the floor. Mary grabbed Cris Junior's arm and pulled him aside.

"I knew you'd have too much sugar," she scolded, dragging her son out of the kitchen by his elbow and toward the side door. Young Walter began to cry but, true to his nature of solemn loyalty to his brother, followed them.

The wails of young Cris faded away, overshadowed only by Mary's harsh words, half in Dutch and half in English.

From her seat on the sofa, Salome pursed her lips, her eyes watching as her two grandsons and daughter-in-law disappeared. Leah and Hannah both shook their heads but remained silent. Feeling uncomfortable, Anna was uncertain whether or not she should leave with Mary. However, leaving after just arriving seemed almost as discourteous as her sister's departure, so she quickly opted to stay.

"It's right *gut* to see you," Anna managed to say with a small smile. "I wanted to visit before the supper hour."

The tension lifted. Sitting at the kitchen table, Leah's arms were stained a reddish-purple, almost matching the color of her work dress, as she stirred the contents of a large metal pot with her hands. Without having to ask, Anna knew that she was pickling beets to be canned for the winter months. The sweet smell of vinegar mixed with raw cane sugar and pickling spices began to fill the room, overcoming the scent of baked cookies, most of which the boys had eaten long ago. Cookies never lasted long in any kitchen when Cris Junior and Walter were around.

"You should stay for supper then," Leah said, a genuine smile on her face. Her straw-blonde hair framed her face and her pretty cornflower-blue eyes sparkled when she spoke. "It'll be a welcome change for all of us, I'm sure."

Hannah agreed and looked at her mother. "We have plenty, ain't so, *Maem*?"

There was no need to nod her head. Instead, Salome smiled and patted a spot on the sofa, indicating that Anna should sit down beside her. "*Kum, kum*, Anna," she said. "Amuse me with your clever stories."

The compliment, unexpected and, in Anna's eyes, unwarranted, brought a flush to her cheeks. "I dare say that I don't have any stories, and if I did, I certainly wouldn't know if they were clever or not!" But she joined the older woman, pleased for the joyful reception from the Musser family.

"The boys are keeping you busy, then?"

Anna nodded. "The boys are a refreshing change from the everyday, *ja*? I'm not certain which one makes me laugh more! Little Cris with his mischief or Walter with his ability to attract dirt to his face, even just after he's had his bath!"

"Bless him, that child!" Salome said, a smile on her lips but some pain showing in her eyes. She lifted her hand to her cheek, gently touching her own skin as if to remember the soft touch of another, from years long gone. "Surely he reminds me so much of my dear Rodney."

A moment of silence blanketed the room at the mention of her deceased son who, almost ten years ago, had been called home to walk with Jesus. Anna remembered the news of Rodney's passing. What had started out as a severe headache quickly escalated into something much worse: a malignant brain tumor. He had only been twenty when he died.

Clearing her throat, Salome lowered her hand and took a deep breath. As she exhaled, she looked at Anna, studying her for a long moment. Finally, she asked, "You are faring well at Mary's, then?"

The shift in conversation, while welcomed by all, startled Anna, mostly because of the curious tone of the question which hinted at more than just polite inquisitiveness.

"Quite well, *danke*," she responded.

"Your calming nature must be a pleasant addition to the household," Hannah quipped. "For sure and certain, *ja*?"

"Perhaps it will linger after you have left," Leah was quick to add, to which Salome cast a stern look in the direction of her daughters.

Anna laughed, uncomfortable with the hidden complaint in the compliment. "One sure does learn to appreciate moments of quiet, that's for sure and certain. But I wouldn't change it for anything in the world. I enjoy those *kinner* so much, I'm afraid I'll be hesitant to leave."

Salome nodded her head, approving of Anna's tact in responding.

"You must miss your *daed* and *schwester*, *ja*?" Without waiting for Anna to answer, she caught her breath and leaned forward, another thought having just occurred to her. "Have you been to meet George and Sara Coblentz yet?"

"*Nee*," Anna confessed. "I have not."

Salome smiled, understanding written on her face. "In due time, I reckon. That must be a disconcerting feeling, to move from your *daed*'s *haus*!"

With all of her being, Anna wished she could speak her mind and tell them that it wasn't a disconcerting feeling to leave her father's house; *that* she could bear just fine, *danke*. And it didn't bother her that someone else enjoyed it now. *Nee*, neither of those two reasons struck her as remotely troublesome. What created unease for Anna was the idea that, should she call upon the Coblentz family, she might run into her past. Instead of speaking, Anna merely lowered her eyes.

Salome hesitated, after glancing at Leah and Hannah, then spoke once again: "We would have come to visit you yesterday, Anna. But we went to welcome them with Bishop Troyer's *fraa*."

This news brightened Anna's mood: a welcome diversion from her thoughts of Freman. Looking up, she smiled. "*Ja*? And how did you find them, then? Were they to your liking? Are they godly people?"

"Oh, heavens!" Salome clapped her hands together and laughed. "Godly? Why, I've never met such a fine woman! That Sara...why!...she'll be the perfect caretaker of your *daed*'s *haus*! She's quite fastidious, you see. Everything is so clean that it shines!"

Hannah dried her hands on a towel and walked over to the sitting area. "They have a visitor coming next week," she said, a light growing in her eyes. At eighteen, Hannah was young and pretty, the slight up curve of her nose giving her face a playful look. Since both sisters were younger than Anna, they ran with a different set of friends. But Anna always had thought kindly of both young women, even if they were more animated and lively than most Amish women.

From the kitchen, Leah called out, "*Ja*, her *bruder*!"

"Her...*bruder*?"

Anna felt her heart skipping a beat as she held her breath for a few seconds and forced herself to remain calm. The last thing she wanted was to appear curious. Surely they didn't mean Freman, for he had left Charm, Ohio, almost immediately after Anna refused his offer of marriage. The grapevine did not speak of his sudden departure, at least not in the presence of Anna. And, given the rest of the Eicher family's tendency to focus on themselves, and not on other individuals that they deemed less interesting, she heard of no scuttlebutt in the community divulging his whereabouts.

That had been years ago.

Hannah glanced at her sister and a secretive look passed between them. "Leah heard his name is Freman and he's quite handsome," she went on, quickly dodging the hand towel that was thrown in her direction.

"Why would you notice, with Caleb calling on you!"

Hannah flushed at the mention of her second cousin, Caleb Wagler. While some Amish youth kept their courtships private until such a time when the wedding was announced by a deacon right after worship, apparently Caleb was not one of them. Not only did he bring Hannah home from every youth singing, but he also had made clear to other potential suitors that he had every intention of marrying Hannah. While she remained silent about her own feelings on the matter, no one doubted that she shared Caleb's sentiments.

"I'm promised to no one!" Hannah retorted quickly but without credence. "I suppose I still may ride home with any young man who asks me!" "Girls!" Salome chastised them with her voice, but her eyes held a sparkle that clearly indicated that she too hoped that the younger brother of Sara Coblentz might come calling on one of her *dochders*. But wouldn't Freman be married by now?

Anna felt as if the walls were closing upon her. The lightness in her head was as intense as the heaviness in her chest. Despite the continuation of the visit, including two more invitations to supper which she declined, her mind remained focused on one realization: Freman was returning to Charm!

It wasn't until later that evening, as she sat upon the edge of her bed, staring at the empty white wall before her, that she became aware of something even more consequential: his physical absence had not lessened the emotional turmoil that she felt, even after so many years, upon hearing his name.

❧ Chapter Three ❧

WHEN HE WALKED into the worship service, Anna Eicher had to catch her breath.

For the past week, she had tried to prepare herself for this moment, the moment when her eyes would fall, once again, upon Freman Whittmore—for the first time in eight years! She had thought herself ready, her inner discourse aimed at rehashing the reasons why, despite herself, she had rejected his proposal: *Daed* thought him too reproachable, and Lydia thought him not worth risking her *daed*'s disapproval. And Anna found their arguments too persuasive.

Yet, nothing could have properly prepared her for when she once again saw his face. She recognized him immediately when his tall form followed the other Amish men walking single file into the room, their Sunday hats casting shadows over their brows so she couldn't see his eyes. It didn't matter. She knew that he wasn't glancing around the room in order to catch her gaze. He probably didn't even know that she was watching him moving through the line of empty pine benches, waiting until the men stopped and sat down, sliding the length of the bench to make room for each other.

He looked the same, she thought, a flurry of emotions coursing through her veins. For the briefest of seconds, she was no longer sitting on a hard, pine bench but was transported through her memory to a time, eight years prior, when she had sat beside him in his borrowed buggy. His strong hands held the reins and he smiled as he talked to her. When he asked her a question and she responded, he nodded his head with approval at her words. Respect. That was what he had offered her eight years ago. Respect and his hand in marriage: two things that, with the deepest sense of loyalty to her family, she had found herself rejecting.

Not a day had passed when she did not think back to that rejection and the ensuing grief that she felt when he, caught off-guard with her denial, had slipped his hat back upon his head and turned to leave. As his buggy pulled away, the dark canopy shadowing his face, she hadn't called for him to return. Oh, how she had wanted to! She had wanted nothing more than to run after him and stop the horse, to confess that it was a mistake and that there was nothing she wanted more than to become his wife.

But she hadn't.

Yes, not a day had passed without thoughts of Freman Whittmore infiltrating her mind. As days turned to weeks, weeks into months, and months into years, she wondered of his circumstances. Where had he gone? What was his occupation? Had he taken a wife?

Now, however, as she snuck another look at him, her heart beat rapidly, for she realized he wore no beard. Was it possible, she wondered, that he had never married after all that time?

As if on cue, once the rest of the unmarried men were seated, all of the men reached up to remove their hats and slide them under their bench. The men in the back of the room stood up and hung their hats on metal hooks that lined the wall near the ceiling. Anna normally used this moment as her reminder to fix her attention on the *Ausbund*, the black chunky book that she held in her hands. It felt old, as she knew very well that it was published some forty years ago. The cover was worn and spoke of an uncounted number of hands that, over the years, had clutched the book during just as many worship services. Today, however, she could not keep her eyes from watching Freman Whittmore, sitting so proper and straight on the bench, his attention fully turned to the front of the room where no one stood yet, but where the bishop would eventually stand for his opening sermon.

The *vorsinger*, the young man who started singing the hymns, began the first syllable of the song, his voice lifting in the air, following an ageless and unwritten tune. When the rest of the worshippers began to sing with him, the bishop and the *g'may's* three deacons stood up and left the room. Anna glanced at them, just for a second, before returning her gaze toward Freman. To her surprise, his dark eyes now stared in her direction, no emotion in his expression. While she felt certain that he knew her, for it had been only eight years, he showed no sign of recognition. At least, not on the surface.

"Anna!"

She caught her breath and glanced at the older woman seated beside her. Normally Elizabeth sat beside her, as she was one of the oldest unmarried women in the church district, second only to Kate Schwartzentruber, another older woman known for being overly righteous and rigid, her hopes of marrying gone with both her youth and her reputation. Today, however, Anna sat next to Kate. Had Elizabeth not gone traveling, she, not Anna, would have sat next to Kate, since the members of the *g'may* always sat in order of their age.

"Pay attention!" Kate hissed at Anna, her steely gray eyes flitting in her direction for just the briefest of moments.

Embarrassed, Anna lowered her gaze to the *Ausbund* and tried to find her place in the hymn that everyone else sang. Even though she knew the words by heart, she continued to follow the words in the book, her mouth moving and the words coming out while her mind wandered back to Freman.

With his dark, curly hair and deep brown eyes, he looked exactly the same as he had eight years ago. The only differences were subtle signs of aging on his face: wrinkles by the corners of his eyes and furrows in his brow. He remained as handsome as she remembered him, perhaps more so, if that were even possible. Of course she knew that memories often took on a life of their own. Surely hers had exaggerated the depth of his feelings, and despite the way her mind raced and her pulse quickened, she tried to convince herself that it had been just a spring romance between them.

"Who is that?"

The soft voice in her ear startled Anna. Without looking, however, she knew who it was: only Leah, who sat beside her, would dare to whisper during the opening hymn.

Not daring to respond, for surely Kate would have complained afterwards, and probably directly to the bishop, Anna merely shook her head, just enough to silence Leah.

Yet from the corner of her eye, she saw the slight movement of the other, younger unmarried women that sat to her left. Their attention was not focused on the bishop but on the newcomer to their worship service. Anna knew she'd have to answer questions afterwards if she indicated that she knew his name.

The last thing she wanted to do was to rehash the emotions and the hurt from so long ago, especially since she had already convinced herself, in just those few minutes, that his affection had been the fleeting fancy of a young man who, clearly, had not been truly ready to settle down. Even Cris had taken her refusal in stride, quickly shifting his attention from Anna to Mary since marriage had been his main intention. For most Amish men love was not necessarily a precursor to proposals. It was more important for both parties to have a good standing in the community, a reputation for righteousness, and a hint of compatibility for the future.

Anna exhaled slowly through her mouth, willing her heart to stop beating so rapidly.

Their courtship had been so secretive. Few people had even suspected that Anna Eicher rode home from the youth singings with Freman Whittmore. In public settings Freman was always the last to voice his opinion, never quick to speak, and so when he did, people listened. As for Anna, her propensity for remaining quiet in group settings was as renowned as her kindness to individuals. Never one for gossip or judgment, Anna was known to be the quintessential Amish woman.

Unfortunately, when she was sixteen, what caused the older members of the community to observe her with respect was the very reason she walked home alone from the singings during those early months of her *Rumschpringe*: her reputation for shyness meant no one offered her a ride home. So she walked alone. It wouldn't have been that way if Elizabeth hadn't refused to attend the singings. She professed to being offended by the fast pace of the chosen songs in the youth group. As for Mary, fifteen at the time, she was too young to accompany Anna. Without either of her sisters, Anna had no choice but to walk home alone, a fact that hadn't bothered her because she was more than comfortable in her own thoughts.

And then, one night, Freman had asked her to ride home with him.

"Kneel, Anna!"

Snapping to attention, Anna looked over at Kate, stunned to realize that everyone was kneeling before their benches, foreheads pressed into clasped hands as they began to silently pray. Quickly, she slipped off the bench and knelt down, the color rising to her cheeks as she anticipated quite the tongue scolding from Kate right after the service. Had she truly been daydreaming for so long that she missed an entire sermon and another hymn?

For the rest of the service, Anna focused her eyes on the front of the room, forcing herself to pay attention to the second (and longer) sermon. When the final hymn was sung, she sang along with the other members of the *g'may*, ignoring the urge to glance in Freman's direction. There was no point in doing so, she told herself. At almost twenty-five years of age, she had lost the beauty and zest of her youth. Her skin was too tan and her hands too callused from working in the gardens. Indeed, she worked so hard that, unlike her two sisters, her hollowed cheeks lacked the cheerful roundness that most of the older Amish women touted.

Nee, like Elizabeth, her time for courting handsome young men was long expired. It would be an older man, most likely a widower, who would come calling now. And Anna knew what that meant: young children to raise and a rigid husband to mind. While she much preferred being married to her memories, she knew that the day would come when she'd have to make a decision to create new memories to replace the old.

"What ailed you, Anna?"

As expected, there had been no escape from Kate's harsh reprimands. With her pinched nose and down-turned mouth, Kate always appeared angry. She wore stern black dresses, even when it wasn't worship Sunday. The dark color of the fabric drained her already pale face and made her appear even more austere. Despite her reputation for being righteous and hardworking, suitors never offered to bring her home after the singings in the evening. Instead, she could often be seen walking, alone, down the road in the gentle evening hours while all of the other young women rode by in a buggy, sharing the company of a single young man or tagging along with a group of friends.

Kate's astute eye and sharp tongue offended many and, as such, rather than be subject to them, others chose merely to avoid her.

Anna, however, was not so fortunate.

"I'm just feeling poorly," Anna offered as a way of excuse. "*Danke* for telling me to kneel."

"You sat there like you were in another world!" Kate's voice carried and, to Anna's dismay, caught the attention

47

of Mary and her two sisters-in-law. "And during worship! My word, I thought you weren't even paying attention, Anna Eicher!"

Anna lowered her eyes, withdrawing into herself as she listened to Kate remind her of her inadequacies.

Fortunately, Leah and Hannah hurried over to join them, leaving Mary behind as the two boys hung onto her hands.

Laughing at something Hannah must have said, Leah smiled as she stood before Anna and Kate. "Good day, Kate!" she said as she reached out and shook Kate's hand.

"Didn't see you before the service," Kate replied, referring to the greeting, a kiss on the mouth, that the women always gave each other in the quarter-hour before worship started.

Hannah nudged her sister. "We'd have been here on time if you weren't so concerned with your new *kapp* strings."

Leah frowned at her sister's teasing.

From the expression on Kate's face, she wasn't impressed with either woman's excuse. When she turned away, the two younger girls leaned their heads together and tittered. There was solidarity in their unity, a closeness that was foreign to the Eicher sisters.

Anna remained silent, too aware that, on the other side of the room, Freman stood with the men, meeting new people and reuniting with old acquaintances. It took all of her willpower to not let her eyes wander in that direction. When she had heard that George and Sara Coblentz would rent her father's home, she wondered if Freman would come visiting. Such a possibility clearly existed since, in fact, they had grown up in a nearby community.

With such knowledge, Anna had prayed for the strength to see him again.

Now it is done, she told herself. The worst is over, I reckon.

"Girls, Anna," a voice said from behind her. Anna turned around, and upon recognizing Salome, she smiled. The woman accompanying Salome, however, was unfamiliar to Anna. From the strange head cover that the woman wore, far more flexible and finer in material, Anna immediately suspected that she was about to meet Freman's sister. "I want you to meet Sara," Salome said as she introduced her daughters, her daughter-in-law, and Anna.

"*Ach*, Anna!" Sara shook her hand in a friendly, warm manner. "I'm so pleased to meet you! Your *daed*'s *haus* is just lovely! We cannot tell you how inviting it is!"

"You've found comfort there, then, *ja*?"

Sara's smile, so soft and gentle, warmed Anna's heart. "Most definitely!" the older woman said. "George did not want to infringe on his sister's family. Their place is rather crowded already." She didn't need to explain; Anna could only imagine how many people resided there. "The peace that greets us after visiting with his sister is a welcome time for reflection and prayer." She gave a slight laugh. "No doubt we'd have lacked that elsewhere!"

Salome regained Sara's attention. "You must come visiting then," she said firmly. Beside her, both Hannah and Leah glanced at each other and beamed as they listened to their mother's invitation. "We *insist* on sharing fellowship at our *haus*!"

With a pleasant nod of her head, Sara accepted the invitation. "George will be grateful, I'm sure, to get to know your husband better as I will you and your *dochders*."

She glanced at Hannah and Leah as if contemplating something. "His company has been limited to my *bruder*, Freman, as of late...at least after he tends his *schwester*. Freman will be staying with us for some time, you see."

Salome immediately glanced in his direction, giving away the fact that she already had noticed Freman's presence. "I wondered when I saw him," she said, although she had clearly connected the tall, unmarried Amish man with the Coblentzes. "He must come visit too. *Mayhaps* for Monday dinner?" She looked at Leah and Hannah. "The girls don't work on Monday."

With the visitation scheduled, Salome and Sara began to talk about other things while Leah and Hannah preened themselves as they tried to catch Freman's attention. Not once did he look in Anna's direction, but rather seemed intent on the conversation in which he was engaged.

While no one watched, Anna slipped out the door and wandered down the lane past the long line of black buggies parked on the grass.

There would be no escaping the fact that she would be in Freman's presence sooner or later. If she had thought she was prepared to face him, she realized how wrong she had been. She took some deep breaths as she moved away from the house, wondering how he would respond to being in her company once again. That thought stayed with her long after she found herself wandering down the road, ignoring the rumble of her empty stomach as her feet led her swiftly toward Mary's home. If her sister were to ask her why she left before the *g'may* meal, she would plead a headache, knowing that Mary—oft ill with headaches herself—would have to accept such an explanation without complaint.

✤ *Chapter Four* ✤

O F ALL THE days to be ill!" Mary plopped onto the sofa, jostling little Cris far too much for Anna's liking. It was Monday, the day of the much-anticipated visit with the Coblentzes, and the poor boy lay ill with a fever. Cris Junior deserved better treatment from his mother. Still, Anna knew better than to speak her mind. Anything construed as criticism, no matter whether or not it was intended that way, would set off her sister, spiraling Mary into the depths of her moods.

That was happening quite often lately. Already, Anna could tell that her sister was teetering on the edge: every little detail in her daily life seemed to set her off, as if everyone in the *g'may*, family included, even her young son, were all conspiring together to make her life miserable.

With a loud sigh, Mary tucked a quilt along the child's small body. He rested on the sofa, his eyes shut and his cheeks pale. Despite the way that Mary pushed the quilt under him, he gave no response to his mother's distressed comment or less-than-compassionate touch. "I'll have to stay home now, won't I?" Mary complained. They had been invited to dinner at the Mussers in order to meet the Coblentzes, an appointment that Mary clearly had anticipated.

Mary stood up and stared down at her son, frustration etched on her face. Unlike her sister Anna, Mary was not the subdued type, her personality neither restrained nor repressed. She was resonant and boisterous, and, to Anna's constant mortification, thrived on being the center of attention as well as conversation. It did not make her a bad person; it just made her a loud person. Missing out on an early visit with the newcomers was definitely not something that sat well with her.

Earlier in the day, Lydia Rothberger had stopped by, spending a few hours visiting with both Anna and Mary. They sat outside, Anna working on her quilting while the other two women crocheted, as the boys played on the rusty swing set near the garden. Despite being autumn, the weather remained pleasant enough, cool during the nights and warm during the days. With the sun on the back of her neck, Anna sighed, content with both the day and the company.

However, that changed rapidly.

Walter began to fight with his older brother. Earlier in the day, little Cris had complained that he felt poorly, his lack of energy a testament to his claim. Now, no matter how much his younger brother tried to encourage him to play, Cris Junior refused. Mary set down the blanket she was crocheting and glanced in their direction.

"Whatever are they fussing about now?" When she made no move in their direction, Anna rose from her seat and walked over to the playset.

Little Cris sat on the swing, his head pressed against the chain as his legs barely pushed himself back and forth. Walter, however, tugged on the other side, eager to encourage his brother to go down the slide with him.

"What's wrong?" Anna asked as she knelt before him. When she reached out to touch his forehead, she realized that he had a fever. "Best get you inside, Cris," she said, taking his hand and leading her willing patient into the house where she situated him on the sofa. He hadn't stirred since.

Now Mary rose from the sofa and stomped back to the kitchen area. She rummaged through the cabinets, found a glass, and filled it with water from the faucet for her son. Her thoughts, however, were clearly not focused on the child's well-being but rather on her own disappointment. She sipped from the glass before heading back to the sofa. "And I was so looking forward to meeting and visiting with the Coblentz family!" she repeated.

"Now, now, Mary," Cris said as he stood in the doorway. He had just come in from his evening chores and still needed to wash up. His dirty boots stood by the doorway and there was dirt on his clothing. He looked tired and evidently not in the mood for an emotional outburst from his wife. Still, he patiently tried to reason with her. "You'll have plenty of opportunities to visit with them while they are staying here. It isn't as if they are leaving anytime soon."

His comment reminded Anna that the Coblentz family, and apparently Freman, were not going anywhere. The latest update about Irma, George's sister, was that her health was quickly deteriorating and the family needed his support. Since George and Sara had sold their home, they had nowhere else to live; George had made clear his intention to stay near his sister's family throughout their ordeal.

As for Freman, while Anna had thought long and hard about his sudden reappearance to Charm and completely understood that he wanted to visit with his sister, the implied duration of his stay simply did not make sense. While she knew that he had been raised north of Berlin, a larger town just ten miles away from Charm, it was her understanding that the rest of his family had moved away five years ago to the distant state of Montana. So why did it look as if he were here to stay for a while?

With a slight tremor in her heart, she focused on busying herself with washing the dishes from earlier in the day, something that Mary had said she would take care of but conveniently had forgotten when, to use her own words, a wave of fatigue had stricken her.

Handing the glass of water to her son, Mary didn't offer the child any further help as she turned to face her husband, hand upon her hip and a frown upon her face. "*Ja vell*," she snapped. "Easy enough for you to say since you are never forced to miss social engagements!"

"Your son could use your comfort," Cris protested in earnest.

"And to think that your *maem* and *schwesters* went to introduce themselves without me!" She went on, ignoring her husband's concern. "They could have at least asked me to accompany them." Her face softened as her mood swung from anger to self-pity, two facial expressions she had become a master at toggling, shifting from one to the other in order to drive home her point. "I get so tired of being home all the time. Even Anna's company can entertain me only so far!"

Anna took no offense at her sister's words, knowing only too well that there was no point. Besides, she knew where the conversation was going and what the outcome would be. There was no point in trying to interject. While she also agreed that Mary should stay with her child, Anna knew all too well that it would not happen.

"*Mayhaps* I could go for just a short time," Mary continued, glancing at the sleeping boy, the glass of water tipped in his hand and the liquid soaking the edge of the blanket by his shoulder. "He *is* sleeping. I dare say he won't awaken anytime soon! A few minutes to meet them, *ja?*"

Cris frowned. "Leave him alone? Now Mary, I don't care for that idea."

Immediately, Mary bristled at the implied criticism. "Of course not, Cris! I'd go over to greet them and you stay with the boys. Then I'll return so you can join them for the meal." Then, with a long, drawn-out sigh, she glanced upwards as if thinking before she added, "Such a shame, though. I know Sara Coblentz will be so disappointed. She has no acquaintances here, and I dare say that I have more in common with her than your two *schwesters.*" When Cris lifted an eyebrow in response to her statement, she quickly added, "Being married and all."

"I see."

Dropping her shoulders, Mary accepted defeat. "I suppose no one would think well of me for leaving the boy." She leaned over and picked up the glass, pausing to push the wet edge of the blanket away from his shoulder. "I was so looking forward to going…"

There it is, Anna thought, listening from the kitchen: the cue for Anna to step forward. Oh, it was a routine that she knew well, for Mary had perfected it in her youth:

playing the martyr in such a way that Anna felt guilty. Only this time, she didn't feel guilty; she felt relieved.

Drying her hands on the dish towel, Anna turned away from the sink and quietly offered, "I'll stay with the *kinner*." *There*, she thought, *the deed is done*. She didn't mind anyway. It was the perfect excuse to avoid meeting Freman again after so many years.

Immediately at the suggestion, Mary brightened, looking first at Anna and then at her husband, a smile forming on her lips. "Why, that's a *wunderbarr* idea!" Gone were the emotions of disappointment, self-pity, and vexation. Instead, she added praise for her sister, a way of rationalizing the decision to pawn off her sick child's care onto another: "Anna's ever so much better at calming the child anyway. I wouldn't be much use at home, no more so than you, I reckon." With a newfound energy, Mary bustled about the room, taking a moment to glance in the small mirror that hung over a wash sink in the back of the kitchen. She touched her hair, making certain it was properly tucked beneath her prayer *kapp*. "I haven't been to visit at the house anyway since...the last time," she offered in her most serious tone.

Cris took a deep breath and shook his head. "I would imagine that's true..."

Mary waved her hand at him. "You know what I mean." Dissatisfied with her dress, for she had worn it more than once since it was last laundered, Mary decided to change. She hurried up the narrow staircase, her bare feet thumping against the steps as she ascended to the second floor.

With a defeated sigh, Cris followed, knowing that he should change from his work clothes and wash up since he was to meet these newcomers for the first time. While he was not fastidious with his appearance, he was not one to desire incurring the wrath of his wife should she feel that he presented anything less than an impeccable image to others.

Anna dried her hands on a dry dish towel near the sink and went over to sit on the edge of the sofa. She brushed the hair from little Cris's forehead. It was cooler than before but still warm. When her hand touched his shoulder, she frowned, realizing that, in her sister's concern for herself, Mary had not considered the fact that the spilled water had seeped through the blanket and dampened his shirt. Without a word, Anna quickly hurried to the closet and retrieved a fresh blanket to replace the wet one that covered him.

It was a gesture no one would notice, she reckoned.

By the time Mary and Cris returned downstairs ready to depart to meet the Coblentz family, Anna was sitting in a recliner. Walter was nestled in her lap as the two of them looked through a picture book about the great Flood. The book's edges worn and the cover torn, it was a book that had passed through many different hands over the generations. It was also a book that Anna had read numerous times to her nephews. She liked to read to them at night, often choosing stories from the Bible. This one was a particular favorite, especially since Anna would pause at the end of each page, asking them to point out the different animals that approached the ark, testing their knowledge of both Dutch and English vocabularies.

In her hurry to leave the house, Mary barely did more than say good night to her sons since she wouldn't return home until after they were tucked into bed. As for Anna,

Mary didn't even pause to express her gratitude, a fact that caused Cris to frown even if Anna didn't give it a second thought. And then Mary glanced, once again, into the hand mirror before she went outside to wait on the front porch for her husband.

Clearing his throat, Cris hesitated in the doorway and cast a compassionate look at his sister-in-law. "I would have preferred that you go, Anna," he said, his tone sounding regretful despite his inability to stand up to his wife. "But Mary was anticipating the visit, so your offer to stay is greatly appreciated."

Anna inclined her head at the acknowledgment. "Anyone would do the same, *ja*?"

He was about to respond but their conversation was interrupted.

"Come along, Cris!" Mary called to her husband from the front porch. There was no need to second guess her impatience. The last thing she wanted was to arrive after Freman and the Coblentz family. "We don't want to be late!"

Taking a deep breath, Cris reached for his straw hat and slid it atop his head. He gave Anna one last encouraging smile before he disappeared through the door.

Anna could hear Mary talking to him, her voice slowly fading away as they walked down the driveway toward the main house. She shut her eyes, just for a moment, listening for the sound of the Coblentzes' buggy about to arrive. She wondered if Freman would ride with them or bring his own buggy; most likely the latter as the former would limit his independence to leave at will.

The sound of young Walter crying diverted her attention. When the adults were talking, he had climbed down from her lap to play.

"*Wie gehts*, Walter?" she asked. He had fallen and bumped his head on the furniture. Wrapping him into her arms, she sat on the floor, rocking him back and forth to soothe him. She never heard the sound of the two buggies that pulled into the driveway, passing the small house in front of its entrance as they traveled to the larger of the Mussers' homes in the back, near the garden.

❧ *Chapter Five* ❧

OVER MORNING COFFEE, Mary sat at the kitchen table, a wistful smile on her lips as she stared at the wall, her eyes clouded over with satisfaction. Her spoon tapped rapidly against the edge of the coffee cup, the gentle noise almost as constant as the ticking of the clock upon the wall.

"I wonder which one it will be," she said dreamily.

Anna glanced up from where she sat on the bench, encouraging Cris Junior to eat his toast. His fever was gone, but he had not yet regained his energy or his appetite. He sat next to her at the kitchen table, his head pressed against his cheek, and shook his head at Anna's patient attempts. Walter still slept, for which Anna was thankful. With Mary in such a dreamy state, Anna knew that it would fall to her to tend to Walter's needs when he awoke. "Which one *what* will be, Mary?"

"Not 'what'! *Who*!" Mary laughed, a childish sound of delight.

"I have no idea what you are talking about," Anna replied.

With a quick rolling of her eyes, Mary leaned forward and said, "Why, which girl has caught Freman's eye!"

Her sister's statement felt like a knife cutting through Anna's heart. Mary never knew of her aborted courtship with Freman, of course. Mary had been both too young and too self-absorbed to pay much attention to Anna and her despondent state. But had she already so accepted that Anna was an old *maedel* that she couldn't even fathom the idea of Freman as a potential suitor for her single sister?

While she had decidedly avoided being in his presence the previous evening, voluntarily offering to sit with the two boys, it never had dawned on Anna that either of the Musser daughters would be considered a match for Freman. Notwithstanding the age difference, a match between Leah or Hannah with Freman would imply a move to another state. Yet Salome's dependence on her daughters was clear to everyone who knew her. And, of course, the idea that one of Mary's sisters-in-law might become Freman's wife rekindled the remorse she felt at declining his offer of marriage.

Cris laughed at his wife's question. "Leah, no doubt. She is a bit high-spirited! I rather think that would be quite a complementary match for Freman, *ja?*"

"*Nee*, you are incorrect!" Mary pouted. "Hannah. She is far prettier…in a plain sort of way. I don't think Leah would suit someone as stoic and proper as Freman Whittmore! Why, he's so serious and practical and godly, I think Leah's silliness would not sit well with him at all."

From what Anna could gather from the bits and pieces of information that Mary provided, the previous day's visit had been rather successful. Sara Coblentz fit in wonderfully well with the Musser women, despite the strange, flimsy-shaped prayer *kapp* that she wore. As for her husband, George, everyone found him much to their liking, enjoying his stories and wise contributions to the discussion.

"It's not everyone who could remain so interested in hearing about your parents' cousins and nephews and whatever else seems to slip off your *maem*'s tongue," Mary said airily. "It isn't as if he knew anyone!"

"A fine addition to our community," Cris agreed, ignoring his wife's slight toward his mother. "A most agreeable evening, *ja*?" As if in an afterthought, he turned to Anna and gave her a quick smile. "Your presence was missed by all."

"All but that Freman, for sure and certain," Mary added dismissively. "He did not speak well of Anna, although he seemed most attentive to me, didn't he, Cris?"

Anna was used to Mary deflecting attention back to herself, whether by changing the subject so that she could be the center of it or by debasing whoever *was* the subject, in this case, Anna. While she normally simply ignored her sister's uncultured approach to socializing, this time Anna looked up and stared at Mary. No words could express the sinking feeling that was forming in her stomach.

"Why, he went so far as to mention how he remembered you from several years ago and that you were now so altered that he barely recognized you!" With no indication that she realized, even ever so slightly, that she may have stepped over the margins of propriety, she laughed, her hand fluttering in the air. "*Pffft*, altered beyond any memory, he said; although I dare say that might not be such a bad thing."

Too aware that Cris watched her, his lips pressed tightly together, Anna excused herself from the table, justifying her rapid departure on the sound of little Walter crying from his room on the second floor.

When she first saw Freman at the worship service, it felt as though time had stood still. She was no longer the young, carefree girl of seventeen. Indeed, at twenty-four years of age (twenty-five in just another three months), Anna knew that her youth had faded and her options were now limited. She acknowledged it privately, unlike her sister Elizabeth, who had no qualms about vocalizing how she accepted—*nee*...embraced!—the fact that she would never marry, having just turned thirty only last spring.

The fading bloom of youth was a bitter pill to swallow, though. Anna doted on her nephews, both by choice and by chance, for Mary was quite happy to relinquish their care to her. As a young girl, Anna just assumed that she would eventually marry and have babies, raise a large family, and surround herself with love, laughter, and life. *Mayhaps* her attachment to her sister's *kinner* was but just a shadow of her intimate desires. Or regrets.

However, Freman had remained even more handsome than she remembered. From what she could gather from her sister, he was also proper in his dealings with people and godly in his behavior. Neither surprised her for she remembered him in the same manner. Still, his words hurt Anna, even if she knew that he had just cause. A broken heart often held scars long after it had mended.

"Anna!"

She had barely gotten Walter changed when she heard Mary calling up the stairs for her attention. As she fastened Walter's pants, she smiled at him. "Seems your *maem* wants me little man, *ja*?"

He giggled and reached out to pull at her prayer *kapp* strings, causing it to shift sideways on her head. "Now,

Walter," she scolded gently as she set him on the floor. "We don't do that. I've told you before..."

But he didn't hear her. His bare feet carried him across the floor as he ran to the stairs.

"Careful!" she called out, knowing that the overly energetic Walter was most likely already halfway down the staircase.

After touching up her *kapp* she returned downstairs to see what Mary needed.

"I have a dreadful headache," she said. "Cris's *maem* wanted to see the boys. Might you take them over there, then?"

Knowing that it was fruitless to argue that Cris Junior was still feeling poorly and, in all likelihood, should not be moved, Anna merely nodded her head. *Mayhaps* the fresh air could do the child some good, she tried to convince herself. And Walter, a spitfire of energy, could certainly use some time outdoors.

They walked down the lane, Cris holding her hand while Walter ran along the fence-line, yelling at the mules. At one point, he tripped over a rock, hidden beneath the tall grass, and fell against the fence before tumbling to the ground. Anna started to rush to his side, but the child stood up and laughed, continuing to run toward his grandparents' house.

"There she is!" Salome welcomed her with a wide smile. "You were missed last night."

"*Danke*, Salome."

The older woman turned her attention toward the children, her focus on Cris Junior more than Walter. "Oh, child," she said softly, bending down a bit and placing her hands on his cheeks and turning his face from side to side.

"You must lie down, Cris. *Kum, kum*," she commanded, shepherding him to the sofa against the far wall of the kitchen. Clicking her tongue, a sound of disapproval, she shook her head as she plumped a pillow before slipping it underneath his head. "Poor lamb."

"He's feeling much better," Anna offered.

"Why, I'm sure of it!" Salome brushed Cris's hair from his forehead. "Under your care, I have no doubt that he is well-attended."

The compliment itself masked a far greater criticism. Anna didn't dare to comment on it.

"Why, these poor *kinner* come here, starving for attention as well as sweets!" She bustled over to the kitchen counter where a large, white container sat. "Speaking of which, I have cookies here and I sure wonder if anyone would like one or two."

Walter ran to her side, eager for the freshly baked cookies, while Cris merely raised his hand, too weak (or too comfortable, Anna suspected) to sit up.

"Really, Anna," Salome said, her voice kindly but firm. "You must speak with your *schwester*. These *kinner*..." She gave her typical disapproving *tsk, tsk* as she shook her head. "A little attention from her once in a while would go a long way to help them, especially when they are feeling poorly."

"I want to see the chickens!" Walter cried out, tugging at Anna's hand.

"Now, now, Walter," Salome responded before Anna could say a word. "I have to go out there and fetch their eggs. Shall we go together then?" She stood up and smoothed down the black apron that covered the front of her dress. "I'll even let you carry the basket."

Anna tried to hide a smile. Little things like carrying a basket or collecting eggs from the chicken coop meant a lot to Walter. His mother, who tended to worry about everything, told him he was too young to take on those responsibilities. She had just cause, for Walter was very rambunctious and became excited quite easily. In those moments, he was prone to dropping things or not doing a chore particularly well. While such little mishaps didn't bother Anna or Salome, Mary preferred to avoid taking chances.

Grandmother and grandson walked to the door, Walter's legs moving faster than Salome's as he tried to beat her to the door without looking too anxious. After all, collecting and carrying the eggs was a task for mature boys.

When the door shut behind the two of them, Anna turned toward Cris Junior. "You poor child," she said. "I'm sorry you must stay inside on such a nice day. But another day of rest will clear up this illness, for sure and certain."

"You reckon, *Aendi*?"

She sat beside him on the sofa and gently patted his arm. "*Ja*, I sure do. God heals all and I've been praying for Him to heal you."

"*Danke*," he replied softly, a hint of a smile on his lips.

"And I am not the only one praying for you to recover," she continued, her voice soft and soothing. "Your *maem* and *daed*, your other *aendis*, your *grossmammi* and *grossdawdi*..."

"All those people?"

Anna laughed. "Oh, *ja*, Cris. All of those people are praying for you."

A look of self-importance crossed his face, and Anna decided to let him have that moment. After all, it wasn't often when the *kinner* were truly the center of attention, at least not from what she had seen. While pride was frowned upon, a little shot of confidence certainly couldn't hurt a child, especially one like Cris.

After a moment, she sighed and brushed her finger over his cheek. He was still pale and his skin felt dewy. "You should rest a spell now," she said.

"Will you sit with me?"

"Of course. If that's what would please you."

Not five minutes passed before his breathing slowed and his eyes closed, a light sleep overtaking him. Anna watched his chest rise and fall, wondering at the miracle of life that her sister, Mary, had been so blessed to witness yet so unwilling to enjoy. Loving the two children, even Walter with his energetic ways, came naturally to Anna.

"Excuse me," a deep voice said from the doorway.

Startled, Anna jumped just enough to display her surprise at seeing Freman standing at the entrance to the kitchen. With no way to avoid his presence, she lowered her eyes for a moment, too flustered by the unexpected appearance of the only person she did not particularly wish to encounter.

He too appeared uneasy and stepped no further into the kitchen. "I thought I might find the Musser *schwesters* here." He hesitated, that momentary pause speaking more than any words might convey about what he was thinking. He turned his body to such an angle that he could look out the door and she could not see his expression. "I...I mentioned I would stop by today to visit."

"I haven't seen them this morning," Anna admitted, surprised at the steadiness of her voice. "But I'm sure they must be around somewhere if they were expecting you."

He cleared his throat, glancing, just once, over his shoulder to look at her. His eyes drifted to Cris Junior, still napping on the sofa. "I do hope the boy is feeling better."

Anna glanced down at Cris, knowing full well that, had Cris not asked her to sit with him, she would have found an excuse to remove herself from Freman's presence. Just being near Freman sent her heart into conflicting waves of emotion. Not knowing how to respond, or, perhaps, not truly wanting to engage in conversation with him, Anna remained silent. The room, however, did not; for Walter raced into the room, slipping by Freman and running over to where Anna sat next to his older brother.

"Don't tease him, Walter," Anna scolded, a quiet gentleness in her tone. "He needs his rest."

Rather than leave the sofa, Walter grabbed at Anna's apron and startled climbing onto her lap. He laughed and tried to reach over to poke his brother in the stomach.

"Walter, you are being very naughty," she said, her voice a little firmer. "And after your *grossmammi* let you collect the eggs! I dare say she won't let you do that tomorrow if you keep behaving like this."

At this comment, rather than retreat, Walter slipped around her back so that she couldn't reach him with her hands unless she turned around which, certainly, would have disturbed Cris's nap. Already Cris Junior was stirring, his brother's laughter and bouncing on the sofa having interrupted his sleep. With great mischief in his giggles, Walter clung to her neck and leaned against her back. Though small, he was heavy enough to knock her forward, and she caught herself on the arm of the sofa.

Just as Anna was ready to scold Walter one last time, she was surprised to feel him suddenly removed from her back. It took her a moment to realize that Freman had plucked the spunky two-year-old from her person and promptly set him down upon the ground. Anna was just about to express her gratitude, as well as her embarrassment that Walter had so misbehaved, when she realized that Freman did not wish to hear such words from her. He focused on the young child, instead, distracting him by swooping him into his arms and whirling him in the air. Walter giggled and forgot about Anna, his joy at having someone's attention, even a stranger's, suddenly much more attractive than fighting for hers.

The kindness that Freman displayed by removing the rowdy child conflicted with his apparent evasion of further interaction with her. The incident left her speechless and agitated to the point of complete silence. Mercifully, the door opened again moments later, this time producing Salome with Leah and Hannah in tow. Her mind was in such turmoil that Anna could not stay to watch the interactions, so joyous and hopeful on the part of the two young women. Instead, she quietly excused herself and slipped out the side door, needing time to reflect on what had just happened and how one small act of kindness had sent her into a tailspin of shame.

❧ *Chapter Six* ❧

IN THE NEXT few days, the frequency with which Freman visited the Mussers' farm quickly dispelled any of Anna's hopes that she might be able to avoid his company. With Salome inviting Anna to visit, or her nephews pulling her next door, Anna could not escape hearing Freman's voice as he chatted with Leah or Hannah. Each day, he brought along goodies from the general store: pickled mushrooms, a shoofly pie, or farmer's cheese. One day he even added some fresh-cut flowers, careful to offer them to Salome for fear that his intentions could be misconstrued by giving them to any other potential recipient.

From what she learned from Mary, who was only too happy to share the latest news with her husband and sister after the two boys went to bed Saturday evening, Freman had returned to the area with one, and only one, intention: to find a wife.

"Clearly we shall have a wedding to attend this season!" Mary gushed. "We should start cleaning the flower beds and make certain to remove the dying petunias. They never did get very bushy."

Cris sat at the head of the table with the two women on either side, a coffee cup by his one hand and a small bowl of popcorn by the other. He was reading *The Budget*, the weekly newspaper to which most Amish households subscribed; it was his only deviation from reading the Bible. "*Ja*, I hear you, Mary," he said as he reached for a handful of popcorn. "This is *wunderbarr* popcorn!" He glanced up, looking first at Mary and then at Anna, one eyebrow lifted in an inquisitive kind of way.

"Brewer's yeast," Anna said softly. "I added brewer's yeast to the salt seasoning."

Despite having initiated the conversation, Mary showed no interest in discussing popcorn. Instead she continued rattling off her list of tasks that needed attention for the upcoming wedding, a wedding she had already scheduling in her mind. "And the front door should be painted, Cris. It took such a beating from the sun and the heat this summer..." She waved her hand in the air. "Dreadful. With a wedding at your *maem*'s, we can't have tongues wagging that we don't care for our *haus*!"

"A wedding? You're putting the buggy before the horse, my *fraa*," Cris said lightly.

Mary huffed at the slight. "Why, I think I know enough to recognize when a man is interested in a woman! And your sisters...why, one of them would be a right *gut* companion for Freman!" She turned to Anna, unaware of the pain she had just inflicted on her own sister. "I heard he has a lovely business in Indiana. A carpentry store that makes sheds. He has a whole staff of people," Mary said. "That's why he can visit for so long, you see. He's become quite successful."

"I see" was the only reply that Anna could muster.

While Mary continued rambling on with various bits and pieces of gossip that she had picked up, Anna retreated within herself. She remembered that Freman had an affinity for carpentry. It was one of the very reasons why Lydia Rothberger had expressed concern for his interest in Anna. Carpentry was not a very successful business for an Amish man, according to Lydia. And after all, Freman did not come from a family that specialized in working with wood. There was no business to pass from father to son. And, even more important, Holmes County was overrun with carpenters, and many of them were out of work.

To Anna, it didn't matter whether or not Freman was successful; at least, not in the way that Mary talked about. Instead Anna felt her heart swell with joy that, despite the doubt that so many people had expressed in him, Freman was following his dream. No one had been able to persuade him otherwise.

If only I had been as brave, she pondered.

She looked up, startled at the harshness of Mary's voice.

"I said could you answer the door! Someone is knocking." She frowned and stared back into her coffee cup. "Would you have them wait, then?"

If Anna wanted to ask why Mary hadn't answered the door herself, she made no such inquiry. Instead, she quickly stood up and hurried to the door, surprised to see Leah and Hannah standing there with smiles on their faces.

"The sun is setting, Anna, just over the field," Hannah said. "We're going to go walk to see it. It's the perfect night!"

"Come with us!" Leah urged.

From the kitchen came the sound of a chair's legs scraping against the floor. Before Anna could respond to the invitation, Mary stood behind her and peered over her shoulder.

"A walk? Why, I'd like to go on a walk! I've been cooped up all day, haven't I, Anna?"

Leah's expression of joy quickly changed to one that was more serious. "It's a long walk to the top of the hill, Mary."

"Long and steep," Hannah added.

Mary clicked her tongue and reached for her sweater that hung on the wall. "Well," she huffed. "I don't think that should stop me at all!"

Gratefully, only Anna saw the look exchanged between Leah and Hannah. Over the past few days, Anna had heard more of her share from both parties in regards to what they truly thought of the other. For Mary, she focused on how often her husband's family slighted her or didn't include her in certain events or outings. For Leah and Hannah, they expressed how comfortable they were around Anna and lamented the fact that it was not she who had accepted their brother's offer of marriage.

To all of this, Anna remained silent, knowing that there was nothing she could add to either conversation that would be remotely useful.

By the time Mary had fetched her shawl, for she claimed fear of catching a chill, Cris too stood outside and waited with Leah and Hannah. Anna glanced up toward the second-story windows, silently wondering about leaving both *kinner* alone in the house. Seeing the concerned look on her sister's face, Mary scoffed and waved her hand dismissively.

"Oh, Anna! They are both sound asleep. We won't be gone more than…what?…thirty minutes?" She gave a small laugh. "A nice walk will do us all good, *ja*?"

Behind her, Leah and Hannah looked at each other, a gentle lifting of their eyebrows saying more than words could express about their thoughts of Mary's behavior. Cris, however, sighed and shook his head. "I best catch up with you women," he said as he started walking toward the house. "I'll fetch Mother to keep an eye on the *kinner*, then."

Mary gave a short, exasperated sigh and started walking in the opposite direction, leaving the other three women behind as she mumbled about Cris worrying so much about sleeping children. Lowering her head, Anna fell into step behind her sister, embarrassed both by the clear disregard felt by Mary for her own children and by her sisters-in-laws' clear disdain for Mary.

The four women walked down the lane, the sun curving in the sky as it dipped toward the hill behind the back fields. True to Leah's words, the incline of the hill was steep. Additionally, the dew upon the grass darkened the hem of her dress. The air, however, remained cool.

Leah and Hannah ran ahead, laughing as they ascended the hill. Anna walked slower, more out of kindness to Mary, who struggled along the forged path.

"My word," she complained, slipping once on the grass. "Is there not any other place to see that sun set? And where is that husband of mine?" She reached for Anna's extended hand and righted herself. "You'd think he'd be here to assist me!"

"He's coming now," Anna said as she glanced over her sister's shoulder. "And with someone else too, it looks like!" She squinted as she tried to see who accompanied him. "*Mayhaps* it's Raymond?"

Mary straightened her dress and looked in the direction of her husband. "*Nee*," she said. "He's too tall to be Raymond." After a brief hesitation, Mary smiled. "Why, that's Freman Whittmore!" She laughed and clapped her hands together once. "I bet he's come calling for Hannah!"

The words tore through Anna and she looked away, ashamed at the way her heart pounded and her palms sweated. *You had your chance*, she told herself. *And you threw it away to please others.* She knew that she had no right to deny happiness to either Leah or Hannah. If Freman was intent on marrying one of the Mussers' daughters, Anna would express her joy and happiness for that union in public, even if she cried in the solitude of her own room.

As Cris and Freman approached, Mary began waving, a wide smile on her face. Anna wondered at her sister's overt jubilation at Freman's presence, especially given her less-than-gleeful mood just moments prior.

"What a *wunderbarr gut* surprise, Freman!"

He nodded his head in her direction, his eyes briefly meeting Anna's before he looked toward the top of the hill. Seeing Leah and Hannah waving at him, he lifted his hand in response before returning his attention to the two women standing before him. "A lovely sunset indeed," he said, his voice flat and emotionless.

Mary laughed, still giddy and behaving like a young girl in a way that brought color to Anna's cheeks. She averted her eyes when her sister gushed, "God blessed us with this cool evening air. A welcome change from the heat, *ja*?"

"Oh, now, Mary, what heat? I would say God's taken right *gut* care of us this summer," Cris countered. "Not too hot and the crops received just enough water."

Anna started walking again, more than eager to put a little distance between herself and the discussion behind her, and noticed Hannah returning to Cris and Mary. Now she wished that she had volunteered to stay behind with the boys.

Clearing his throat, Freman mumbled, "Excuse me," and quickened his pace. With more energy in his step, he passed them and hurried ahead to join Leah, who stood on the crest of the hill.

Despite not wanting to, Anna's eyes trailed after him, watching his back as he walked up the incline. His broad shoulders certainly spoke of his work ethic; no man who lazed about could be so strong and muscular. The straw hat that sat atop his head looked new, the brim perfectly maintained, an indication that he did not work outdoors. Farmers frequently removed their hats to wipe the sweat from their brows, damaging them in the process. Since replacing hats wasn't always practical, farmers were easily identified from those Amish men who worked mostly indoors.

At the top of the hill, already waiting for the others, Freman and Leah stood facing the setting sun. Engaged in admiring the beautiful colors that filled the horizon, neither one noticed Anna. Not wishing to interrupt them or be viewed as eavesdropping, Anna stood slightly apart from them, wishing that the others would hurry up and finish their ascent. Despite the distance between herself and the couple, Anna could not, however, avoid overhearing their conversation since their voices carried on the evening breeze.

"What a lovely view," Freman said, his hands behind his back as he stared toward the sun. "I have missed such beautiful sunsets. I believe that God paints Ohio's skies with a special brush."

Leah glanced up at him, a look upon her face that Anna couldn't help but observe: adoration. Clearly Anna was not the only one who had noticed that Freman was particularly partial to Leah Musser. As far as Anna knew, the young woman had not courted before, and as she was almost twenty-one, the thought of marriage would certainly be at the forefront of her mind.

"Ohio is rather spectacular," Leah said.

"Have you traveled outside of the state?" The question was asked with genuine curiosity. "Indiana? Pennsylvania?"

She shook her head. "*Nee*, I have not."

Anna glanced over her shoulder, seeing Mary slip on the grass, her flat-bottomed shoes not providing enough traction. Luckily, Cris was close enough to catch her.

"It's nice to see other places," Freman said. "Of course, there is no place like home."

"It must be nice for your *schwester* to return to Ohio after so many years away," Leah stated.

"Ah, Sara." He smiled, glancing down at Leah, and for the briefest of seconds, noticing Anna standing apart from them. "She is most content to be wherever George is, I assure you."

Leah sighed. "Home is where the heart is, *ja*?"

Another glance in Anna's direction preceded his reply. "For most, although some may believe that the heart is where home is, instead." He didn't wait for Leah to comment nor did he look at Anna to see her reaction. Instead, he glanced at the sunset once again. "George and Sara had yet to return from his sister's *haus* when I left. I pray they have caught this glorious gift from God, although I should worry more about that new horse of theirs. He's apt to upset the carriage."

"Prone to spooking, then?" Leah asked.

"Indeed." Freman shook his head. "It's a wonder my *schwester* is willing to ride with George at all, being knocked about so!"

To this, Leah smiled and, in a gesture so unexpected and rare, caught his attention by touching his arm. "Oh, Freman, you might look at it as being knocked about and riding within a cloud of danger, but I can assure you that if I felt the same way about my husband as Sara feels for George, I'd never want to be left at home, either." She tilted her head and looked toward the sun so that her eyes were downcast. "I'd want to be by his side always. There would be no amount of persuasion to convince me otherwise."

Anna fought the urge to do more than glance at the couple. Their intimacy now quite apparent, Anna forced herself to walk a bit farther away, but not before she heard Freman respond.

"Is that so, Leah? Why! I find that most honorable!"

The combination of her words and his response, coupled with his previous statement about the home being, for some, where the heart is, cut straight through her. Her memory flashed back eight years prior, to the long discussions Lydia had with her regarding Freman's position being too precarious for her to consider marriage at such a young age as well as her father's insistence that not one of his daughters would marry a penniless Whittmore, regardless of whether or not he was in good standing with the Amish community.

Her hands shook and her cheeks turned red, embarrassed at her imprudent decision to have permitted herself to be persuaded to follow their counsel, not paying any mind to how much she had disagreed with it. She had used him ill, abandoning a man she cared about despite the understanding that they would wed. *Oh*, she thought, making a fist with her hands so that no one could notice her reaction, *if only I had shown greater fortitude...*

"It's getting cold!" Mary's complaint broke Anna's concentration, for which she was, actually, most thankful. "And my hem is wet!" She glanced at the sky. "And there's a dark cloud rolling in from the east! Why, this was a horrible idea. I'll be sick again before the morning sun rises!"

"It's not going to rain," Cris reassured her. As if to emphasize his statement, he gestured toward the sunset. "Just enjoy the beautiful colors for a moment, Mary. That is why we all went walking, *ja*?"

Ignoring his words, she continued to fuss. "I'm not prepared for rain! I haven't brought an umbrella!" With pursed lips and creases in her brow, she turned to face her husband. "Cris," she proclaimed in front of everyone, "I would like to return home immediately."

He sighed. "I do believe you know the way."

Anna thought she saw Hannah snicker at the rebuke from her brother to his wife.

Mary found it less than humorous. "I would think that you would take my arm and help me. That incline..." She gestured over her shoulder. "Why, I could slip and fall again!"

Without further argument, Cris took ahold of her elbow and guided her back down the trodden path that their shoes had made on the trek to the top. Hannah seemed content to stay, but a fierce look from Leah quickly convinced her otherwise.

"Come, Anna," Hannah said, her tone cheery despite realizing that Freman's attention focused on her sister and not herself. "Let's go down together. We can help each other!" Without waiting, however, Hannah started down the hill, her steps quick and sure in complete opposition to Mary, who, even with Cris's help, struggled with each move she attempted.

Realizing that Leah wanted time to walk down alone with Freman, Anna quietly proceeded down the slope. While her distance from the couple was great, the breeze carried their voices, and she could not help but overhear their discussion as they slowly meandered down the hill behind her, obviously not in any hurry to reach the bottom.

"She's good-natured in many ways, that Mary," Leah said, the intonation of her voice indicating that there was more to her statement than a compliment. "Her self-regard, however, does vex me at times." She sighed. "How we so often wish that Anna had accepted Cris's offer! She's much more suitable to our family."

Freman seemed taken aback. "Anna refused him? When did this happen?"

"Oh, I'm not quite certain. *Mayhaps* a year before he married Anna." Leah laughed nervously, clearly put off by his interest in Anna. "*Maem* and *Daed* were disappointed. *Maem* blames that Lydia Rothberger. She has such a hold over the family and apparently felt that Cris didn't suit, being that he's not as principled as Anna." Another laugh. "She is rather well-tempered and irreproachable in nature."

Freman hesitated before he said a soft, "Indeed."

Anna heard no more.

At the bottom of the hill, just a quarter mile from the farm, Cris and Mary stood beside an open-top buggy, conversing with the occupants who, in the dim gray of evening, Anna could not quite identify. As she approached, however, she heard a joyful Sara Coblentz call out her name.

"Such a refreshing night," Sara said as she reached down to take Anna's hand in greeting. Her eyes flickered over the group's heads. "Why, there's my own *bruder*! What are all of you young people doing?"

Anna did not respond, presuming the question was intended for Hannah or Leah, who approached them from the meadow beneath the hill with Freman following just a few paces behind.

With her mood much improved, Mary took it upon herself to answer. "We went walking to see the sunset over the hill."

Sara nodded her head, and with a half-turn toward her husband, said, "We saw the gorgeous colors in the sky, didn't we, George?"

"*Ja*, sure did."

Freman approached the side of the buggy, glancing at Anna as he passed her. The look could have gone unnoticed but for what happened next. He leaned over and mumbled something to his sister before asking George about his family. No sooner had George finished catching everyone up-to-date with his ailing sister than Sara moved over in the buggy and patted the seat next to her.

"*Kum*, Anna," she said. "You look peaked. Come ride with us."

The request startled Anna. While she was fatigued, especially since she had been up early that morning, she felt discomfort with the attention. "*Nee*, it's just a half-mile, but *danke*."

"I insist," Sara said, a smile on her face as she, once again, touched the empty space beside her.

To Anna's surprise, Freman reached for her arm, his touch sending a shiver throughout her body. If the close proximity in which he stood to her didn't unsettle her, the physical contact with him did. He guided her toward the carriage. Speechless, Anna followed. Truly, she had no choice. Wordlessly, he placed his hand out, gesturing toward the buggy, quietly insisting that she oblige Sara's request.

Stunned, Anna stared at him as she settled into the carriage. His perception that she had been tired from the walk and his resolution to tend to her needs left her wordless. How was it possible that, despite his apparent resentment and disdain on account of the pain she caused him so long ago, he still remained sensitive to her unspoken needs?

She stared at him as George clicked his tongue for the horse to start trotting down the remainder of the lane toward the farm. He, however, did not look after her, for he had already returned his attention to Leah and Hannah. No one seemed to think twice of Freman's gesture; however, Anna knew that it spoke of a remaining sentiment that, while lost to another now, still indicated a degree of unstated friendship and spoke highly of his fine character.

"I do believe," Sara said to her husband, obviously unaware of Anna's thoughts, "that we shall have a wedding soon, *ja*?"

"You women! Always trying to guess what's on a man's mind." George laughed at the expression on his wife's face. "It's a wonder anything is left to privacy at all!"

"George!"

Sobering, he reached over and covered her hand with his, the teasing clearly over. "Although I do admit that he does seem intent to call on one of those Musser girls."

Unable to mask her dismay, Anna stared straight ahead at the house as the buggy approached it. While Freman's interest in the two sisters, particularly Leah, was more than apparent to her, Anna couldn't help but feel a tightness in her chest when George spoke his opinion. Those words! So direct and candid. A truth spoken was more bitter than a truth suspected.

Before George turned down the driveway, Anna tried to change the subject. She noticed a light from the kitchen glowing through the front window. She pointed toward it and changed the subject. "It's later than I thought if the lamp was lit. I do hope that little Cris and Walter didn't give Salome any troubles," she managed to say, eager to disembark from the carriage.

After thanking them for their kindness, she quickly retreated into the house to relieve Salome. She was grateful that, being tired herself, the older woman did not stay to visit. Instead, she bid Anna good night, obviously eager to return to her own home. For Anna, it was a relief to shut the door and lean against it, catching her breath from the conflicting emotions that raced through her.

Had he returned to Charm already married and with *kinner*, surely she could have borne that in much grander style, *mayhaps* even joy! But to watch the unfolding of a courtship right under her nose? It was more than she could bear, although bear it she had to for there was no alternative. Choices had been made, even if she now recognized the coercion and ugly prejudice from both Lydia and her *daed*. She did not blame them; *nee*, she only blamed herself. After all, she had lacked the fortitude to stand up to them or to suggest to Freman that they should wait patiently until he had established himself and proven his viability as a carpenter. But not knowing how to navigate the stormy waters between two men she cared so much about, father and fiancé, she had thought it better to follow her father's wishes. The hurt that she had felt at her breakup with Freman was almost as great as the hurt from the idea of having to attend his wedding to Leah Musser.

She heard voices approaching, the high-pitched shrill sound of Mary's words mercifully countered by the soft, gentle baritone of Freman's voice. When Anna heard the group nearing the house, she suspected that they would sit inside to visit. Alarmed, she hurried toward the stairs.

The comfort of her small room beckoned her, its darkness a shield from the pain that she felt in her heart. Despite knowing that it was not quite adequate, she also knew that it was the only safe harbor for the emotional storm that brewed inside of her.

❧ *Chapter Seven* ❧

L ANCASTER?"

Anna wasn't certain if she had correctly heard Leah and Hannah. It was Monday morning and they had just burst into Mary's kitchen, laughing with glowing faces. They both talked at once as they practically jumped up and down, looking more like schoolchildren than young women of eighteen and twenty. Anna laughed at their jubilation, especially when little Cris followed their example, bouncing on his feet and knocking into Walter. When the younger boy fell to the floor, Anna was quick to pick him up and make him giggle before he could think of complaining.

"Heavens to Betsy!" Mary scowled. "Such a ruckus! And what an example you are setting for Cris and Walter!"

No one listened as Leah took a hold of Cris's hands and spun around, both laughing. Walter, quite content to sit on Anna's lap, clapped his hands. Hannah sat down at the table, a big smile on her face as she watched her older sister.

"If you happen to think about calming down," Mary said, "*mayhaps* you'll tell us what brought on this childish display. What is this about Lancaster I hear?"

"Freman is headed there to visit his cousin," Leah gushed, her eyes glancing in Hannah's direction at the mention of Freman, a look of advantage in her eyes. "His cousin, Benjamin Esh, suffered a great loss recently, and Freman intends to visit him before the weather changes."

"A loss?" Anna asked.

"*Ja*, he intended to get married this November, but his girl…" Leah's voice trailed away.

"Oh, mercy!" Anna knew what remained unsaid. Whether it was a farming accident, illness, or collision on the road, young people were not immune to the tragedies of life. "How sad."

Mary stared at Leah in disbelief. "I fail to see what is so joyous about that, Leah!"

"It happened in May," Leah said, as if that should, somehow, make the situation less painful for Benjamin. "Anyway, we are going with him!"

Before Anna could make sense of what Leah had just said, Hannah interrupted her sister. "A van is headed out that way! Apparently, when Freman told *Daed* about this trip, *Maem* suggested to Freman that we should also go along!" Both young women tittered at this and bounced joyfully on the balls of their bare feet. "*Daed* said we could!"

This time, it was Leah interrupting Hannah. "Isn't that just *wunderbarr*! Lancaster County! Why, I've always wanted to go there!"

"Why on earth would he permit the two of you to travel to Lancaster?" Mary's off-handed comment, singed with more spice than sugar, was ignored by the two enthusiastic young women.

"We're to visit with *Maem*'s cousins, the ones that live in Leola."

"The Blanks?" Mary made a face. "What on earth for? Salome hasn't seen them in...oh, what?...twenty-plus years, I suppose!"

Leah frowned at her sister-in-law. "That's not the point!"

"And I seem to recall your *maem* thinking unfavorably about one of the Blanks. The mother, I reckon."

Sighing, Leah rolled her eyes and returned her attention to Anna. Once more, she became joyous again. "We're leaving on Thursday in the morning and will return Tuesday. It's just for a few nights, but we'll attend worship and fellowship there! And then they are having a special youth gathering on Sunday! Won't that be fun to visit with *Maem*'s cousins, meet new people, and see how they worship? I do wonder if it will be much different than *our* services."

Hannah didn't wait for Leah to catch her breath before she added, "You must come, Anna. It simply wouldn't be complete without you!"

Both the news and their request were completely unexpected and caught Anna off-guard.

All afternoon, she had been sitting at the kitchen counter, peeling apples for making applesauce, a staple at the table since both little Cris and Walter often ate three helpings of it, especially when the vegetables weren't to their liking. And, unless Anna was the one to cook, the boys often wrinkled their nose at the overcooked, limp vegetables that graced the table.

"I don't know what to say," she stammered. She had never left Ohio. In fact, she had never left Holmes County. What was the need? Her family and life were here; she never had any reason to travel outside of the area. The thought of traveling so far away unnerved her. "Where would we stay?"

"*Maem*'s cousins live in Leola, but we are to stay with the Esh family."

"Leola?" Anna had never heard of such a place. "And why the Esh family? I'm not familiar with any of these people."

"It's nearby. The Esh family are Freman's relatives, and their son is his good friend. Apparently the Esh family has a large farm there. A farm that the son is to inherit." Leah stole another look at Hannah as if to suggest something.

"Oh, please!" Hannah waved away Leah's insinuation. Everyone knew that she courted Caleb, even if an announcement had still to be announced. Still, under the cloak of evening shadows and in the privacy of her own home, Mary often wondered out loud why he hadn't spoken to Raymond and Salome yet, speculating that it wasn't a definite marriage.

Apparently, Leah felt the same way. "Think about it, Hannah! I hear that Pennsylvania's winters aren't half as horrid as ours! You'd do quite well living in Pennsylvania with their cute little heart-shaped prayer *kapp*s!"

Ignoring Leah's teasing, Hannah reached for Anna's hands. "Say you'll join us!"

Before she could answer, Mary stepped forward and interrupted the conversation. "This is outrageous! I fail to see why Cris and I couldn't join you too!" She looked at Leah, her mouth pressed into a firm and clearly dissatisfied line. "It's as if we aren't allowed to experience anything out of the norm, just because we are married! There is no reason for omitting us in your invitation. We are family too, ain't that so?"

At this comment, the joy evaporated from the air. For just a moment, Leah and Hannah stood there, the former with her mouth hanging open and the latter with a dumbfounded expression on her face. The silence hung heavy between them. Hadn't the girls learned anything from their sunset walk a few nights ago? They should know by now that, upon learning of any social event or adventure, their sister-in-law would insist upon participating, regardless of her responsibilities with her home and children.

Wishing she was anywhere but there, Anna bent her head over the apple in her hand, focusing her attention on peeling it in the hopes that she wouldn't be called upon to respond.

That responsibility fell upon Leah's shoulders.

"Why, Mary," Leah said. "Little Cris and Walter—"

"—Can stay with your *maem*!" Mary quickly added, interrupting Leah. "I've never been to Lancaster, and with just these two small ones, this might be our last opportunity to travel alone."

Leah laughed. "I fail to see your reasons for that statement, Mary! People travel with their *kinner* all the time."

Mary looked at Anna, drilling her with her eyes. "If you go, I most certainly need to go. After all, you are staying here to help me. You know how sick I have been."

"I really do not have to go," Anna offered, her voice sounding meek against Mary's.

Ignoring her sister, Mary began to think out loud. "And Cris should accompany us too. I mean, honestly, how much do we really know about this Freman Whittmore?" With great purpose, she looked at each of the three women, taking her time to assess their reactions. "Hmm? And I certainly don't think young women traveling alone with a single man are going to lead to anything except gossip anyway!" She straightened her apron, a prim expression on her face. "A chaperone. That's what you need. Someone older and more...responsible, to guide and oversee you."

Leah lifted her chin and stared at her sister-in-law, the muscles tightening in her jaw. Anna held her breath, watching and waiting for what she presumed would be an interesting, if not deliberately hostile, response.

"I highly doubt that the bishop would welcome any such gossip in his *g'may*, indeed," Leah said in an even tone. "Especially since he is to accompany us on this journey."

Stifling a laugh, Anna bit her lower lip and returned her attention to the apples.

Mary, however, gasped and put her hand on her hip, staring down at Leah. "*Ach*!" she said sharply. "You never mentioned that this was a retreat of any type! For shame, Leah, not telling me that! And with the bishop attending, it's even more dreadful of you to not include us!"

Hoping to redirect everyone's attention to a more peaceful topic, especially since Anna was firmly convinced that Mary would now occupy a seat in the van that would take Leah and Hannah to Lancaster, Anna changed the subject. "It's a lovely time of year to travel, I'm sure. However, I best stay here with the *kinner*."

To Mary's chagrin, Hannah immediately went to Anna and grasped her shoulders. "*Nee*, Anna. Leah and I are most determined that you should go with us! It's only for a few days and you, of all people, need the change of environment."

"You've never been there, ain't so?" Leah asked.

With the focus of the discussion on her, Anna knew that Mary's temper would flare again. To her credit, her sister contained it as best as she could, choosing not to respond with words but demeanor. With a loud huff, she stomped out of the kitchen and disappeared through the door, most likely to track down Cris and share the news of an upcoming trip.

Her absence was barely noticed, such was the excitement from Leah and Hannah. Their enthusiasm to talk meant that Anna did not have to contribute to the conversation. For that, she was grateful.

But truth be told, the last thing she wanted was to travel for so many hours in a van with Freman Whittmore. The close proximity to him would surely cause her more pain than she felt able to bear. Still, she could scarcely say no to the two young women who begged and pleaded with her, saying that they too would stay home if Anna did not accompany them. While Anna tried to make her point that the two young children would need her, especially considering Mary's determination to travel along, both Leah and Hannah stood strong, neither one willing to hear an argument against having Anna's companionship on their journey.

With great reluctance, Anna could do nothing more than acquiesce. Their perseverance and their reasoning outweighed her objections. As the two young women discussed what they would bring and wondered what Lancaster would look like, Anna managed to pick up another apple, eager to push this upcoming journey into the furthest corners of her mind.

While the thought of traveling in a van for so many hours, Freman seated just mere feet from her, brought her dread, she also knew that she had only herself to blame. Time and distance had not healed that wound. At the time, Anna didn't know how to argue against the people who guided her through life. Her *own* life.

With a heavy heart Anna realized that, eight years later, she still did not have the strength to stand up to the decisions made by others on her behalf.

❧ *Chapter Eight* ❧

THE EXPANSIVE FARMS sat in low valleys between the hills as they drove down the main street in Leola, Pennsylvania, a scene quite different from the towns in Holmes County, Ohio. Due to the flat nature of the valley, the fields flowed in a way that Anna had never seen before. In Ohio the hilly nature of the farms meant that farmers had to compartmentalize their fields so that crops were often grouped together and separated by fences. Not so in Lancaster, Anna observed. But in both places the first shade of autumn—yellow—had colored many of the trees, with the first burst of reds and oranges not far behind. Leola in early October promised to be as splendid as Sugarcreek in that regard.

With eyes large and curious, she stared out the window, seeing the white barns with open planks and large tobacco leaves hanging from the rafters. Such a beautiful vision, she thought. In one field, a man, his beard long and gray, sat hunched over on a corn binder, four cream-colored Belgian draft horses pulling the piece of machinery along the rows of brown corn stalks. As the van passed, the man lifted his hand and waved to the driver and the occupants.

At the top of the next hill, the driver turned left and drove down a long, straight road. Anna's eyes searched the fields, taking in the large houses, often expanded multiple times to accommodate new additions to the family, looking strangely out-of-proportion to the barns. In many cases, the houses were three times the size of the other outbuildings. Unlike Holmes County, Ohio, the Amish of Lancaster County seemed to build additions onto their houses, almost as if the family lived in a small community. With land being so expensive, and disappearing at an alarming rate, Anna understood the need to have several generations living under the same roof or on the same property. However, she much preferred the smaller houses of the Amish in her native Holmes County in Ohio.

The bishop had slept for most of the journey, although his companion, another bishop named Wilmer Kaufman—who lived in a nearby *g'may*—seemed content to talk with Freman for most of the journey. Since Freman sat beside the driver, Wilmer leaned forward as he talked. While the discussion mostly focused on crop rotation and Scripture, it appeared to Anna that Wilmer conducted most of the conversation, voicing his opinions as facts and ignoring the emotionless expression on Freman's face. As neither a farmer nor an evangelist, Freman certainly had little to contribute, a fact which apparently pleased Wilmer. Within one hour of their journey, it was clear to Anna that this Wilmer enjoyed speaking almost as much as he enjoyed hearing himself.

Behind the two bishops, Cris and Mary occupied the middle row of the van. For the duration of the long drive, Mary fussed and fidgeted, occasionally complaining that the seat was uncomfortable and her back ached from sitting for so long. To his credit, Cris offered his sympathies and, at one point, offered to switch places with her on the off chance that his seat was more comfortable.

The remaining three women occupied the rear row of the van. Anna sat by the window, which afforded her the opportunity to either watch the scenery unfold or sneak fleeting, undetected looks at Freman. The giddiness with which Leah and Hannah had embraced the idea of the journey seemed to wear thin when they had been in the vehicle for over three hours and with another three hours still ahead of them. Yet, unlike Mary, neither one complained. They merely shut their eyes and let sleep overtake them, which, to her relief, had left Anna alone with her thoughts.

"Here's our place," Freman suddenly indicated, pointing to a large farm at the next driveway, a long one that cut between two large fields. In the distance Anna thought she saw a pond glimmer under the sun.

As the van pulled down the driveway, she turned her attention to the house. It was more contemporary than the other farms they had driven past. With a wide front porch that wrapped around the south side of the house, Anna imagined that Jonas and Rebecca Esh might often pause to observe glorious sunsets from such a vantage point. It was something she, herself, would certainly do should she be ever so fortunate as to have such a view from her own home.

There were numerous flower beds in front of the porch, planted with hardy mums and ornamental cabbage to reflect the change from summer to autumn. To the north of the house was a large two-story barn. The double doors at its entrance were wide open, and she could see a horse standing in a stall, its ears perked forward at the noise of the vehicle coming up the driveway.

"Hello there!" a voice called from the depths of the barn as they disembarked from the van. A man emerged through the doors, a large black dog at his heels. He was a short man with bright blue eyes and a gray beard that was trimmed in such a way that it just touched the top button of his shirt. His black trousers had four horizontal buttons just under the waist, and he wore large clunky boots upon his feet. He seemed pleasant enough, and Anna knew at once that she would like him.

"Freman! Right *gut* to see you!" He extended his hand to shake Freman's before being introduced to the others. From the expression on his face, Anna also knew that he was genuinely pleased to welcome them to his farm.

The two older men, however, and in particular Bishop Kaufman, seemed anxious to continue their journey, for they were headed farther east to Pequea. Bishop Kaufman stated as much to Jonas Esh and abruptly turned toward the van. Bishop Troyer, demonstrating more manners and grace, cleared his throat before confirming with Freman that the group would be retrieved on Tuesday morning at four. Slipping a piece of paper into Freman's hand, a note that contained a phone number to reach him in Pequea, the bishop bade good-bye to the rest of the group and returned to the van, assuming the front passenger seat while Bishop Kaufman returned to the backseat.

Jonas Esh led the group to the house. "Rebecca has been baking all day," he said, smiling as they climbed the steps to the porch. "So excited for company."

"I hope we didn't trouble her," Anna said softly. "Five people for company might be more than she anticipated."

He laughed. "Nonsense. A home is happiest when there are lots of people in it to share fellowship! We raised our *kinner* here and plan to raise lots of grand-babies here too!" He opened the door and pushed it open. "Providence just didn't provide them for us." He winked at her. "Yet." Stepping aside, he gestured for everyone to enter before him.

The downstairs of the house was large and open, the floor plan having been designed with an Amish family in mind. Anna soon learned that Jonas and Rebecca Esh had six children, four married daughters who lived in neigh-boring towns, and two sons, Benjamin being the one set to inherit the large farm and Jacob, who had not felt moved to become a baptized member of the Amish church.

When she learned this, Anna glanced at Rebecca. With her rotund face and pink cheeks, she reminded Anna of her grandmother on her mother's side. The memory warmed her insides, and once again, Anna was struck with an immediate sense of ease in their company.

Within minutes, Benjamin entered through a back door, having seen the van arrive from the fields where he had been working. With dust on his face and freckles on his nose, he looked younger than his twenty-three years. He wiped his hands on his black pants before he greeted the visitors. Unlike his parents, he did not smile, nor did he have bright, sparkling eyes, a fact that caught her off-guard.

There was an aura of dullness about him, one that star-tled Anna, for it was a look that she knew all too well. While Freman introduced everyone, Anna studied the young man, wondering at the depths of his pain and why more than six months later, he could still be so intensely mournful for a woman who had not even been his wife.

However, as soon as she thought that, she reproached herself. Eight years after her own loss, she too was still grieving. Why should she expect that Benjamin could regain his spirits so soon after the death of his intended?

And yet, she knew, despite his pain and sorrow, he would find another to replace his lost love. He was a young man with a grand future still ahead of him: not every young man could offer a bride such potential sustenance. So, while she recognized the depth of his grief, she remained dubious as to the eventual breadth of it.

Shortly after five o'clock, they sat for the supper meal, one that was far larger than Anna suspected was normal for the Esh family. The larger farmer's table, however, fit them nicely. After they were situated, Jonas bowed his head for the silent prayer over the meal, the others immediately doing the same. A long minute later, he looked up and the rest of the group finished their prayers. With a big smile, Jonas reached for the plate of warm ham and began to dish it onto his plate.

During the meal, Jonas told stories about how he had grown up with Freman's mother before she married and moved to Ohio. Rebecca smiled during his stories, laughing at all of the right moments of conversation while she kept an eye on everyone's plates. If she saw that someone's dish became even slightly empty, she began passing around food items to refill it.

"And then Freman came to live with us," Jonas said, with a look of admiration at the man who sat across from Benjamin. "When was that, now?" He tugged at his beard and looked at the ceiling as if counting in his head. "Oh, I'd say eight years now?" He waited for affirmation from

Freman, who merely inclined his head. "*Ja*, just about eight years, I reckon."

Anna almost gasped aloud. So this was where Freman had retreated when she had refused his offer of marriage? Now she understood better. It was no wonder that he had been so concerned about Benjamin. If he had lived with the Esh family, his cousin would seem more like a brother to him. Unable to stop herself, she looked at Benjamin and wondered how much Freman had confided in him. If so, surely Jonas and Rebecca knew too. That realization caused her a moment of panic: What on earth must they think of her? While she knew that it was not in the nature of the Amish to judge others, she also knew that the reality of their culture often spoke otherwise.

"Stayed for five or so years, ain't so?"

"Pass the potatoes down to Cris," Rebecca said softly as she nudged Anna with the bowl.

"Stayed until the wind blew him off to Indiana. Guess he had enough with the strictness of the Pennsylvania Amish!" He laughed when he said it and sent a wink in Hannah's direction. While stricter with their religious practices, they were certainly not lacking in humor.

Freman turned his attention to Benjamin. "I heard of a new carpentry shop not far from here. A Miller's Woodshop?"

"*Ja*, I know John Miller."

"*Mayhaps* you might take me to see it tomorrow?" He gestured toward the women. "They will be visiting with their cousins, and my time would be better suited seeing how this Miller is making out with his new business."

His cousin nodded.

Anna saw a look pass between Freman and Benjamin's mother. It was a look that she did not need interpreted. Suddenly she realized that it was no accident that so many people had descended upon the Esh family. Yes, Freman had traveled to Lancaster out of concern for his cousin, but undoubtedly his aunt had contacted Freman out of concern for her son. By bringing the others, Freman intended to lighten Benjamin's mood, instilling him with a new sense of life.

He knows the sense of loss as deeply as Benjamin and I do, she thought, realizing the bitter irony of her own presence at the Esh home.

"Perhaps after we help clean the supper dishes," Anna heard herself say, staring directly at Benjamin, "you might take us walking?" She smiled at Leah, who sat next to him. "I'm sure we all would benefit from stretching our legs and seeing the country a bit, *ja*?"

It was after six o'clock when they finally set out upon their evening walk. To no one's surprise, Mary had begged to be excused, claiming that what she needed most was to lie down and rest. Without her participation, the rest of the group paired off, Hannah enjoying the company of her older brother without any interference from his overly opinionated wife, Leah falling in beside Freman, and Anna walking beside Benjamin.

While they walked, Benjamin pointed out different farms along the road. However, given that the road was flat and the farms so spread apart, he had soon shared all that knowledge before they had traveled very far. For a few moments, Anna walked silently, wondering how to start a conversation with a man so clearly distraught over the loss of his fiancée.

"Freman told us of your loss, Benjamin," she finally said. "I am very sorry. Losing someone you care for is never easy."

Benjamin took a deep breath and kicked at a loose stone in the road. "'The Lord is close to the brokenhearted and saves those who are crushed in spirit,'" he said, quoting from the book of Psalms. "Do you believe that, Anna?"

His question surprised her, and she couldn't help but look up at him in wonder. Out of the corner of her eye, she noticed that Freman slowed his pace, his eyes scanning the horizon as if mesmerized by the change of scenery, despite having lived there for so many years. It occurred to her that he might have intentionally modified his pace in order to overhear her response.

"I do believe that," Anna replied, her voice carrying in the air. "I too have suffered a loss." She paused, just enough time for Benjamin to gasp. Lifting her hand, she stopped him before he offered his condolences. "*Nee*, it was many years ago—my mother. But a lost love is difficult too."

"Such a tragedy to lose your mother," he mumbled, shaking his head.

"It is only through my faith in the Lord that my spirit is lifted at all," she continued. "After all, Jesus bore our grief and carried our sorrows so that we wouldn't have to. I take great comfort in that thought. Even with a heart that remains torn in two."

He sighed. "We might suffer together, I reckon."

As a gray-topped buggy passed by, Benjamin lifted his hand to wave. By this time, Freman and Leah were in front of them, and as such, the four of them walked together. Anna listened to their conversation with only partial interest. They spoke of people that she didn't know and places she had never visited. She did, however, notice that Leah hung on every word, appropriately smiling when Freman told a pleasant recollection and carefully shaking her head when Benjamin shared a sorrowful one. There seemed to be a careful balance between the two men, and toward the end of their walk, both appeared more relaxed, whether from the company or the conversation, Anna could not tell.

Over an hour had passed by the time they returned to the Esh farm, the sun having set and the sky turning a grayish-blue color. The stars hadn't come out yet, but Anna could tell that the sky would not be as full of them as at home. Despite the darkness, there was a glow from the *Englische* houses and nearby cities that would certainly drown out the crisp twinkling of lights in the night sky.

As they filed into the kitchen, the women removed their shawls and sweaters while the men hung their straw hats on hooks near the door. Jonas sat at the kitchen table, reading the paper, while Rebecca leaned over the open door of the oven. A sweet scent filled the kitchen as she removed a baking sheet of fresh, baked cookies. Using a quilted pot holder, she set the tray on a cooling rack before she turned around, smiling as she greeted them.

"Refreshing walk, then?" She glanced at Benjamin, her eyes lighting up when she noticed the change in her son's demeanor.

Without being asked, Anna went to Rebecca's side to help her wash the dishes.

"*Danke*, Anna." Rebecca wiped her hands on her black apron. "Thought I'd send some cookies over for your *aendi*," she added, directing this to Hannah and Leah.

"Haven't seen her in a while and I would so love to go visit. Unfortunately, I'm already committed to help our neighbors with making applesauce." While her words spoke of regret, Rebecca did not look completely remorseful in Anna's opinion. And she suspected she knew why.

"Mayhaps Anna might accompany you?"

The suggestion surprised her just as much as the person who offered it: Freman.

"Oh?" Rebecca raised an eyebrow and looked at her. She too seemed surprised by Freman's words. However, from the sparkle in her eyes, so dark and warm, the idea was not unpleasant to her. "That would be lovely." She paused, a quick glance cast in Mary's direction before she added, "Would you like to go along, then? I'm sure you may enjoy it." As if an afterthought, she quickly added, "That is, unless you'd prefer to visit with the Blanks."

Words escaped her. For what seemed like an eternity to Anna, she stood there, too aware that everyone watched her and waited for her response. While she wanted to speak, her mind was focused, not on what she wanted to say, but on the fact that Freman had obviously suggested an alternative in order to ensure her enjoyment of the day.

"I..." Her eyes flickered from Rebecca, who waited expectantly, to Freman, who merely lifted one eyebrow as he watched her. The expression on his face, so serene and calm as if he had not just said anything at all, made her catch her breath. Had she just imagined that he spoke? Yet, when she returned her attention to Rebecca, she knew that she had heard correctly. "I...should like that very much," she managed to say at last.

No one appeared to notice that anything was amiss. Rebecca seemed delighted, and since plans were now arranged for Friday, everyone else began to discuss their plans for Saturday. The men discussed the potential of attending a horse auction in a nearby town. Mary quickly stated that she too would like to go. Before anyone could object, both of the Musser sisters readily voiced their enthusiasm for the idea.

Anna, however, was left standing by the sink, dumbfounded as she pondered the meaning behind Freman's words.

Hours later, under the cover of darkness, her mind still raced. She lay on a twin mattress in the bedroom that she shared with Leah and Hannah, listening to their soft breathing as they slept. She, however, couldn't stop thinking about his words and remembering the expression on his face. Under the cover of darkness, she still could not make sense of it.

Clearly his behavior conflicted sharply with his words. Since his reappearance in Sugarcreek several weeks ago, he had barely paid any attention to her. Even that very day, despite traveling for hours in the same van, he directed no questions toward her. And, just moments before, when the group had been outside for their walk, he seemed to purposefully focus his attention on conversing with Benjamin or Leah. However, when he made the suggestion that she accompany Rebecca to the neighbors, it was clear that this was not a random proposition; he had obviously given thought to this matter before he spoke.

This left her with a burning question: what had driven Freman to propose such a thing?

❧ Chapter Nine ❧

WHEN SHE HEARD Leah and Hannah whispering, their voices low and hushed so as not to wake her, Anna's eyes fluttered open. At first, she couldn't quite place where she was. Sunlight streamed through the window near the foot of her bed. The brightness in the room felt warm and welcoming, unlike the darkness that usually greeted her when she awoke at Mary and Cris's home. Focusing on the slanted ceiling hanging quite low over her head, she frowned: everything felt unfamiliar, including the sounds of other people in the room.

And then she remembered where she was.

"Did we wake you, then?"

Anna looked across the room at Leah. She was already dressed and leaning against the door, a pretty picture with her hair pinned back and her blue dress matching the color of her eyes. Having arisen earlier than her sister, Leah waited patiently while Hannah sat on the edge of the double bed that they had shared, brushing her long hair as it hung over her shoulder. She too was already dressed.

"Oh, help!" Anna cried softly as she quickly pushed back the sheet and quilt to get up. "Have I slept *that* late?"

Leah laughed at her concern. "*Nee*, Anna," she offered as a reply. "It's just a quarter to seven. You've plenty of time to dress."

Quarter to seven? Anna blushed, embarrassed that she had slept so late. That was certainly not like her.

She turned around and slipped the white nightgown over her head and quickly changed into the same dress that she had worn the previous day. Unlike Leah, she had only packed two extra dresses: one for work and one for worship. Since her burgundy dress, the one that she wore yesterday, had not gotten soiled, she saw no reason to dirty another one.

Downstairs, the enticing smell of freshly baked bread and fried potatoes greeted the three young women. With the table already covered with a green and white checkered tablecloth and set with dishes, the kitchen seemed to welcome them.

Rebecca smiled when she heard their soft footsteps on the stairs. "Did you all sleep well, then?" she asked as she sliced a loaf of bread on a wooden cutting board.

"*Ja*, *danke*, some of us even better than others," Leah replied, eliciting a smile from Hannah and a slight blush on Anna's face even though Rebecca's back was turned to them.

"Let me help you," Anna offered as she hurried to the counter. Her unfamiliarity with the Eshes' kitchen did not counter her familiarity with morning routines. Momentarily the men would come inside, having finished morning chores. With a long day ahead of everyone, they'd be hungry for a hearty breakfast.

Rebecca pointed to the top of the refrigerator at a plastic blue pitcher. "Just the water."

The other two women made themselves busy, even though there was truly not much for them to do.

"It's such a pleasure having people around the house," Rebecca said as she placed the basket with still-warm bread onto the table. "With everyone married and living elsewhere, it gets awful quiet here sometimes." Placing her hand on the counter, she gazed out the window, staring without seeing at the fields.

Anna wondered what she was thinking about, whether it was her own grown children having moved away or the broken dream of Benjamin's marriage and the sound of grandchildren that now would not be running through the house. Either way, she felt a tug at her heartstrings and wished she had words of solace for the kind woman now hosting them in her home.

The silence in the kitchen ended when the door opened and three of the men entered, stomping their feet to kick off any dirt that remained on the soles of their boots. Each man removed his hat and hung it on the wall near the door before approaching the table. Anna noticed that Benjamin, once again, seemed morose and withdrawn, with the dullness to his eyes that she had first observed upon her arrival. After their walk the previous evening, some life had returned to these eyes, only to disappear once again after what she hoped had been a good night's sleep.

"I dare say there's a chill to the air this morning!" Jonas announced, a smile on his face as he rubbed his hands over his arms. "Shall I put on the heater, Rebecca?"

"For me?" Rebecca laughed, making a light sound as she shook her head. "Heavens, no! I'm just fine, Jonas."

"*Mayhaps* the other women, then?" He peered at them, anticipating their answer.

When Anna realized that neither Leah nor Hannah would respond, she stepped forward and thanked him. "That's very kind of you," she said. "But we shall all be leaving soon. I don't think a little cool air will harm anyone. It would be a shame to waste the propane."

"How considerate!" Rebecca smiled her appreciation while Jonas nodded his head in approval.

Not used to compliments, Anna averted her eyes and, staring at the breakfast table, noticed that it was set for seven, not nine. "Oh! Is there a missing place setting?"

Everyone's attention turned to the table and Rebecca quickly counted, "...five...six...seven. That's right, seven."

"But Mary and Cris..."

Freman made a move to sit at the table, Benjamin following, as he explained, "Cris has gone walking. He wanted to assess the streams behind the pond for fish. As for Mary," he said, pausing to clear his throat. "She's not well this morning, apparently."

Anna looked up. "She's ill?" She started to make her way to the stairs in order to check on her sister.

"Anna," Freman called after her. At the sound of his voice saying her name, she froze and turned around. "She's fine. You should sit and have breakfast with the rest of us." He gestured toward the table.

Stunned once again at his thoughtfulness, Anna stood there, her feet unable to move while he looked at her. She couldn't read any emotion in his eyes, yet his kindness was more than apparent.

He swept his arm, once again, toward the other side of the table where he was seated.

Without further invitation, Leah and Hannah pulled out the bench opposite the men and sat down, Leah making certain that she positioned herself across from Freman. She kept her hands folded in her lap but smiled when she caught his attention. Quietly, Anna slid onto the bench beside Hannah, feeling uncomfortable and awkward sharing a morning meal at the same table as Freman. She tried not to look at him and kept her attention focused on her plate. Leah, however, was quite content to be the focal point of his vision.

Once everyone was seated, Jonas bent his head and the others quickly did the same. Anna prayed silently over her food, thanking God for His many blessings and asking that He help her sister feel better. When she lifted her head, she noticed that she was the last to do so.

Hands reached across the table, picking up serving bowls and dishing hot, steaming food onto their plates. The sound of spoons hitting against the side of porcelain replaced words while everyone served themselves.

"I'm sure you are looking forward to meeting your *maem*'s cousin," Rebecca said as she passed the butter plate to her left where Benjamin sat. Her statement, however, was directed to Leah and Hannah.

"*Maem* insisted that we visit with her," Hannah volunteered. "They haven't seen each other in years!"

"Not since her *dochders* were younger," Leah added. "I do wonder what our cousins are like, don't you, Hannah? I barely recall having met them so many years ago. It was a wedding, I believe."

"You were only ten or eleven at the time," Hannah reminded her. "I recall the younger *dochder*, Mary, was rather bookish."

"Bookish?" Leah gasped and turned to Anna. "Such a shame you won't be going. You love to read! You'd get on quite well with her, I reckon."

Hannah laughed. "No doubt! Anna gets on well with everyone, after all."

Both of the young women radiated happiness, excited to meet their *maem*'s extended family. But, from across the table, a look passed between Rebecca and Jonas. Anna recognized the look and thought she saw a hint of a smile on Rebecca's lips. Remembering Rachel's comments about the Blanks, Anna suspected that the mother's reputation for inane and senseless behavior was just as well known in Leola as it was in Sugarcreek.

Benjamin, however, lifted his head and studied Anna for a long moment. When she realized that she was being watched, she fought the urge to squirm in her seat. He soon ended her agony when he asked, "You like to read, then?"

"I do, *ja*," she answered.

He inhaled deeply. "As do I. 'For whatsoever things were written aforetime were written for our learning, that we through patience and comfort of the scriptures might have hope.'"

Anna smiled. "The Book of Romans. One of my favorite in the New Testament." When she paused, she sensed Leah giving Hannah a nudge with her knee under the table. Trying to focus her attention on Benjamin, she ignored the two women beside her. "Do you prefer the poetic verses to the prose? I do."

"*Nee*," he said, shaking his head, the light rapidly fading from his eyes. "David's lyrical poems speak to my heart, and, as such, remind me too much of Fanny."

A silence fell over the table and Anna chewed on her lower lip, embarrassed at having reminded him of the one thing that she suspected his parents wished him to forget.

After an appropriate pause, Jonas asked for more potatoes, and the noise of breakfast returned to the room.

As she passed the jam to Rebecca, Anna forced a smile and addressed her directly. "Do tell me about your neighbor," Anna asked brightly, redirecting the conversation to a safer territory.

"Oh, *ja*! The Kings live just down the road a spell," Rebecca responded. "You'll adore the *kinner*. The oldest one is most likely at market today. She goes to Maryland on Fridays and Saturdays."

Leah gasped. "Maryland! So far!"

Freman chuckled. "*Mayhaps* from Ohio, Leah, but it's only a two-and-a-half-hour drive from here."

Rebecca continued, eagerness showing in her tone of voice. "Rachel King has six *kinner* and, from the looks of it, another one on the way. The two youngest *dochders* are so dear, always trying to help their *maem*." She smiled and clicked her tongue: *tsk, tsk*. "Such sweet angels. I do so miss having little ones around."

Pointing across the table with his fork, Jonas interrupted her. "You have plenty of little ones that run around!"

"Only when Susan's or Becca Ann's come visiting!" Rebecca retorted in a gentle tone, referencing her two daughters who lived nearby.

Another unsafe subject, Anna feared. She wondered if Benjamin was reminded of his Fanny and how, if they had married in November, they might have been blessed with a child by August of the following year. The thought weighed heavy inside of her chest, and she wished that she could help him through his pain.

Shortly after breakfast was finished, Benjamin and Freman excused themselves. The two men had a lot of catching up to do, and Anna suspected that Freman wanted some quality time with his cousin. While Rebecca hurried upstairs to make the beds and finish her morning chores so that she and Anna could depart, Anna stood at the sink washing the breakfast dishes. She was drying the last one when their buggy pulled down the lane toward the road, the black horse's mane and tail fluttering as it moved.

She must have sighed for Leah walked up behind her, peering over Anna's shoulder to see what she was watching. Glancing at the younger woman, Anna smiled and leaned, just slightly, against her. "So intriguing," she said softly.

"Benjamin?"

Turning around, Anna stared at Leah, taken aback by her quick reply. Immediately, as she realized what Leah had inferred, color flooded her cheeks. "I was actually referring to the differences between Sugarcreek and Leola."

Leah tried to hide her smile.

"The gray-topped buggies," Anna continued. "And the larger houses. Even Jonas's neatly shaven beard. It's interesting to me, Leah." Setting the dish towel on the counter, she leaned forward and whispered, "Not…Benjamin!"

With a soft laugh, Leah covered her mouth and turned away, which only added to Anna's embarrassment.

That was twice that Benjamin had paid special attention to her. She thought well enough of him, so far anyway.

However, when Leah teased her, Anna was mortified that anyone might have conceived the idea that she was interested in anything beyond friendship with Benjamin Esh. While she enjoyed talking with him, especially about Scripture, for his recollection of Bible verses appeared most impressive, she found him dark and foreboding—as if he might be melancholic in general and not just because of Fanny's death.

An hour later, the Musser sisters and Cris stood in the kitchen, waiting for Mary to finish getting ready. After Anna brought her breakfast in bed, Mary had suddenly recovered and dressed, eager to ride with Hannah, Leah, and Cris to meet their family.

"Now how will we all ride over to the Blanks?" Mary fussed as she looked in the small mirror hanging over a wash sink, retying the thin white ribbons that hung from her prayer *kapp*. "We can't all fit in one buggy, now, can we?"

Cris tapped his fingers on the counter while he waited for his wife to finish her primping. "I have the directions and Jonas is lending us *his* horse and buggy."

Anna peered out the kitchen window. "The horse is already hitched to the buggy, Mary. You needn't even wait."

"Where is Hannah? We can't leave without her! And if she doesn't hurry, we'll be late!" She frowned at Cris. "What will your *aendi* think if we are late because of your *schwester*?"

By nine o'clock they were on their way to the far side of Leola while Rebecca and Anna walked down the road in the opposite direction. There was a slight incline before the Kings' mailbox. The field closest to the driveway was

115

already cleared of cornstalks, and in the distance, Anna saw a man working on cutting the growth. With his hat tilted forward upon his head and the sun in his face, he didn't notice them. Rebecca waved anyway.

The Kings' farmhouse was older than the Eshes'. However, Anna noticed that, once again, the downstairs kitchen, combined with a sizable sitting room, was large enough to accommodate not just the King family but extended relations and visitors. When they arrived, the women were already busy peeling apples at the wooden farmer's table. Their heart-shaped prayer *kapps*, so different from the stiff, cuplike *kapp* that Anna wore, framed their faces in such a way that they appeared delicate and dainty.

"*Wilkum*!" A convivial older woman greeted Rebecca and Anna at the door. "You must be Anna Eicher!" With her brown dress held closed with tiny straight pins down the front, Linda King seemed plain enough. Her three daughters, busy at the sink washing and drying canning jars and lids, also wore darker clothing; however, two wore a fabric that had patterns in it, so minute that Anna wouldn't have noticed if she hadn't been looking. *How different*, she thought, smiling while Linda introduced her to each of the girls and her two sisters who sat at the table already.

"Benjamin and Freman stopped by on their way out visiting, to see if Abe wanted to ride along," Rachel said as she returned to her seat at the table. "Abe was put out to think he couldn't go." She laughed good-naturedly and glanced at her daughters. "Wasn't he now?"

The younger girls merely smiled and nodded their heads.

Anna and Rebecca joined the other three women at the table. Within minutes, a paring knife in her hand, Anna's fingers worked at peeling the apples, a sweet, juicy aroma filling the air. She listened to the older women talking, sharing recent news about people that she didn't know or places she had never been. The one thing she did know was that it was a warm and inviting environment. Unlike her home growing up or Mary's home, there was no tension in the air, and a feeling of happiness pervaded the room. Even the children, so wide-eyed and shy, wore an expression of genuine peace.

"Your *schwesters* are here too ain't so?" Linda asked, breaking Anna's train of thought.

Looking up from the apple she held in her left hand, Anna nodded. "My one younger *schwester*, *ja*," she answered. "She went with her husband's two *schwesters* to visit with their cousins."

"Oh?" Rachel seemed surprised and glanced at Rebecca. "I wasn't aware that there was family in the area."

"It's her husband's family," Anna pointed out.

Rebecca kept her head bent, her focus on peeling the apples as she added, "The Blank family."

At this announcement, Rachel pursed her lips and leaned back in her chair. "I see" was her simple response. But from the terse tone in her voice, it was clear that her opinion of the family was less than favorable.

Nothing further was said about the Blank family.

The conversation shifted to more mundane topics related to the people they knew from their church district while Anna continued peeling her apples. On the stove were three large steel pots, all with steam escaping from under the tops. Rachel was quick to cut her apples into eight pieces before tossing them into the boiling water. Anna knew that, after thirty minutes, the apples would be soft enough to drain and then mash, with just a hint of cinnamon added to the mixture, before the smooth liquid would be spooned into the waiting jars. The jars would then be added to a hot water bath in order to seal their tops. They would repeat the process at least three times that day in order to fill all of the empty jars waiting on the counter.

Working in the kitchen was a chore that Anna liked, and she rarely complained about any particular tasks. However, when there were other women—especially friendly and cheerful women like Rebecca and Rachel— to work alongside, canning food was no longer a chore; it became a social event.

Even though Anna did not know the people that Rebecca and Rachel mentioned as they told stories, she laughed with them and felt a camaraderie that she so often missed back in Ohio.

Unfortunately, her sister's day did not travel the same course.

Later that afternoon, when the Mussers returned from visiting her husband's cousins, Mary took the opportunity of being alone in the sitting room with Anna to share her less fortunate experience.

"My word!" Mary plopped her weary body down on the sofa and leaned her head back against the soft cushion. Even though they were alone in the room, Mary lowered her voice when she said, "I've never seen such a place! Not tidy at all; and that woman!"

"What of their *maem*?"

Mary exhaled sharply and shook her head in disgust. "Such a ridiculous creature! It's a wonder that Salome would want us to visit her!"

Not certain how to respond to Mary's statement, Anna remained silent.

"And not one son! No wonder the place is in shambles!"

Anna wanted to remind her that there were only daughters in their immediate family too. But she quickly saw that Mary wasn't looking for contributions to the discussion, merely sympathy as she complained about her husband's relations.

Placing her hand on her forehead, Mary sighed. "I've such a headache from listening to her ramble on and on about her *dochders*." She opened one eye and peered at Anna as if to make certain she was listening. "They seemed fine enough, especially the two older ones. But it's no wonder they aren't married! I'd be quite unhappy if one of my boys married into that family."

"Mary!"

"*Vell*!" She lifted her head and stared at Anna. "It's the truth, ain't so?"

"'Pleasant words are a honeycomb,'" Anna quoted softly.

"And with every honeycomb is a hive of bees!" Mary snapped back, an intense look on her face.

Anna highly doubted that the visit could have gone as poorly as Mary suggested. However, when the rest of the Mussers joined them, there were no lively discussions from Leah or Hannah about their cousins. Kind words were mentioned in regard to the two older daughters, Jane and Lizzie, but that was where the discussion ended. Neither Rebecca nor Jonas pressed the issue; neither did Freman.

Mayhaps Mary was right, Anna thought. If so she couldn't help but wonder why Salome would have insisted upon the visit. Regardless, Anna remained quite pleased with her own day and secretly felt rather thankful that Freman had made the suggestion to begin with.

After the supper meal, Anna and Hannah helped Rebecca with the dishes while Mary retired to nurse her headache. The four men sat in the small sitting area, Leah joining them, to listen to Freman's description of his visit with Benjamin to the carpentry store.

"A fine operation that John runs!" His voice relayed how sincere the compliment was. "He uses an assembly-line-type method for construction. I often wondered about the benefits of that system, and I can see now how effective it truly is."

"Not surprised," Jonas said. "His *grossdawdi* started that business, and John's expanded it substantially. He's a *gut* man with an even better reputation."

"Can't ask for more than that," was Freman's response. "A man who stands by his word and does the right thing is almost certain to have a successful business."

"Speaking of success," Jonas said, turning his attention toward his wife. "How was your time making applesauce?"

Rebecca was wiping down the table when he asked the question. "Eighty quarts canned," she replied, hardly able to repress a smile despite the hint of pride it would indicate.

Whistling, Jonas seemed impressed. "That's a lot of apples!"

"I think Linda said she bought six bushels!" Rebecca told him. "Although we didn't quite peel all of them, did we now, Anna?"

"*Nee*, not quite all."

"Curious that Linda seemed to know Anna was coming," Rebecca remarked as she shook out the dish towel over the sink and hung it on the side. "Didn't she make that comment, Anna? That she had heard you were coming?"

Before Anna could reply, Freman cleared his throat politely before he spoke. "*Ja*, we stopped by on the way out to let Linda know that Anna would be joining you." He didn't look at her as he said this, but Anna caught the inflection in his voice. Clearly stopping by the Kings' farm had been his idea, not Benjamin's, for she couldn't imagine Benjamin being so inspired or thoughtful.

"That was good of you," Rebecca said. "I should have thought to ask you to do that." She smiled at her nephew, clearly pleased with his attention to such details.

Anna too was moved—not just that he had gone out of his way to alert Linda but that he had done so on her behalf. While the men continued talking, she remained in the kitchen, half listening to their conversation and half thinking about how Freman seemed so attentive to what most men wouldn't even consider more than a triviality. Even now, as she contemplated this, his attention to include Leah in the conversation was admirable.

Once again, Anna had a fitful sleep, confused by the seconds of concern Freman showed for her well-being that seemed to live in the shadows of the minutes of intense focus on Leah.

For a moment she pondered if Freman was focusing his attention on Leah as a way of testing whether or not there would be some apparent reaction on her part. *Mayhaps* a reaction of regret, or even jealousy? And *mayhaps* the fact that he still showed some obvious concern for her well-being indicated that his interest in her was not a thing of the past but merely needed to be rekindled? Yet as soon as these thoughts crossed her mind, Anna immediately felt ashamed, the heat coming to her cheeks. *Am I letting myself believe that he would actually play Leah and me against each other*, she pondered? Immediately, she chastised herself for entertaining such a thought. Freman simply was not capable of such a ploy. While not overly talkative during the trip and in the days preceding it, he had been a perfect gentleman so far.

It took Anna a long while to fall asleep, disconcerted by the fact that, if only for a moment, she had actually entertained the thought that his intentions and attentions may have been less than honorable.

❧ *Chapter Ten* ❧

THE SATURDAY MORNING drive to the horse auction, which took almost thirty minutes by van, wound through a series of small scenic back roads toward the south of Strasburg. Rows of Amish buggies filled the parking lot, and toward the back, Anna saw the trucks with long, metal trailers that had transported the horses to the auction and that would deliver them to their new owners' farms later on.

As they approached the main building, two young Amish boys, no more than fourteen years of age, led a brown horse toward a wide door. The horse lifted its head. With wild eyes and twitching ears, it looked around nervously, appraising the unfamiliar surroundings. One of the boys tugged on the blue lead rope that was clipped to the tie ring on the halter. Immediately, the horse stopped walking and jerked its head backward in a defensive gesture.

Anna looked away.

When she was younger, she had always wanted to go to a horse auction. Her father, however, never took her. Later, after her mother died, he often took his three daughters to equipment and farmers' auctions, but never to an actual horse auction.

As she grew older she often heard whispers about these auctions, as if discussing an ugly secret. Indeed, she soon learned that some of the auctions were nothing more than places for meat suppliers to buy unwanted horses. From that point forward, her desire to attend one vanished. The idea of a "kill auction" brought a terrible ache to her heart, and years ago she had once confessed to Freman that she could never attend such an event.

This auction, however, surprised her. Instead of being filled with *Englischers* who intended to purchase old, lame, or ill horses to sell to the slaughterhouses, the seats were filled with Amish. She breathed a sigh of relief and felt the muscles in her shoulders relax. Despite the fear in the eyes of the horse she had just seen outside, she could immediately tell that these horses were to be purchased by other Amish people for practical purposes.

To her further surprise, Freman noticed the change in her demeanor. As she passed by him to sit down, the other women already seated on folding chairs near the side of the room, he leaned over and, with a low voice, said, "I would never take you, or anyone else for that matter, to one of *those* auctions, Anna."

She stopped walking and looked at him, noticing that he stared directly into her eyes. "I...I didn't know what to expect," she admitted, stumbling over her words. Regaining her composure, she glanced at the horse, the same brown one she had just watched. One of the young Amish boys led the horse for all the people to view, running up and down a fifty-foot track surrounded by metal fencing. "I am pleased, though, to see that these animals look healthy and well-cared for."

No further words were spoken. He merely gestured toward the seats, indicating that she should join the others. Without waiting for her to move, he turned and walked in the direction Jonas and Benjamin had disappeared.

Settling into her seat, Anna watched as the horse, calmer now, ran back and forth, lifting its front legs high in the air. Two men were bidding on the horse, indicating their bids by lifting up a paper with a red number printed on one side. On the other side of the track, four men sat at a table on a platform.

One of the auctioneers held a microphone and spoke into it, uttering a staccato of words in a singing tone, practically impossible for Anna to decipher. His hands moved, gesturing towards the two bidders, enticing them to raise their stakes against each other, as he chanted a litany of numbers followed by "going once, going twice" only to be followed by a resounding "yup" as he turned, alternately, towards each of the two men. The longer she listened, the more she became mesmerized by his fast-paced, songlike words.

"Who'll give me a six hundred dollars? Six hundred dollar bid, beautiful mare, six hundred dollars, six, now seven, now seven, will ya give me seven? Seven hundred dollar bid!" He pointed to another man. "Now, eight, now eight, now eight hundred, will ya give me eight? Even your women can drive that eight-year-old! Eight hundred? Seven and a half, seven-fifty. How about seven-fifty? Fifty? Fifty? Fifty? I got it!" The original bidder had lifted his paper and the auctioneer pointed in his direction. "How about eight hundred? Eight? Eight? Will ya give me eight? I've got seven-fifty. Eight? Eight? I got eight! Eight hundred!"

This continued until the bidding stopped climbing, each man outbidding the other. The auctioneer slammed the gavel down on the table and yelled, "Sold! Nine hundred and fifty dollars to Abe Stoltzfus, here, bidder number 107!" Within seconds, the Amish boy led the brown mare off the track, someone crossing off the number on the horse's croup with a thick red marker, while another horse was led in.

Hannah leaned against Anna's arm. "I can't understand one single word that he said!"

Anna laughed. "You need to really listen. It's rather interesting, I think."

Mary was quick to offer her opinion. "Sounds like jibber-jabber to me!"

There was no more time for talking as the auctioneer began again, describing the horse, a black Morgan cross with a flowing mane and easy gait. Once again, the rhythmic chant began, and within seconds, white cardboards began to signal bids.

Enthralled, Anna watched the gorgeous horse as it pranced along the track, neither pulling on its lead rope nor pushing against the boy. Its muscles rippled as it moved, and a thin layer of sweat made its coat shine. Anna thought it was the most gorgeous horse she had ever seen.

"Sold!" The gavel slammed down once again and the auctioneer pointed toward an Amish man seated in the front row.

When the men returned, six other horses had already been auctioned. Jonas handed each of the women a thick package of papers, each stapled in the corner. It was the listing for the horse numbers and descriptions.

Thanking him, Anna accepted it before she eagerly looked up at the horse that was currently pacing the track.

"Enjoying yourself, then?"

Anna smiled at Jonas. "Oh *ja*!" Her eyes flickered back to the auctioneer. "It's like listening to and seeing poetry in motion all at the same time!"

Jonas laughed at her words as he sat in the row behind the women. Benjamin took the seat directly behind her while Freman moved farther down the aisle, sitting behind Hannah. Cris, however, had not returned with them.

Mary scanned the crowd, searching for her husband. "Where did he go?" she asked, irritation showing in her voice. Her eyes continued searching, but to no avail. As for the others in the group, no one responded to her inquiry, wisely choosing to pay attention to the auction and not her complaints. When she realized that she was being ignored, she huffed and quickly got to her feet, her quest to find Cris more important than the activity around her.

If anyone noticed or minded Mary's departure, they did not comment about it. Instead, Freman explained to Hannah about how the auction worked while Leah talked with Benjamin about the list of horses.

"A Dutch Harness horse!" Benjamin exclaimed. "Number two thirty-seven!"

His excitement caught Anna's attention. "Is that a special horse?" she asked.

Turning his attention away from Leah, Benjamin nodded, leaning over the back of the folding chair so that she could hear his words over the din in the large room.

"A fine breed of horse, indeed! They are high steppers and quite smooth under harness. Even under saddle."

Anna smiled at his enthusiasm. "I should like to see that one, then!"

"Ah, high steppers," Freman said. "I should not be so affected by a horse's gait, no matter how poetic it may look, especially when the manufactured gait can often lead to issues with the hooves at a later stage. Their temperament is much more important to me."

Anna tore her eyes away from the prancing horse that was currently being auctioned. "Manufactured?"

Freman nodded. "*Ja*, manufactured. Some trainers use painful chemicals on their hooves to teach the horses how to lift their front legs. A horrible practice called soring. It's been outlawed but..." He hesitated and looked at the other two women. "It's still being used, no doubt."

Benjamin nodded, then added, "Others simply attach chains or put really heavy shoes on the horses' hooves to force them to lift their legs higher, something they eventually do out of habit, then. It's a bit more humane, don't you think?"

Anna thought no such thing. "Oh, how awful!"

Both Hannah and Leah nodded in agreement with Anna, expressing their own dismay at the description of such a practice. For such a fine animal, one of God's creations, to be purposefully put in pain, strictly in order to have a pretty gait, was a horrible thought for all of the women. Anna doubted she would ever again look at a high-stepping horse without thinking about what Freman and Benjamin had just told them.

While she was still pondering this, Cris and Mary returned, their arms carrying trays filled with sodas and bagged snacks for everyone.

"What do we each owe you, then?" Jonas said, reaching into his pocket for his wallet.

Cris held up his hand. "*Nee*, Jonas. It was nothing, especially after all of your generosity."

Jonas shook his head, taking out a few single dollar bills and thrusting them at Cris. Benjamin and Freman did the same. "*Nee*," Jonas said. "Fair is fair. Take the extra for the women, *ja*?"

It was the way of the Amish. *Fair was fair.* Had Jonas not offered, Cris would have thought nothing of it. However, once he had handed the money forward, Cris had no choice but to accept it. Anna understood the foundation of fastidiousness for fairness that flowed under every exchange: nothing was given or accepted for free. It was a token of goodwill and kept disagreements over money at bay.

For the next hour, the small group watched the auction, some with more genuine interest than others. Anna remained transfixed, watching the horses with an intensity that made Jonas laugh, teasing her that she might want to purchase one for herself. Blushing, Anna smiled and returned her attention to the front of the room.

Occasionally, she would look at the people surrounding her. While most were men, all dressed in black pants, white shirts, and black jackets, there were a few women beside them. Anna noticed a young man and woman, clearly not married, for the man wore no beard upon his chin, seated toward the back. She wondered if they were courting. With the wedding season so near, they might have snuck away under the guise of attending the auction to spend some time together before their betrothal would be announced in another few weeks.

In the row next to them, a woman in a dark green dress with gray rubber shoes on her feet held a baby. Dressed in a little pink dress, her blond hair tucked under a tiny white prayer *kapp*, the baby couldn't have been more than a year old. Her big blue eyes stared back at Anna, and upon realizing that she was being watched, the baby smiled and squirmed, struggling to push up so that she could peer over her mother's shoulder. Anna laughed, and when the mother glanced in her direction, curious to see what her daughter found so amusing, they exchanged smiles.

"Such a cute *boppli*," Leah said.

Anna nodded. "Oh, *ja*, she's a precious little one, indeed."

After several hours had passed, Anna sensed that the other women were ready to leave, although no one would have suggested such a thing. For Anna, she could have stayed there all day and well into the evening. She suspected that the men too were enjoying themselves. A few times, Jonas had excused himself to greet someone that he knew: a friend, neighbor, or relative. Always, he would bring the person back to introduce his son's guests.

"Oh, look, Anna!" Leah nudged her gently. "Is that the horse you wanted to see?"

Anna glanced at the white numbered tag on the horse's croup and then checked it against the paper. "Number two thirty-seven! Oh, look how beautiful she is!" For the moment she forgot the controversy over high-stepping horses. The black mare trotted down the track, her mane braided along the arch of her neck into tiny, rosebud-like plaits, her front legs lifted high in the air.

Benjamin leaned forward and pointed over her shoulder at the horse. "She's a nice-looking mare. Look at her conformation!"

Not wanting to admit that she wasn't familiar with what a horse's conformation should or shouldn't be, she merely nodded.

Unlike the previous horse, which was auctioned for only six hundred dollars, this horse created a stir among the attendees, and as the bidding began, new energy and excitement filled the atmosphere.

"What say you, Freman? Four thousand?"

All of the women gasped.

Freman, however, leaned back in his chair and shook his head, laughing. "*Nee*, Benjamin. For just four thousand, I'd buy her myself and ship her back to Indiana!"

"Then what will be the high bid?"

For a moment, Freman stared at the horse, his eyes gazing over Anna's head toward the front of the room. While all of the other women waited expectantly for his response, Anna felt the color rise to her cheeks, uncomfortable in his line of vision.

"For such a godly creature," Freman said slowly, his eyes momentarily flickering to Anna's before he turned to look at Benjamin. "Just under seven. Sixty-eight hundred."

At this announcement, Cris balked. "That's a king's ransom."

"Indeed," Freman replied. "And worth every penny." He paused as if thinking of something. "There is no value to be placed on a faithful partner that will carry you along many a journey. In addition, she will produce many nice foals."

Hannah and Leah shot amused glances at each other as Jonas clapped him on the shoulder. "Well said, Freman. Now, let's see which of you fellows is right and which one will have egg on his face."

Anna focused on the rapid-fire words that the auctioneer spoke into the microphone, his voice droning into a lull-like, hypnotic leitmotiv. Hands with white papers were being raised on both sides of the room, quickly at first, the auctioneer pointing toward them as he sang numbers. Slowly, as the amount of the horse increased, the volume of rising hands decreased. When the bidding passed four thousand, Benjamin leaned forward as if anticipating the offers to cease. But to everyone's amazement, the bids continued until only two men were left in the competition.

"Oh, I hope the better man will win the horse," Anna said, more to herself than to anyone else.

Jonas, however, had heard her words. "They're both right *gut* men, Anna," he reassured her. "And for this kind of money, that horse will be well cared for, that's for sure and certain!"

"Sold!" The auctioneer's gavel slammed down on the table and he pointed toward the man seated to the right of the room. "Sixty-six hundred dollars to bidder eighty-six, Gid Peachey!"

A murmur went around the room and heads nodded, clearly expressing pleasure, not just with the purchase itself but with the free entertainment that the bidding war had provided.

It was close to four in the afternoon when they all returned to the Eshes' farm. While the men tended to chores, the women offered their assistance to Rebecca.

The table, however, was already set and the food already placed upon the white tablecloth, pieces of aluminum foil covering the heated items.

Instead of helping her, Rebecca insisted that the women sit and tell her about the auction.

"Oh, my word! Sixty-six hundred dollars for a horse?" She shook her head, a look of disapproval on her face. "Such extravagance!"

Mary immediately agreed with her. "Seems a bit prideful to me...driving around with a fancy horse when any Standardbred will do!"

"Oh, Mary!" Hannah said. "It's a personal preference, no doubt!"

"*Ja vell*, that's not for me!" Her hand fluttered in the air dismissively.

Anna wondered if she might remind her sister of her generous offer to purchase her own father's new buggy, complete with the self-generating battery and fancy mahogany dashboard, despite already having one.

Over the supper meal, the men relished retelling the stories from the day, Jonas making certain to update his wife about all of the people he had caught up with. But the highlight of the day was, unanimously, the story of the Dutch Harness horse. Benjamin took his time to describe the mare and the bidding war that ensued in great detail. There was, undeniably, a sparkle in his eyes, one that hadn't been there before that day. For the first time Anna understood that, beneath the layers of mourning, there was a lively young man hidden there. And, from the joy that radiated from his parents, she suspected that he was long overdue to unlock the door so that his true self could be freed.

After supper, over pecan pie and homemade vanilla ice cream, plans were discussed for the following morning. Jonas suggested that they leave no later than a quarter after seven. The worship service would start promptly at eight o'clock in the morning. Since it was being held at a farm not too far from theirs, he also suggested that they walk.

"It's our last service before the autumn baptism," he added. "Four youths are taking their kneeling vow in two weeks."

A moment of reverent silence fell over the group, each person undoubtedly thinking back to the day when they too had knelt before their own *g'may* and acknowledged that Jesus was their Savior. Additionally, they had agreed to forego conformity to the world, to reject worldliness, and to live a plain life.

Once undertaken, the vow could not be reversed...at least not easily. To leave the church after accepting the baptism meant being shunned from family, friends, and community. So the seriousness of the decision was understood by all of those who had already made the same commitment.

And, of course, two weeks after the baptism service would be the autumn communion. Anna knew what that meant: a flurry of weddings would soon follow.

She suspected that Hannah and Caleb's announcement would take place shortly after Communion Sunday. She had long ago noticed Salome's garden, full of growing celery plants—always an indicator that a wedding was being planned. But as she sat at the table, listening to the men talking and hearing the women laugh, she wondered if there might be another match at the table.

"Now, you women head on up to bed," Rebecca said as she stood to clear the dessert plates. "It's after eight o'clock. You've had a long day and we've another one that starts early tomorrow."

While Leah, Hannah, and Mary bid their good nights to everyone, Anna refused to let Rebecca wash all of the dishes on her own. Even though she knew that she needed to get up at six o'clock in the morning, Anna also knew that she couldn't, in good conscience, let someone else clean up all the dishes, plates, and utensils alone.

"Many hands make light the work," she said to Rebecca. Without another word, she grabbed a towel and began drying the plates and pans after they were washed. In silence they worked, but it was comforting to Anna. She had grown to like Rebecca, her light-hearted nature and quick smile reminding her of her own mother, someone she missed very much. While no one in the community spoke about Anne anymore, Anna often wondered how her absence had impacted her development. Perhaps, had her mother not passed away, Anna would have received different advice so long ago, advice that would have taken into consideration the deepest desires of her heart.

That night, she lay in bed, her eyes adjusting to the dark as she stared out the window. Darkness blanketed the outdoors but she could make out a few twinkling stars. After two almost sleepless nights, she hoped she would soon fall asleep, for the next day was a worship Sunday, and she did not want to risk dozing off during the long, three-hour service. Lunch and a long day of visiting would follow the service, and she wanted to be rested enough to enjoy all of the new sights and people.

As she shut her eyelids, her breath deepening, her last thought before succumbing to slumber was how much she was actually looking forward to worshipping with the Esh family and their *g'may*.

❧ *Chapter Eleven* ❧

WHAT DO YOU mean you're going to leave me here? And all alone!" Mary's shrill and boisterous voice cut through Anna as she emphasized the word *alone*.

With her back to her sister, Anna shut her eyes and said a silent prayer to God for an extra dose of patience. Her usual ability to remain calm and composed, under even the most stressful of circumstances, was being stretched today, and it wasn't even 7:15 a.m. Although she always rose to the occasion to tend to the ill or injured, Anna felt resentment building inside of her, causing her to count to ten and actually let out a sigh before she could address her sister.

When she had awoken that morning, Anna had felt refreshed and vibrant after finally sleeping soundly through the night. Her dreams had taken her back to Charm, to the creek that ran behind her father's property along the dip of the neighbor's property. As a child she had often walked barefoot through the water, looking for small frogs or pretty salamanders. Until her mother passed away, she often played with Elizabeth and Mary. But when their mother died and their father put so much responsibility on Elizabeth's shoulders, their personalities had changed and their relationships divided. Elizabeth became more matronly, almost a psychological replacement for their mother; Mary became the helpless, hapless youngest child. Lost in the middle, was Anna.

In her dream the three Eicher girls walked together, no differences or role delineations separating them.

Shortly after awaking, however, reality returned. She was not a young girl and her sisters were no longer her playmates and friends.

"Anna! You can't leave me. I'm sick!"

Slowly turning around, Anna managed to maintain an even tone as she responded. "I've been looking forward to attending the worship service. I'd be ever so disappointed if I missed it, Mary."

She had arisen early and taken great care to properly pin the front of her black church dress before combing her long dark hair so that it shone. When she twisted it into a neat bun at the nape of her neck, not one hair was out of place. Her black prayer *kapp*, the one she wore only to worship, rested comfortably on the back of her head. Everything about her appearance spoke of her desire to attend the service with the others. Unfortunately something was missing—there was not one ounce of sympathy on Mary's face.

"Must you have someone stay with you, then?" Anna asked. "I'm sure you'll feel much better in a few hours. Most likely you'll sleep, anyway."

Smoothing the sheet around herself, Mary pursed her lips and scowled. Clearly the idea of being left alone was not to her liking. Anna should have known better. Her sister wasn't one to sit in the shadows without being noticed. When they were children, Mary loved the attention of adults and pandered to their laughter. As she grew older and was no longer the cherubic toddler, she resorted to tantrums and tears. While their mother had known how to handle her, she had been the first and the last to do so.

"You know how I've been feeling, Anna. Especially in the mornings." Mary rested her hand on her stomach, the slight bulge underneath the sheet visible, indicating what she hadn't acknowledged yet. "I'm in a strange house and might need something. I wouldn't even know where to look!"

Anna gave a short laugh. "As if I would?"

"You know what I mean. Besides, you are, after all, the most reliable person for tending people's needs."

Immediately a cloud hung around Anna's shoulders, a formidable fog of disappointment. There would be no sense in arguing with Mary. She never did, for Mary always won; persistence trumped selflessness every time. Taking a deep breath, she tried to clear her mind, hoping to think of a counterargument against her sister's request. Unfortunately, her mind went blank. With a deep sigh Anna acquiesced and agreed to stay at the Eshes' farm in case Mary needed her.

"Let me go tell the others," she finally said. "They're waiting for me."

She shut the bedroom door behind herself and headed down the stairs. She knew that everyone was waiting in the kitchen. They had been ready five minutes ago when Anna realized that Mary was not among them. Cris had started to walk up the stairs to fetch his wife, but Anna offered to go in his place. She knew that, in her delicate condition, Mary often fought off the morning sickness.

At the bottom step she paused and forced a smile. Six pairs of eyes stared back at her, each one dressed in their Sunday best: a sea of black dresses and suits. "She's not feeling well and won't be attending the service."

"Poor lamb." Rebecca shook her head, genuinely expressing sympathy. "She did look a bit peaked yesterday after the horse auction, I must say."

Leah and Hannah exchanged a look, ignoring Rebecca's concern.

Likewise, Cris gave an exasperated sigh. "Reckon I'll need to stay with her too, then."

"*Nee*, Cris," Anna said quickly, holding up her hand to stop him. "She's requested that I stay. I don't mind." She knew it wasn't true, but she also knew that God would forgive her for saying so. She didn't want anyone else to feel as if they should sacrifice attending the worship service.

Despite Anna's words, Hannah stepped forward. "Oh, Anna, you were so looking forward to attending worship! Let me stay in your place," she offered.

But Anna knew better than to agree to Hannah's offer. If Mary requested that Anna nurse her, it was best to oblige her. "*Danke*, Hannah, but no," she replied, noticing Freman scowl as if finding her words distasteful. Without a word, he turned his back on the group and silently slipped out the door. Anna wondered at his reaction but kept her attention focused on the others. "It's better if I stay...since that's her wish."

Less than fifteen minutes after they left, walking to the service since it was nearby, Anna settled into a chair, her own Bible in her hands. Since Mary was no doubt sleeping and most likely wouldn't even call upon her, Anna sought comfort in the Psalms.

> The transgression of the wicked saith within my heart, that there is no fear of God before his eyes. For he flattereth himself in his own eyes, until his iniquity be found to be hateful. The words of his mouth are iniquity and deceit: he hath left off to be wise, and to do good. He deviseth mischief upon his bed; he setteth himself in a way that is not good; he abhorreth not evil.
>
> Thy mercy, O LORD, is in the heavens; and thy faithfulness reacheth unto the clouds. Thy righteousness is like the great mountains; thy judgments are a great deep: O LORD, thou preservest man and beast. How excellent is thy loving kindness, O God! therefore the children of men put their trust under the shadow of thy wings.
>
> They shall be abundantly satisfied with the fatness of thy house; and thou shalt make them drink of the river of thy pleasures. For with thee is the fountain of life: in thy light shall we see light. O continue thy loving kindness unto them that know thee; and thy righteousness to the upright in heart. Let not the foot of pride come against me, and let not the hand of the wicked remove me. There are the workers of iniquity fallen: they are cast down, and shall not be able to rise.

She shut her eyes and leaned back in the chair for a moment, reflecting on the words. Oh, how she wanted God's mercy. She tried to walk in His light and knew that, like every other person, she was a sinner. Even that morning, when Mary had requested that she stay to comfort her, Anna's initial thought had been self-centered instead of philanthropic toward her sister's morning sickness.

Even the previous day, when she had watched Freman talking with Hannah and Leah, she envied his attention. Instead of yearning after what she had so carelessly thrown away, she should focus on being satisfied with her own lot in life, the one that a loving and kind God provided to her.

With her eyes shut she silently prayed for Mary's health and also for her own salvation. She wanted to walk in the light and not with the wicked. *Only then*, she thought, *might I rise to righteousness and please God.*

An hour later she set aside her Bible and went about preparing a light broth for Mary. She glanced at the clock and knew that the worshippers were most likely listening to the first preacher of the day. She tried not to think about what message he was giving to the congregation. Instead she hummed one of the hymns from the *Ausbund*. The words kept her mind preoccupied as she poured the broth into a large coffee mug.

Anna climbed the stairs and peeked around Mary's door. Seeing her sister's eyes were open, she slipped into the room. "Are you awake now? I've brought you some broth."

With a great deal of effort, Mary sat up and positioned a pillow behind her back. "*Danke, schwester.*" She reached for the coffee mug and for a moment seemed puzzled. Then, in a rare moment of pleasure, she smiled. "How clever of you! A coffee mug for broth!" Puckering her lips, she blew on the liquid before sipping it. Another smile. "See, Anna? You are more conscientious than anyone else!

How could I have anyone else tend to me when I'm feeling so poorly?"

The compliment was almost as rare as her smiles.

"Are you feeling better then?"

Mary shook her head. "*Nee*, I'm not. But the broth will help settle my stomach." She took another sip then handed the mug to Anna to set upon the nightstand. "I do believe that yesterday just took its toll on me, all that time at the auction and with such noise."

"*Mayhaps* more sleep might help?"

Mary slid back down and nestled her head into the pillow, shutting her eyes. "*Mayhaps*," she mumbled. "I do so hate these first months of pregnancy! You have no idea how dreadful it is to feel so sick!"

No, Anna thought as she stood by the bed and stared down at her sister. *I do not.*

There was a bitter taste in her mouth as she quietly exited the room, her sister's words echoing in her head and hurting her heart.

Certainly after the worship service, the Eshes and their guests would stay for the fellowship meal. Afterward Benjamin and Freman would visit with the young men, introducing Cris, while the women helped to clean up the plates. On their way back to the Esh farm, if they did not stop to visit with another neighbor along the road, Freman would certainly walk alongside Leah, for Cris tended to favor his younger sister, Hannah, when Mary was not around.

The clock on the shelf in the sitting room ticked, the sound loud in the silence of the house. There was not much for Anna to do. On Sundays women were not permitted to quilt or crochet since it was an activity that did not focus on fellowship or God. Her eyes already ached from having read the Bible all morning, and her stomach rumbled from hunger.

By noon, she needed to get out of the house. The early-morning chill had gone from the air, and the afternoon promised the warmth of an Indian summer. Anna opened a few windows as well as the front door to let in fresh air. Then, after checking on Mary, who still slept soundly, Anna slipped outside and wandered toward the barn.

Not having grown up on a farm, she found the atmosphere of a dairy barn both interesting and relaxing. While the Eshes derived most of their income from farming the land, certainly a nice income came from the thirty black and white cows that lined the barn.

There was a pungent odor in the barn, but she didn't mind it. It reminded her of Charm and the farms surrounding her father's house. It was a musky smell with a sharp hint of ammonia to it. She knew that most of the tourists wrinkled their nose at the smell and commented about it. Back in Charm, the Amish often made remarks about how the *Englische* enjoyed the fruits of their labor without appreciating the actual labor itself. The remark stuck with Anna, for she knew it to be true.

Careful that she didn't get any manure or dirt on her dress, she leaned forward and tugged gently on a cow's ear. It looked at her, its deep brown eyes so soft and gentle. Never once did the cow stop chewing, its pink mouth moving in a steady rhythm: *chomp, chomp, chomp*. Anna laughed, a soft sound that caused another cow to lift its head and stare at her.

"Am I interrupting you, then?"

She jumped at the sound of Freman's voice. Spinning around, she pressed her hand to her chest and took a step backward. "You scared me!"

The corner of his mouth twitched as if he wanted to smile.

"You are back already, then?"

He nodded his head. "Leah and I walked back to see how you fared. When we couldn't find you in the house, I offered to see whether you had gone out to the barn. She brought a plate of food for you, in case you were hungry."

"That was kind of her." With a final glance at the cows, she started forward and walked beside Freman toward the barn door. Outside, the sun warmed her face and she squinted in the light until her eyes adjusted. "I trust the service was nice?" she asked as they strolled towards the house.

He nodded. "A good preacher, Deacon Lapp. I've missed his sermons."

She had forgotten how long Freman had lived in Leola. He would be used to the different style of sermon which, she had heard, focused on how their daily behaviors needed to mirror God's Word. Bishop Troyer, however, tended to preach about the sacrifices Jesus made for their salvation.

"We do become so used to the familiar that we aren't often open to new or different things," she said absent-mindedly. "But I would have liked to have heard his sermon anyway."

"Even if those new or different things are not pleasing to others?"

There was a peculiar look in his eyes, almost a gleam of curiosity. Anna wondered what he found so curious about her statement and his question in response. "I imagine it would depend, then," she said slowly, thinking carefully about her words. "We have a duty to please certain people, even at the risk of making ourselves unhappy, I suppose. Take the issue of cell phones. I've heard tell that some communities are having problems with their youth not wanting to give up their cell phones when they become baptized members of the church."

"A frivolous trifle," he commented.

"I agree." She paused at the steps that led to the wide porch at the Eshes' house. "And, as such, I would have no problem supporting the *Ordnung* for any *g'may* which won't allow the cell phones."

"When would you stand your ground, Anna?"

The way he spoke, her name rolling off of his tongue as if eight years of separation had never happened, brought her back to a time long gone. For a moment, she was a teenager again, sitting beside him in the buggy, talking as they rode home from a singing. Immediately, she understood what his question truly meant: he referenced her inability to stand up against her father and Lydia's opposition to their marriage.

She lowered her eyes, feeling heat rise to her cheeks. "A young woman might find it uncomfortable, even unseemly, to stand for anything if others disagree." She bit her lower lip and forced herself to speak the following words. "However, as a mature woman I see the folly in that and, as such, know there are certain things I would adamantly support, even if I were to offend those who so often guide me and offer advice."

Out of the corner of her eye, she saw him nod, as if pleased with her response. But he had no time to comment, for the sound of Leah's voice announced her approach and interrupted their conversation. Anna took advantage of the distraction to mount the steps and enter through the screen door.

"There you are!" Leah laughed as she bounded down the stairs and stood next to Freman. "I've checked on Mary and she seems quite content to stay in bed all day. She asked me to reheat the broth for her."

Anna reached for the empty mug that Leah held. "*Nee*, I'll take care of it." Swiftly she retreated to the kitchen where the pot of broth still rested on the stove. In the distance came the sound of an approaching horse and buggy. The familiar clip-clop of its hooves on the pavement carried strongly in the stillness of the air. People were returning home after the fellowship meal that had followed worship.

Moments later, Anna joined Leah and Freman at the table, where they were discussing that morning's worship service. They paused a moment in their discussion to allow Anna to pray silently over her noon meal. On the plate before her Leah had put two slices of bread, small salted pretzels, a few slices of cheese and bologna, coleslaw, and two pickles. It was enough to sustain her until the supper meal. Sunday fare was always lighter than other days, usually prepared in advance so that no one would need to cook. Leftovers might be reheated for the evening meal, but on that day women did not generally cook for the family.

"What a gorgeous day!" Leah exclaimed, her eyes shining and bright. "Anna, we walked a spell after worship and you won't believe what I did!" Her laughter filled the room. "I climbed on a felled tree by the road and..."

She paused and glanced at Freman. He lifted an eyebrow, perfectly arched, with an amused expression on his face.

"And what, Leah?" Anna asked, conflicting emotions flooding through her. Leah's happiness and joy was delightful to see, yet Anna felt pain at suspecting the cause of it.

Covering her mouth with her hands, Leah giggled, a noise that seemed far too young for her age. "I jumped!"

Freman's expression changed, a more serious look upon his face. "Indeed you did. And not once but twice." He glanced at Anna and shook his head. "I warned her not to do it."

"Oh, Freman!" Leah gushed. "It was so liberating! I'm not certain when I last did such a thing."

He took a deep breath and returned his attention to Leah. "I should not have caught you the first time! It encouraged you, I fear, to do it again."

Anna's heart beat rapidly as she realized what Freman implied. Had Leah openly flirted with him by jumping into his arms? Such behavior, Anna thought, was uncomely, even for Leah, who was the more energetic and lively of the two sisters.

"Perhaps," Anna started, hoping to change the direction of the conversation, "you might tell me about the service."

As she picked at the food on her plate, she listened to Leah and Freman talk, discussing the sermon and how the deacon had informed the congregation that they were not doing enough to help others. He had related stories from the Bible, often quoting Scripture from memory to support his sermon.

"I found it rather powerful," Leah said. "It's quite different than the sermons we hear in Sugarcreek, don't you think?"

"And from Indiana, as well," he agreed. "The sermons here seem more conservative than elsewhere…with the exception of the Schwartzentrubers and Nebraska Amish, of course."

Anna looked up, curious at the statement he had just made. "But they, themselves, are not so conservative," she pointed out. "Seems that they rely heavily on the *Englischer* tourists."

"How so, Anna?"

Freman's pointed question shifted the discussion in her direction. She hadn't meant to interrupt them, but the conversation had caught her attention. "*Vell*," Anna said as she took a breath to collect her thoughts. "When I helped with the applesauce canning, those jars would normally be for the family, ain't so? But Linda stated that half of them would be sold at a store in town that the *Englische* visit."

"That is true."

"And when we drove through town to the auction the other day," she continued, "the entire town seemed to cater to the tourists. Why, the exposure to worldliness would tempt more than a few youth, I imagine." She shook her head. "I dare say that the quaintness of Charm and Sugarcreek appeals far more to me."

He seemed to consider her words for a moment, but did not comment further. He didn't have to for the sound of voices approaching the house interrupted the small group. Anna stood up to clear her plate and wipe the table so that everything was tidy upon their arrival.

For the rest of the afternoon and after the light evening meal, the four women played Scrabble while the men discussed the price of tobacco. At some point Mary descended the stairs, dressed in a plain navy blue dress and with her hair pinned back under her *kapp*. As was to be expected, everyone fussed over her, Rebecca quick to abandon the game in order to make Mary a cup of peppermint tea.

"*Danke*, Rebecca," Mary said as she accepted the teacup. "I am so sorry to have missed the service. But I *am* feeling better. So much activity yesterday must have just worn me out."

"That's understandable," Rebecca sympathized. "You just relax and rest. The best cure for most ailments."

It did not, however, surprise Anna that Mary sat at the table, watching the game of Scrabble. She peered at Hannah's tiles and clicked her tongue when she laid down a word. "You could have doubled your points," she said, pointing at two letters in Hannah's tray.

"*Mayhaps* you might wish to play in the next round?"

Anna detected a touch of sarcasm from Hannah, but Mary viewed the question as a proper invitation. "I would indeed!"

Leah volunteered to sit out, and when the time came for round two, she excused herself to sit with the men. Again. She sat in the rocking chair, gently pushing it with her bare toes. In the chair next to her sat Freman, who leaned his elbows against his knees as he talked with Jonas, Cris, and Benjamin. While Leah contributed little to the conversation, she seemed to enjoy sitting there, listening to the men talk. Anna suspected it had more to do with being near Freman than a genuine interest in the actual discussion.

By the time that they finished their third round of Scrabble, the sun having long ago set behind the tree line on the horizon, Jonas stood up and stretched, announcing that he would be retiring for the night. "Early to bed, early to rise..." he teased. Unlike people, cows demanded a schedule that did not allow variation. While his herd was small, he still needed to rise at 4:30 a.m. to attend to the first of the day's two milkings.

The rest of the group quickly followed suit, the only one alarmed at the sudden end to the evening being Mary. But, with tomorrow being their last day in Lancaster (and an early morning departure schedule for the morning after that), a good night's sleep was in the best interest of everyone. Anna knew that she, in particular, was looking forward to returning home, even if the vision of home residing in her head did not match the memory of the home in her heart.

❧ *Chapter Twelve* ❧

ON MONDAY, GOOD weather together with the realization that their short venture to Pennsylvania was rapidly drawing to a close, sent the group outdoors to spend an afternoon relaxing by the large pond on the Eshes' property. It was tucked away in the backfields behind the farmhouse, visible only at the entrance of the driveway, for a small gathering of trees blocked it from view when proceeding farther up.

On the far side of the pond, a stream trickled into it, the water gently cascading over several large rocks as it fed the larger body of water.

Cris took advantage of the peace and quiet to fish, having borrowed a pole from Jonas. While he caught only a few stream trout, his serene composure displayed how content he was on this glorious Monday afternoon. The other two men had stayed behind, Freman offering to assist Benjamin with fixing a rotting beam in the ceiling of the hayloft.

Leah and Hannah ran through the meadow, collecting pretty leaves that had already fallen from nearby trees. Since the farmer didn't use this particular field for growing crops, there were several downed trees tucked into the high grass. Both Leah and Hannah reminded Anna of small children as they climbed atop the fallen trees, their arms outstretched as they walked along the top of the logs. Once, Hannah stumbled, and grabbing onto Leah's arm, they both tumbled to the ground.

Swatting at an ant that crawled across the blanket, Mary sighed her disapproval. "It's outrageous!"

"What is?" The gentle breeze that rustled the leaves of the trees lulled Anna into a peaceful mood. She couldn't imagine anything about the afternoon that even Mary could find to her dissatisfaction.

"Sitting here." She gestured at the tall grasses surrounding where they sat. The gentle chirp of crickets filled the air, and flies buzzed past, enjoying the last of the good weather. Soon enough it would turn, and when the vegetation died for the season, they too would be gone.

"It's lovely here, Mary. Considering the long drive ahead of us and how poorly you felt yesterday, you should try to enjoy the warmth of the sun and the fresh air."

"How can I? There are bugs everywhere!" She swatted at a fly to make her point.

Irritated, Mary looked in the direction of her husband and his sisters. Cris stood at the end of a wooden dock, one that probably had been used frequently when the Esh children were younger, his face toward the sun as he held the fishing pole. The water of the pond reflected the sky, soft ripples occasionally breaking the placid surface when a frog jumped from one place to another. Just beyond him, Leah and Hannah sat atop a tree, their arms bared as they basked in the sun.

With a wave of her hand, she added, "And we sit here while they just traipse around. Not a care in the world, I reckon. I'm not even sure why we are here! It's an affront to be ignored in such a manner."

Anna tried to smile, even though she found it hard to constantly listen to her sister's stream of complaints about every perceived slight and personal injury. There was no response that she could offer to appease Mary, even if she put it forward with sincerity. So, as she had been taught at a young age, first by her mother and later by Lydia, silence was the best recourse.

Yet the silence was quickly broken by the sound of deep voices that approached from behind them. Laughter and then more conversation followed. Curious, Anna turned around, lifting her hand to shield her eyes from the sun. She was not surprised to see Freman and Benjamin walking across the field in their direction. As they neared, her eyes flickered once again in their direction, just enough so that Mary noticed that the men were joining them.

Immediately Mary's demeanor changed. The frown previously worn upon her face was quickly changed to one of joy and welcome. She quickly jumped to her feet, the meddlesome insects forgotten as she greeted the two men, both of whom she envisioned would be her future brothers-in-law. "How right *gut* to see you!" She shook their hands and gestured toward the log where Leah and Hannah sat, their heads tilted together as they talked in a way that only sisters can do. "The girls are over there." Without waiting for anyone to respond, Mary waved her arm and called out, "Leah! Hannah!"

Lifting their heads from their private conversation, both women stared at the group, taking a moment before they recognized Freman and Benjamin. It was Leah, however, who smiled first and jumped down from the log, taking a moment to adjust her *kapp* that had slid back onto her neck. Hannah followed, and both of them ran across the field, laughing as they did so.

"Leah!" Mary scolded. "Both of you! Running like schoolgirls!"

Leah waved her hand at her sister-in-law, still laughing. "Oh, Mary! You sound like an old woman! *Mayhaps* it would do you *gut* to have some fun once in a while!"

Hannah leaned against her sister, laughing with her. A strand of hair fell from beneath her prayer *kapp*. When Leah reached to fix it, Hannah's own *kapp* fell off. The white prayer *kapp*, so light and airy, fell gracefully as Hannah reached up, trying to stop it. She turned around, her hand grazing the top of the *kapp*, just as Anna managed to catch it.

"Oh, help," she muttered, her cheeks flushing red, as she took it back from Anna.

As decorum dictated, Freman turned his head, his eyes scanning the field and seeing Cris standing at the edge of the pond. "Why, there's a good idea," he said to no one in particular. "Fishing. A calming hobby. Allows a person to relax, enjoy nature, and reflect on all of the blessings God has bestowed upon us."

"Indeed! Fishing is a *wunderbarr gut* idea. If I had known, I'd have brought another pole to join him," Benjamin added. "Nice size fish in the pond too. I think I shall stroll over there to see what he's caught."

With a nod of his head, Freman approved of the suggestion. "We should all go, *ja*?" He glanced at Leah, his eyes barely skimming past Anna. The answering flush on her cheeks and glow in her eyes told Anna all she needed to know: the pairing was finalized and she need speculate no further regarding which of the Musser sisters interested Freman. Clearly Leah and Freman were courting.

The group began to walk toward the pond, Leah walking beside Freman and Hannah lingering behind. Despite her discomfort, Anna was left to walk with Benjamin. Just as they had the other day, they walked with an uneasy silence between them for a few paces. While others might have found his far-too-public (and lengthy) mourning a bit morose, Anna felt a kinship with Benjamin. After all, they had both lost in love and suffered greatly because of it.

"'I loathe my life; I would not live forever. Let me alone, for my days are but a breath.'"

Anna blinked and turned her head to stare at him. "I beg your pardon?"

The hint of a smile, one that was filled with sorrow and grief, touched his lips. "The Book of Job?"

Recognition flashed through her mind. "Ah, Job 7:16." Yet, she could not help but wonder at his word selection. "That does not sound like the King James Version, however." Searching her memory, she stared into the sky. "*I loathe it: I would not live alway...*"

"What is *it* anyway?" Benjamin replied. "Did you ever wonder about that? One word with no clear, definitive explanation. It is left open, for each individual to interpret. To fill in their own meaning."

Anna laughed. "That's an interesting observation, Benjamin!"

"For me, *it* is *life*."

"Oh, Benjamin," she said softly. "Loathing life is not the answer. Life is God's gift to each and every one of us. While losing someone you love is never easy, it is part of the journey that each of us faces. God has plans for you, and even though they seem bleak now, I can assure you that something glorious awaits you, if not here on earth then in heaven when we join Him."

He remained quiet as they walked, his hands clutched behind his back. She wondered if he was reflecting on what she said. She certainly hoped so. Her belief in those words had sustained her through many rough years, years filled with sadness and heartache. Even now, as she saw Freman beside Leah, she felt the all-too-familiar pangs in her heart.

Finally, he broke the silence. "I'm quite impressed that you recognized not just the verse number but the version of the Bible."

Stepping over a large rock, Anna shrugged her shoulders at his statement. "It is not so impressive when you realize that we only read the King James Version of the Bible." She looked at him again. "It sounds as though you are reading another?"

He nodded. "I read different versions, *ja*. I find that some verses are written just slightly different, helping me to better understand God's Word."

"And your bishop permits that?" Anna could hardly imagine Bishop Troyer's reaction if he learned that anyone in *his g'may* read other versions of the Bible. Still, she admired Benjamin's curiosity as well as his determination to satisfy it by reading other versions of the Bible. God's Word was God's Word; as long as people read it, He must be pleased.

This time, it was Benjamin who shrugged. "I never thought to tell him." There was a slight pause in the conversation as they continued walking after the others.

Leah ran ahead, her laughter lingering in the air behind her. Anna couldn't help but think that she had never seen Leah so gay and lighthearted. Nor had Anna seen her demonstrate such a whimsical attitude toward life. Clearly she was intending to impress someone, the emotions of her heart overtaking the control of her head.

As they neared the pond, Leah jumped onto the trunk of a large tree that had fallen by the edge. The massive roots torn from the ground indicated that the damp earth and a recent rainfall most likely contributed to its collapse. She held out her arms for balance as, with as much dainty poise as one could muster atop a tree, she walked the length of the tree trunk.

"Be careful, Leah," Mary snapped.

Mary's warning seemed to fall on deaf ears. Hannah paid no attention, having paused to admire the view. A nearby farmer had recently shocked his tobacco, and the long, even rows of drying leaves created a landscape the likes of which was never seen in the hilly fields of Holmes County. Freman, however, appeared concerned and quickened his step as he approached the tree, his hand raised for Leah to take.

"Now, Leah," he said solemnly. "You'll get hurt if you fall. There are rocks everywhere."

She spun around and laughed again. Stretching out her arms, she shook her head. "I won't get hurt," she replied. "Not if you catch me!"

Before he could respond with a firm "Don't!" she leapt from the tree toward him, just as she had the previous day. Only this time, her foot became entangled with a thin branch and she stumbled. Instead of landing in Freman's arms, she tumbled to the ground. There was a sharp crack, and even though the tall grass hid her fallen body, the noise alone made it clear that her head had struck a rock.

"Leah!"

Freman was the first to get to her side. He fell to his knees and lifted Leah from the ground, cradling her head in his lap. His silence, coupled with the expression on his face, spoke of the agony he felt for not having been firmer in discouraging her behavior the previous day. "She's not moving!" he exclaimed.

Seeing the accident, Cris dropped his pole and came running, followed closely by Hannah. Meanwhile Mary wrung her hands and cried, "She is dead! She is dead!"

Upon hearing Mary's words and seeing Freman's agony, Hannah sank to her knees and began weeping into her hands. Both Benjamin and Anna were quick to approach her, lifting her up so that she could be comforted properly.

"What have I done?" Freman mumbled, his eyes staring into Leah's face. "If only I had caught her!" The desperation of his words caused another round of screaming from Mary, who collapsed into her husband's arms. Hannah sobbed openly.

Anna turned to Benjamin and motioned toward Freman. "Help him with Leah. Check her pulse. I can handle Hannah." Without a question, Benjamin did as she instructed, taking Leah's limp wrist and bending over it intently. Everyone held their breath while he checked for a pulse, then sighed in relief as he nodded, indicating he had found it.

Anna continued. "Rub her hands, talk to her. See if you can awaken her!" Again, Benjamin followed her instructions, rubbing Leah's hands and murmuring in her ear.

Anna turned to Cris. "We must move Leah to a more comfortable position."

Disengaging himself from Mary, an act which increased rather than softened her wails, Cris nodded and hurried to join Benjamin. Together, they lifted Leah and transferred her to a grassy patch while Freman staggered to his feet, watching Leah's lifeless body.

"Her parents!" he said, his voice thick with grief. "What shall I say to them if she...?" His words faded, the sentence left incomplete.

Leaving Hannah's side, Anna turned toward the men. "A doctor!" She clapped her hands, trying to get one of them to focus on what she had said. "We must fetch a doctor!"

Immediately Freman snapped out of his shock. He nodded his head at the wisdom of her words. "A doctor! I shall go at once!" he said. He started toward the farm.

"Freman!" Anna called out. "Would it not be better if Benjamin went?"

Her words stopped Freman, and he quickly turned back toward the group. Although Freman used to live in the community, Benjamin knew the area best and could fetch the proper people to help Leah. Without further instruction, Benjamin relinquished his hold upon the injured woman and ran as fast as he could toward the farm on the far side of the fields. Anna hoped the doctor lived nearby, or that he could be summoned quickly from the phone that was shared between the neighbors' farms.

Mary fretted as she paced behind Leah. "I told her not to run! I told her that she would fall!" Mary reached for Anna, clinging to her as she sobbed into her sister's shoulder. "Why would she not listen to me? She never listens to me!"

Quietly Anna held Mary, whispering softly to the young woman, partially to comfort her and partially to stop her from rambling. Freman returned to Leah, taking Cris's place and supporting her head in his lap, his eyes staring into her pale face, his lips pressed together in a tight line. Worry was etched on his forehead and he briskly chafed her hands as Anna previously instructed.

Cris rubbed his chin with his hand, a look of distress upon his face as well. The older brother of both Leah and Hannah, he always felt a strong need to protect them. Clearly he felt as if he had failed. With Hannah and Mary lost to hysterics, he seemed torn between comforting his wife and youngest sister and helping Freman with Leah.

"What shall we do next?" Cris asked, the question directed toward the most rational thinking member of the party: Anna.

Surprised by the question, Anna stumbled over her words, but not before she felt the heat of Freman's eyes flicker from Leah to her. It took all of her willpower to focus on the injured woman and not lift her eyes to meet his. She wondered what he was thinking and why, in a moment when his intended needed his care, he would spare her a second's consideration.

"I...I suppose we might carry her to the farmhouse," she suggested softly. "It does not look as if her neck is injured."

"I will carry her." Freman quickly offered. "Cris, see to your *fraa*." He wasted not one moment and lifted Leah into his arms. Gently, he shifted her weight. Just then, a soft moan escaped the woman's lips.

Mary gasped, reaching for her husband. "She's coming to!"

Shortly after they managed to carry Leah back to the farmhouse and settle her onto the couch, a van pulled down the lane with an older, non-Amish man seated in-between the driver and Benjamin. The latter leaped out as soon as the van stopped and held the door open for the doctor. Rebecca stood on the porch, concern and worry etched in her pale face. The man hurried inside, a big brown leather bag in his hand.

Not wishing to crowd around Leah while she was being examined, the remaining members of the party gathered on the porch, Cris still comforting Hannah, who seemed in shock at the sight of her lifeless sister. She wept into his shoulder. Mary continued her pacing but, thankfully, her cries had ceased upon realizing that Leah was indeed merely unconscious.

Anna waited with them. She leaned against the house by the door, her eyes shut as she silently prayed for Leah's recovery. Seconds turned to minutes and the silence of the group led her to believe that she was not the only one praying.

The door opened again, the harsh noise of a rusty hinge disturbing her prayers. Anna looked up and saw Freman pass through the door, intent on joining them.

"What says the doctor, then?"

He shook his head, an indication that he did not have an answer yet.

For what seemed like hours, the small group waited in silence on the porch of the farmhouse.

"A concussion," the doctor announced as he pushed open the screen door. "No injuries to her body save a blow to the head. She will be fine but needs rest for a few days."

"Thank you, Lord!"

Anna felt the intensity of Freman's gratitude in those three words that he uttered. His tone, so filled with relief and grief, would not soon be forgotten by Anna. Such emotion could only confirm what everyone already suspected regarding Freman's feelings toward Leah.

Pushing those thoughts aside, she joined the rest of the group as they stood in a circle, their heads bent once again in a silent prayer, thanking God that He had spared Leah from a more serious injury.

❧ *Chapter Thirteen* ❧

WITH THE *ENGLISCHE* doctor suggesting that Leah not travel for a week, perhaps longer, a discussion immediately ensued regarding the travel arrangements for the group. Because the hired driver was scheduled to arrive in the early morning hours, and some of the group needed to return to Ohio, it was clear that not everyone would depart as planned.

Sitting next to Leah as she slept, Anna listened to the discussion on the other side of the bedroom door. After the doctor left, Rebecca had suggested that Leah be moved from the sofa to recover in her own bedroom, a larger room located on the first floor. Besides being able to accommodate the women tending to her needs, the room was also more convenient for bringing food from the kitchen to the patient. When Leah tried to refuse, her voice weak and the side of her head swollen from being knocked on the rock, both Rebecca and Jonas insisted.

"It will be better for everyone," Rebecca explained softly, her hand placed gently on Leah's arm. It was a motherly gesture, one that spoke volumes for the care that she had taken in raising her own six children. "Let me just change the bedding for you and then the men can help move you, *ja*?" she pursued in a kind, yet firm tone of voice.

"I'm such a bother," Leah moaned, shutting her eyes and turning her head away so that no one could see the tears welling in her eyes.

The doctor had left some medicine for her, a home remedy to address the inevitable headache that would accompany Leah's injury. Because it would make her drowsy, he also recommended for someone to sit by her side, at least for the first twenty-four hours, and gently wake her every few hours. Immediately Anna volunteered to stay with her while the others tried to figure out what to do.

Now, while Anna sat in the straight-back chair, she listened to the voices right outside of the door. She could make out Cris, Hannah, and Freman, each one speaking softly and their words almost inaudible. Benjamin, who had been surprisingly quick in fetching the doctor, had appeared visibly shaken by the whole incident, pacing outside as they waited for the doctor's prognosis. She presumed that now, knowing that Leah was injured but would recover, he was busy assisting his father with the evening chores.

"We should call *Maem* and *Daed*," Hannah said, a pleading tone to her voice.

Upon hearing those words, Anna nodded to herself, wondering why no one had done so yet. Who had made the decision to wait to inform the girls' parents? Surely they would want to know, she thought.

"*Nee*," Cris firmly objected. "*Maem* would panic and that would do no good for anyone. She needs to be reassured that Leah is fine first. A phone call would surely do nothing more than worry her, and undoubtedly, they'd arrive just as the van is coming to retrieve us. *Mayhaps* Leah herself, when she feels up to it, should be the one to make the call."

Anna heard Freman clear his throat. She could imagine him standing there, his hands clasped behind his back, his composure regained and his leadership restored. "Someone must accompany the others back to Sugarcreek to inform your parents," he said firmly. It was an obvious statement but one that had not been addressed as of yet. "They will have questions and need answers in order to be confident that Leah will be fine." He paused. "I believe either you or I must tell them."

The statement must have been directed toward Cris because she heard him mumble something in response to Freman, the exact words remaining unclear to Anna.

Rising from her seat, she quietly crossed the room to the door. Not wishing to disturb Leah while she slept, Anna slipped from the room to join the others. Carefully, she shut the door behind them just in time to hear Freman's next words.

"So then it is settled," he said. "You shall stay, Cris. She is, after all, your *schwester*. And I will accompany your sister home and speak to your parents. And, because we agree that only one woman needs to remain behind to tend to Leah's needs, I suggest that no finer care could be given to her than by Anna. You saw how quick she was to take charge when Leah was injured. I'd feel more comfortable knowing she looked after Leah."

Startled by his suggestion, she must have made a noise for, in unison, the others turned in her direction.

"Anna!" Surprised to see her standing against the closed bedroom door, Freman took a step in her direction. There was a desperate look in his face and she realized how concerned he truly was for Leah's recovery. "You will stay, *ja*? To take care of Leah and nurse her back to health?" His words, spoken with deep feeling, revealed respect and admiration, emotions that brought back memories from many years ago. She had seen that look before, and for just a brief moment, she caught her breath; she had never thought to see it again. The only problem was that the emotions were reserved for Leah, not for her.

"I'll tend to her, *ja*," she readily agreed.

Freman tipped his head toward her, an acknowledgment of his grateful appreciation for her sacrifice. Then, returning his attention to Cris, he said, "I shall go make the arrangements then," and hurried to leave the room. She suspected that he was going across the road to borrow the neighbor's phone because the Esh family did not have their own. Freman would want to contact Bishop Troyer and his companion to alert them about the situation.

"What's this about, then?"

All eyes turned toward Mary as she descended from the second floor and saw the three of them gathered together. Pausing at the bottom step, she looked from one to the next to the next. Her eyes narrowed and she pursed her lips, an indication of her dismay at being excluded from their discussion and decision-making process, but for once she remained silent.

Cris took a deep breath before he moved in her direction. "We've been discussing our plans, Mary. It has been decided that Anna will stay to tend to Leah," he said. "I shall stay too."

Her feet stopped moving and Mary stared at him as if he were speaking in a foreign tongue. "I don't think I understood you correctly," she said. Her statement was clearly rhetorical. "Why on earth should *you* stay?"

"I am, after all, her *bruder*."

"And I her *schwester* and your *fraa*," she quickly added, taking that last step so that she no longer stood on the staircase.

"Why would I go home without you?" Her eyes darted to Anna. "And why should Anna stay? She is nothing to Leah! Not like me. If anyone should stay, it should be me! I am her sister too!"

Anna watched the rising of Cris's chest as he took a deep breath. Clearly Mary was trying his patience. Again. "Now, Mary, it makes perfect sense that Anna should stay. Hannah can hardly walk into Leah's room without bursting into tears. Besides, *Maem* will need Hannah to comfort her."

"So you have decided...behind my back, nonetheless!...that I should return to Ohio without you? You would leave me to myself, to sit and worry about our dear Leah?" She wagged her finger in the air. "I think not!"

"Mary..." Cris attempted to calm down his wife, but she would have none of it.

Lifting her hand, she stopped him before he could say another word. "I find this a grave injustice. Once again, decisions are made without my consultation and my consideration...*nee*, my emotions...are not taken into account! How could I possibly walk away from that injured dove with any sense of conscience?"

"The *kinner*—"

"—Are just fine in the care of their grandparents," she interrupted. "And they prefer Anna's company anyway to mine! They'll be just fine if she tends to them while you and I nurse Leah back to health!"

Anna shook her head. For once, she felt compelled to stand up to her sister. "*Nee*, Mary, you should go home to little Cris and Walter."

"I insist upon staying!"

"I do not have a good feeling about this." Anna felt herself weakening under Mary's vehemence.

"Frankly I would find it rather inappropriate for you to stay here anyway!" Mary added, casting a glare in the direction of her husband. "Without a female chaperone in a house with a single man?" She clicked her tongue as she crossed her arms over her chest. "Scandalous, to say the least."

"Rebecca is here," Anna countered, a bit more forcefully than she usually spoke. "I dare say she is married, *ja*?"

Mary lifted her chin and stared at Anna, clearly unappreciative of her sister's defiance. "Married or not, Rebecca is not Leah's family." She narrowed her eyes and added, "And since you are neither married nor family, you cannot stay here with her."

And with that last cutting remark, a hurtful reminder of what Mary liked to make so obvious, Anna looked away. She resigned herself to the fact that Mary would, once again, get her way. Forcing herself to bite her tongue and hold back from replying, Anna said a silent prayer that God properly watch over Leah, because she doubted that Mary would.

Indeed, Rebecca kept watch over Leah till midnight. Then, through the early hours of the morning, Anna sat by Leah's side, praying fervently for her well-being. She prayed that God would guide Mary to focus her attention on the young woman, and not herself for once, while Leah healed. She felt a pain in her stomach knowing that, already, Mary was being negligent to her proclaimed sisterly duties. Instead of taking a night shift, Mary had quickly voiced her intentions of getting a good night's sleep, telling Anna to wake Cris when she left at four o'clock in the morning.

In the hush of early morning Anna heard Jonas and Rebecca awake and move about the kitchen, speaking softly to avoid disturbing their guests. When the smell of freshly brewed coffee began to permeate the house, Anna heard the kitchen door open, likely Jonas heading to the barn for morning chores. She also heard footsteps overhead and suspected that Hannah and Freman were awake, preparing for the journey back to Ohio. A few minutes later she heard a man's footsteps on the stairs, and once again the door opened and closed. Certainly, she thought, that was Freman, ever so thoughtful to offer his assistance to Jonas.

A half hour later, Anna heard the sound of an engine and tires rolling over the gravel outside, then the muffled thump of van doors slamming. The driver must have arrived. After leaning over to plant a soft, unseen kiss upon Leah's forehead, Anna rose to her feet and departed the room, her already packed suitcase in hand.

Freman stood in the living room, his own travel bag at his feet. Upon hearing her footsteps, he turned.

"Where are Hannah and Mary?" Freman asked as he stood there, confused by the presence of Anna with a suitcase. "Why is your bag packed?"

It dawned on Anna that, the previous evening, he had returned to the house after the decision was made for Mary to stay. Clearly, no one had thought to update him on the plans.

"Hannah must be upstairs still. Getting ready." She paused and lowered her eyes. "Mary decided it was best if she stayed in my place to care for Leah."

He appeared confounded by her simple explanation. "That wasn't what we agreed upon." The sharpness of his words lacked the warmth from the previous day. "You had stated *you* would stay."

His displeasure more than apparent, Anna wondered if he thought that she had intentionally abandoned Leah. "Mary was rather adamant," she offered meekly.

"Indeed."

Knowing that he was dissatisfied with the situation, and no words from anyone would change that, Anna excused herself and tiptoed up the stairs to awaken Cris and tell Hannah their driver had arrived. Her heart felt heavy as she returned downstairs.

In the kitchen Rebecca pressed a bag of sandwiches into her hand, "for breakfast or lunch," she said. Benjamin and Jonas took a break from the milking to see their visitors off. With quick hugs and tears of good-bye, Anna left the Eshes' home and headed to the awaiting van. Moments later Hannah joined her in the backseat, but after making a few comments about the journey ahead, she fell silent, exhausted by yesterday's events and still worried over the health of her sister.

With the sun not yet up, and most people still asleep except dairy farmers and early morning travelers, the driver headed down mostly empty roads. In the front of the van, the bishops talked to Freman, inquiring further about Leah and her condition. Anna sighed and pressed her head against the window, staring outside at the darkness. While it had been a wonderful visit and a welcome interruption to her daily life, the memory of Leah's accident—her lifeless body in the middle of the field—lingered in her mind.

She wondered whether as a result of the accident Freman might have realized the value of a persuadable mind. Had Leah listened to the others, permitting them to convince her that her reckless actions might be harmful, she might have escaped injury as well as the inconvenience forced upon her companions.

For a moment, Anna felt a sense of absolution for having a persuadable temperament, even if she regretted the emotional depths of pain it had inflicted on both parties. But to what extent could one allow oneself to be persuaded to act this way or another without compromising one's free will and personality, both considered, after all, unique gifts from God?

Years back, she had been shopping at the local fabric store when she overheard two *Englische* women commenting that Amish women were so *submissive and obedient*. That remark had stayed with Anna ever since. At the time, she had felt resentment swelling within her chest and wished she had the courage to address their incorrect observation, for contrary to the belief of the outside world, Amish people, including women, were not made from a cookie cutter. However, despite the ridiculous nature of their perception, Anna knew that reacting to it and addressing the women would be more than just plain rude (and certainly not an Amish thing to do); it would also convey a sense of pride, something Anna would not tolerate in herself.

But now, she was not so sure anymore. Had she been too *submissive and obedient* when she rejected Freman's proposal so many years ago? Or had she done so out of respect for the opinions of her elders? She had been so young at the time; how was she to know that her father and Lydia's opinions might be prejudiced? That their opinions were meant to persuade her to do something that benefited them more than her?

Then a new thought dawned on her: Was she just afraid of or uncomfortable with saying "no"? If so, she wondered if that was a flaw in her character as a result of her upbringing. Even worse, and the very thought of it tormented her, had her religion and her profound devotion to Scripture made her overly submissive, unable to stand up for what was right and good? Her experience with Mary seemed to say so. Not only did Mary always demand her own way, Anna always *let* Mary have her own way, even when it hurt someone else, like Leah, when she did so.

No wonder that, earlier that morning, Freman had viewed her actions with dismay and even disgust. She had not stood up for Leah, allowing Mary to get her way, once again. Surely it had reminded Freman of her inability to stand up for him so many years ago. The realization of how so much of her life had been guided by the coercion of others caused her cheeks to flush with shame. Tears burned at the corner of her eyes, and she turned her head to look out the window, blinking rapidly in the hope that no one would notice the tears that threatened to trickle down her cheeks.

❧ *Chapter Fourteen* ❧

THE RETURN TRIP felt much shorter than their previous journey from Holmes County, Ohio, to Lancaster, Pennsylvania, perhaps because the excitement and anticipation of the previous Thursday were now replaced with worry and silent prayers. While Anna was looking forward to returning home, anticipating the comfort of a regular routine and having missed the two boys, she remained anxious about having left Leah behind.

While she felt confident that Leah would recover in no time, Anna spent the majority of the drive fretting over having left the injured woman in the care of Mary. Silently Anna was forced to admit that she worried because of Mary's inability to think of others before herself. For so many years Anna had quietly excused her sister's behavior, since Anna's personality shied away from confronting or arguing with others. She was, she realized, a pleaser; a person who wanted nothing more than to keep others happy, and with that, she had lost the ability to stand up for her own opinions for fear of offending others—especially her own family. Now Anna recognized that this gave her family the power to easily persuade her to do their bidding rather than seeing to her own needs or desires or the needs or desires of others outside the family.

What Anna had once viewed as heroic unselfishness, mirroring her own mother's personality, she now suspected might actually have become a fatal weakness.

Rebecca had packed a bag of sandwiches and some fruit for the travelers so that they would not have to stop along their return trip for a meal. Anna had lost her appetite and declined to take one of the sandwiches. Only at Bishop Troyer's insistence had she finally accepted. Without having to stop, except to refuel the van, they made much better time. Indeed, Rebecca's thoughtfulness was greatly appreciated when, well before noon, the van pulled off the main road at a clutter of mailboxes and drove down the driveway to come to a stop in front of the Mussers' house.

Anna glanced at Freman, knowing that he was bracing himself for relaying the news of Leah's injury to the Mussers. He had been especially quiet during the long drive, his face turned toward the window and his hand pressed under his chin. She hadn't been able to read his expression, but she knew that his thoughts were focused on Leah. His concern remained deep and his mood dark. While he had not said such in so many words, she could tell he had been greatly upset at learning that Mary, and not herself, was to stay behind to tend to Leah.

She saw Freman take a few deep breaths before he reached for the door handle and swung the door open to exit the van. Hannah, who still was prone to weep for her sister, leaned against Anna, both of them watching as Freman walked up the front steps, Bishop Troyer trudging along behind. They had all agreed that the bishop's presence would help reassure Salome that Leah had not sustained any long-lasting head injuries.

While the two men informed Salome, for Raymond was still out in the fields working, Anna and Hannah quietly stood outside, watching as the driver removed their luggage from the back of the van. They waited until Bishop Troyer and Freman reappeared, their faces pale and drawn from the stress of dealing with an upset mother.

"She'll be fine," Freman said to the two women before he returned to his seat in the van. "But you best go to her. She's quite shocked with the news."

Anna nodded and started walking to the house, pausing to wait for Hannah to catch up. She understood Salome's reaction; it was frightening to have a child, no matter how old, injured. And, of course, it was not uncommon to hear of head injuries that were fatal. The Amish grapevine often spoke of a child killed after being kicked by a foul-tempered mule or high-spirited horse. Occasionally an adult would be the one who died after falling from a high place while doing maintenance on a house or barn.

As expected, Salome wanted to immediately travel and tend to her daughter, her distress only heightened when she learned that Mary, not Anna, had stayed behind. With both Anna and Hannah to comfort her, however, she finally calmed down, if not for her own sake than to avoid alarming the two *kinner* who, upon hearing the van in the driveway, had run through the fields back to the house. They had been helping Raymond with dragging the fields, their job to run ahead of the mules and pick up any rocks or sticks in the way. They had happily abandoned their work to greet their returning aunts.

Neither seemed particularly disturbed that their parents had not returned with their aunts. Instead, they clambered onto Anna's lap, both vying for her attention, a welcome distraction from Salome's tears of concern for Leah.

After ensuring that Salome was fine, Anna focused her attention on little Cris and Walter. She took them back to the house and set about preparing their noon meal while they played inside with a set of wooden farm animals. Their laughter and chatter warmed Anna's heart, even if she found it surprising that they didn't ask more than once about when their parents might return. Despite her vague answer, for she truly didn't know the exact date, neither child reacted negatively.

As Mary had correctly predicted, their favor toward their aunt far exceeded that of their mother, a realization that saddened Anna when she thought of what Mary so carelessly neglected. What Anna would have given for her mother to still be with her!

Even though she knew that heaven had welcomed her mother, Anna missed her dreadfully, especially at times like these. Sometimes Anna found herself fighting anger over a life cut short far too soon, especially for such a kind-hearted and loving woman as her mother had been.

Anna thought of her often, sometimes reliving the memories that she had, memories that she cherished and the only comfort she had left of her mother.

She remembered spending the cold winter months seated by the wood-burning stove at the small house in Charm. Entire afternoons were occupied by embroidering linens or quilting small blankets, items that would be given as gifts to brides during the next season or offered to new mothers for their babies. Sometimes, if there was an excess of items, Mother would take them to a local store, leaving them there on consignment so that the store owner could sell them to tourists during the season. But there wasn't a lot of money in that, nor did the Eichers' *g'may* support the idea of pandering to tourists.

Each season seemed to have its own memories, for in the springtime, they worked together to plow the family garden and plant vegetables. Anna had loved walking out to the garden in the evenings, after supper was finished and before her bedtime prayers, to see how much the seedlings had grown. Her mother usually accompanied her and they would stand, in silence, at the edge of the garden to observe its progress.

During the spring and well into the summer, the plants would grow and produce food that would be harvested and canned, food used to feed the family for the rest of the year. Most of the work usually took place in late summer and early autumn, the kitchen absorbing the smell of whatever food they were canning: tomatoes, cauliflower, chow chow, beets, and apples. Like the day she had spent with the King family, helping to can the apples, it was a joyous time with all three of the daughters working alongside their mother. No one complained. In fact, Anna suspected that, like her, both Elizabeth and Mary had always looked forward to that time of year.

Of course those wonderful days spent together as a family, enjoying each other's company as they worked, may have been common while her mother was still alive, but such days would happen no longer. The family had been dispersed, and the house in Charm was now occupied by another: Freman's family.

With her father and Elizabeth having moved down to Pinecraft, Florida, a place that Anna had little to no intentions of visiting, Anna suddenly felt as if everything in her life was in disarray. She missed the daily routine that she had become so accustomed to, even if it meant listening to *Daed* and Elizabeth's conversations that so often centered on their respected place in the community, a fact proven erroneous by the change in their circumstances. She felt as if she were homeless, wanting neither to live in Florida as a third wheel nor to remain in Sugarcreek for the sole purpose of serving her sister, Mary. She had no place in the world to call her own, and the thought created a cloud of sorrow to linger over her head.

To make matters worse, Lydia stopped by to visit on Wednesday morning, having heard from Sara Coblentz about what had happened.

"Such a terrible mess," Lydia said while they sat on the porch watching the two boys chasing the barn cats in the driveway. "Whatever was she thinking?"

Anna often wondered that herself. In hindsight, Leah's carefree, and careless, behavior had caused the situation. The change in the young woman's behavior while in the presence of a suitor had not escaped Anna's attention. If only Leah had just behaved like herself and not worked so hard to attract Freman's attention, none of this would have happened.

"Sara told me that Freman was quite upset over the entire matter," Lydia added. "Felt as if he were to blame."

"To blame?"

Lydia nodded. "*Mayhaps* he feels he might have been able to prevent it, that's what I think." She sighed and stared toward the horizon. "Young men often feel the need to protect others, I suppose, especially women. His worry is an admirable quality and speaks highly of his character."

Anna fought to maintain her composure at this last comment. After all, wasn't it Lydia herself, together with Anna's father, who had spoken against the Whittmore family years ago?

"Sara told me that no sooner had Freman returned to Charm than he turned around and left again!"

Anna gasped at this unexpected news. Quickly, she tried to regain her composure, hoping that Lydia did not notice her reaction. The last thing that Anna wanted was anyone to suspect that her interest stemmed from anything more than casual curiosity. "Left again? Did she say where he went?"

Lydia shook her head. "*Nee*, but she suspects he went back to Lancaster. He's been quite open with her that he intends to return to Indiana with a bride. His determination to settle down at last and his concern for Leah can mean only one thing. Sara's convinced he's intent on having that young woman as his wife."

If only Lydia knew how her words cut through Anna! Oh, the irony! It hurt to hear Lydia discuss Freman's fine qualities and suggest that he was more than suitable to marry Leah Musser when, eight years ago, she had asserted that he was not a good enough man to marry Anna.

Later that evening, after Anna had put the boys to bed, she sat alone at the kitchen table staring at a small spot upon the table top as she reflected on Lydia's words. His behavior toward her in Lancaster had softened, and for a moment or two, Anna had doubted his interest in Leah.

What she had then seen as a glimmer of hope, Anna now viewed as the afterthought of a forgiving man who saw her as a future member of his extended family. It would not do him any good to harbor hard feelings toward his future wife's relations.

If she had wondered at how little Freman knew Leah, she knew that, if he was about to sit at her bedside during her convalescence, there would be more than enough time now for the two of them to become better acquainted. With each passing day, Anna felt more and more despondent, her grief magnified when she heard nothing more about Leah, Mary, or Freman.

Not willing to succumb to her grief, Anna forced herself to focus on the little things around the house in order to take her mind off of the inevitable. She gave Cris Junior and Walter her undivided attention and soon developed a daily routine. In the mornings she made a game of cleaning the dishes and straightening up the kitchen. Afterward they walked down to the barn to offer assistance to Raymond. Without Cris, he was tending the chores alone. If nothing else, an hour or two of help would lighten his burden as well as occupy the boys' time and spend their endless energy.

Anna noticed that, without Mary and Cris around, the boys behaved much better, showing a sense of calmness and respect for authority that Anna had never witnessed before. She found that, rather than vexing her nerves, the *kinner* often provided her with much-needed smiles and laughter.

In the afternoons Salome and Hannah often came down to visit, the three of them sitting outside behind the house while the two boys played on the swing set or tossed a ball back and forth.

Anna enjoyed the adult camaraderie but found the discussions to be dissatisfying, especially since the main topic of conversation often focused on two things: the certainty of Leah's recovery and the likelihood of Leah's wedding.

"Indiana! What on earth will Leah do moving to Indiana?" Salome could barely focus on her needlework. It was four days since the accident, and with the news that Leah's recovery was progressing nicely, Salome had moved on to a new worry.

"*Maem*, you don't know that to be the case," Hannah responded, causing Anna to wonder if she was slightly put out that it was her sister, and not her, that Freman had chosen. But then of course, Hannah had Caleb, so any discontent on her part didn't make any sense. Instead, Anna chose to believe that Hannah wanted to be the first to marry.

Salome sighed and turned her face toward the now empty fields. There was a despondent expression on her face, and she looked as if she had aged overnight. "It was bound to happen that one of you would move away from us. Just the realization that it could be so soon…" She left the end of her sentence hanging.

Anna tried to shut her ears to the conversation.

Hannah too seemed bored with the constant attention being paid to a sister who wasn't even there to appreciate it. Leaning forward, she gently tapped her mother's knee. "*Maem*, tell Anna about the letter."

"The letter?"

Hannah nodded. "*Ja*, from Elizabeth."

Now *this* was interesting news, Anna thought. Not once since her father and sister had left for Pinecraft had Anna received a written word from either one of them; rather, her father had directed his brief notes to Cris. It was to be expected, she realized with not the least bit of jealousy, for she had never been of the same fiber as those two. However, propriety dictated that some communication would be shared with the Mussers, a way of indirectly letting Anna know of their circumstances without burdening themselves with writing multiple letters.

"Oh, *that* letter!" Salome smiled and turned her attention to Anna. "Seems they are having a *wunderbarr gut* time in Florida, the weather being most agreeable to your *daed*. Elizabeth wrote that she too is enjoying her time there and finding Pinecraft much to her liking."

Hannah sighed loudly. "Not *that* part, *Maem*! The part about Willis!"

"Willis?" Now Anna's full attention was focused on the discussion.

"Your *daed*'s nephew's son has been round to see them."

At this, Anna gasped. "I almost don't believe you! *Daed* has disowned him ever since Willis came calling on Elizabeth before marrying another!"

Happy to have some riveting news to share, Salome nodded her head. "It's true, *ja*. His wife died, poor thing. She was sick for so long and refused treatment from *Englische* doctors. She wanted holistic treatment, instead." The way that Salome said the word *holistic* spoke volumes for her opinion about that decision. "I heard they even traveled by train to Mexico for some treatment!"

"Mexico!"

Salome nodded. "Now that she's passed, he is alone and childless. He went visiting his parents who live down there now. His *daed* has arthritis too. In his joints." The reference to the arthritis reminded Anna that her father and Elizabeth had used that excuse as the main reason for leaving Charm in the first place. Leaning forward, Salome lowered her voice so that the boys couldn't overhear her as she continued with her story. "Elizabeth says that Willis comes round almost every evening to visit with them. Your *daed* has forgiven him and restored him to the family's good graces. It seems he has matured quite a bit over the past years."

At this part, Hannah interrupted. "He's to visit here to check on the property," she said, a gleam in her eyes.

Without saying it, Anna knew what that meant. If Willis were to marry Elizabeth, the family could be restored to the farmette. A young man could work the ten acres, possibly even lease some adjourning land to expand the crop yield. No wonder that Elizabeth sounded so joyful in her letter to Salome.

"She wrote that he's to stop by here to visit when he returns," Salome announced, picking up her needlepoint once again. "His *aendi* lives in between Charm and Sugarcreek, you know."

"Do you expect him soon then?" Anna was only half interested in meeting her distant cousin, but wondered what Willis could have possibly said to gain favor with her father after so many years.

"I suspect by the weekend," Salome said. "The letter was dated three days ago. And, if a wedding were to be announced, it would be within the next few weeks. After communion, anyway, wouldn't you think?"

Anna chose not to think at all. The realization that, quite possibly, not just Leah and Hannah could be married within the next two months, but Elizabeth as well, caused her a moment of angst. With everyone married, she would be the lone unmarried *maedel* in the family.

That was a thought that lingered long after Salome and Hannah returned to their house. If she never married, Anna knew that she would become a burden to the families, floating from house to house in order to care for *kinner* and *bopplies*. Then, when her services would no longer be needed, she'd be forced to move in with her father down at Pinecraft, the one place she did not want to live. He'd need someone to care for him, and with two of his three daughters married, that responsibility would fall on her shoulders.

The entire situation had become so complex in the past few weeks that Anna felt it was best to simply push it aside and deal with the situations at a later time.

After a nearly sleepless night, her mind racing with images of being forced to move to Florida, Anna faced the morning with a new determination: to think less about the future and focus more on the current day. *Who am I*, she scolded herself, *to challenge God's plans for me?*

Before the two boys awoke, she sat down at the kitchen table, a cup of steaming coffee set before her as she bent over a pad of paper making a list of things to do. While Mary was away, Anna was determined to be more productive than ever, and she would start by doing the very things that Mary neglected. Just the previous evening, she had noticed that the pantry was missing essential ingredients to make bread or even pancakes. Anna knew that

Mary detested going to the market, so she listed that as the first order of business for the day.

Shortly after breakfast Anna harnessed Cris's horse to the buggy and loaded the two little boys inside of it. They were excited to accompany her but even more enthused to learn that Anna intended to make fresh bread and sugar cookies in the afternoon. She listened to them chatter to each other, first about who would help Anna knead the bread, an argument that was quickly resolved when she informed them that she would make two loaves, instead of one. Satisfied, their attention drifted to watching the different cars that passed them, little Cris favoring the trucks while Walter preferred a red sports car instead. At one point, she let each boy hold the reins so that they too could drive the horse. To her relief, and secret pleasure, neither child misbehaved once as she guided the horse and buggy down the road.

The market was not busy for a Saturday, and the boys ran ahead to look at the candy section. Anna had promised them each one piece if they would behave, the reward carrying enough weight so that they'd followed through on their commitment to do so. She pushed the cart down the narrow aisles, pausing to kneel down and examine a large bottle of aloe vera water. With colder weather upon them, a daily dose of the liquid would help ward off colds and the flu, so she picked one and started to stand up.

A man stood behind her, reaching for something on the top shelf. When Anna turned around, she knocked into him and, startled, dropped the plastic container.

"Oh, help!" she muttered, kneeling once again to retrieve it. Thankfully the plastic had not cracked.

He too had knelt down to fetch the container and, upon doing so, their hands touched, ever so briefly.

Anna stood up again and took a step backward. "I'm sorry," she said softly, her eyes downcast as the color flooded to her cheeks.

He remained silent for a moment, his eyes studying her. And then he broke out with a smile. "Cousin Anna?"

Lifting her eyes, she tried to recognize his face. While not as striking as Freman, the young man was handsome in a more cherubic way with straight blond hair, cut in a simple manner across his forehead, and dark brown chestnut-shaped eyes. His skin was tanned, most likely indicating that he was a farmer. While, like most Amish people, she had plenty of cousins, this was one that she did not know. "Are we familiar...?"

He extended his hand, and when she reluctantly accepted it, he grinned. "Cousin Willis at your service." He bowed, just slightly, an awkward motion that embarrassed her enough to be thankful that the store was empty. "I'd recognize you anywhere. You bear a great resemblance to your mother."

She gasped. "I do?"

He laughed at her reaction. There was something contagious about his happy-go-lucky attitude. "Oh, *ja*! I met her twice before she passed away. I reckon you don't remember that family gathering?"

Immediately, she knew which reunion he referenced, for it had been just months before her mother had died. Certainly her mother must have impressed this Willis Eicher more than he impressed Anna, for she did not recognize him at all. Her manners, however, dictated that she not admit as much to him. Instead, she changed the subject.

"I had heard that you were coming here from Florida," she said. "Is that where you live now?"

He shook his head. "*Nee*, I was just visiting my parents. They too have recently moved down there, you see."

Anna nodded. It was increasingly popular for older Amish couples to purchase small houses in the Pinecraft community, mirroring the *Englische* trend of retirees from the northern states moving down south in search of a better climate. Many people only stayed there during the harsh winter months, migrating south like the robins and finches. That was why her grandparents had originally purchased the house. Other Amish, however, were finding the climate and activities in Florida more to their liking and stayed there year-round. Without having to tend to horses, farms, or other responsibilities, their time was freed to attend Bible study, visit friends, or simply sit outdoors and enjoy the year-round sunshine. And most everything was just a battery-operated golf cart ride away, a far simpler mode of transportation than having to hitch up a horse to a buggy every time an errand was required.

At least she finally understood how the reunion between her father and Willis had occurred. With the community being so small, it would have been hard, if not impossible, for the two men not to encounter each other...whether at church or at a store or even walking down the street! And, of course, neither her father nor Elizabeth would have wanted anyone to question the reasons behind their dislike for a member of their own family. Reconciliation was the logical answer in order to avoid uncomfortable situations that might result in unwanted speculation.

And, of course, with Willis being a widower without any offspring, he certainly would be keen to remarry. Rekindling the relationship with Elizabeth was, no doubt, an easy progression for him on his journey to find a new wife and rebuild his life. However, Anna wondered how he could rekindle such a relationship if he was standing here, in a store located in Ohio.

A moment of awkward silence fell between them. Despite being related, distantly at that, Anna realized that they were, in fact, complete strangers.

"I suppose you have heard from your father, then?"

His question interrupted her private thoughts. She flushed, too embarrassed to admit that he had not written to her personally. "I hear he's doing well," she finally settled upon as a response, figuring it was not a misleading statement. After all, hadn't Salome received a letter just that week?

"Indeed he is! And your *schwester*, Elizabeth too." He chuckled at the memory. "It was quite surprising to run into them."

Anna could only imagine. After so many years of *Daed* insisting they have nothing to do with Willis, something must have transpired to change his mind.

As if reading her thoughts, Willis continued. "Her friend, Martha, invited my parents and me to supper after church one day. It was *wunderbarr* to reconnect with your family. I would like to hope we have moved past our differences, for we parted on friendly terms."

"So Elizabeth wrote," Anna admitted. Another awkward silence fell between the two of them. She had never been one to speak for the mere sake of idle conversation. Now, however, she felt the pressure to do so. According to Elizabeth's letter to Salome, Willis might, after all, become her brother-in-law soon. "I hear you are visiting your *aendi* and checking on *Daed*'s property," she managed to say.

He nodded. "*Ja*, I am. And I heard you were tending to cousin Mary's two boys."

She glanced at the floor, feeling uncomfortable in his steady gaze. While he seemed pleasant enough, she wasn't used to engaging in casual exchanges with people she didn't know. And given his history with the family, she wasn't certain what else to say to him. "Speaking of the boys, I best go find them." She started to back away, adding, "It was nice to run into you, Willis."

His response was a simple smile and wave of his hand.

She hesitated and then waved back before turning around to continue walking down the aisle. At the end she glanced back and, to her surprise, saw him still standing there, watching her. The color rose to her cheeks and she hurried away, uncertain whether she was more eager to find Cris Junior and Walter or to simply get away from Willis.

❧ *Chapter Fifteen* ❧

T HE SHOUTS COMING from the direction of the Mussers' house startled Anna.

After a long weekend, an off-Sunday when they did not have a worship service to attend, then several days of watching the boys, Anna was enjoying her Wednesday morning working in Mary's garden. Salome and Hannah were entertaining the boys, giving Anna a welcome respite. The chill in the air that morning warned of the upcoming winter quickly approaching, and she wanted to enjoy as much time as she could outdoors, basking in the afternoon sun. Soon the weather would change and the joy of outdoor work would be dampened by the need for heavy coats, mittens, and scarves.

Mary's garden was smaller than the one at the Charm house. It was also not as well tended. With a heavy rake Anna removed the dead remnants of plants and weeds. Once it was cleaned and raked nicely, she would cover the dirt with a fine layer of straw, a way of protecting the soil for the winter as well as creating fodder for next year's garden.

Just moments before, she had paused to watch as Hannah raced little Cris to the mailbox, Walter's smaller legs leaving him too far behind to be in the race. Knowing that he'd lose, he lost interest and disappeared into the barn to climb the rafters and jump on the hay bales, a favorite pastime that he wasn't allowed to do when his mother was home but that Anna willingly permitted. She too had fond memories of playing in her father's hayloft when she was a child, although theirs had been much smaller than the Mussers'.

While Anna had watched Hannah and Cris's race on their way to the end of the driveway, her back had been toward them when they returned to the house with the day's mail in their hands. A thick vine had caught her attention, and using the rake as leverage, she had bent over to give it a strong tug.

The moment it broke free from the soil was the moment that she heard the shouts coming from the house. With the wind blowing in her direction, the loud noise of the commotion carried on the breeze.

Quickly Anna stood up, leaning against the rake's handle as she tried to ascertain whether the shouts were from joy or despair. Her heart beat rapidly and she had to take several deep breaths to calm her nerves. It had been over a week since Leah's accident. While Cris had called a few times, updating the family on her recovery, not one letter had arrived from Mary since Hannah and Anna returned.

With Leah on the mend, a letter was certainly expected, if for no other reason than to provide details about when they would all be arriving home. For that reason, Anna doubted that a letter had arrived with bad news. Certainly, if something had happened, Cris would have called.

Ruling out bad news, there was only one conclusion that came to mind: the contents of the letter surely must contain news that would be happily received by everyone...everyone, that is, except for Anna. And that surely meant that a wedding had been announced.

Regaining her composure, she set down the rake on the side of the garden and dusted off her hands on her dirty apron. She took one last breath as she prepared herself to hear the unimaginable. Over the past eight years, she had wondered about his life and where he had settled. In the quiet of her room, she had shed many tears when she thought of him happily settled with a wife and children. Upon his return to Holmes County, when she had learned that he never married, the gratification she felt could never be described.

Now she wondered at the irony of those feelings. Would it not be better if Freman had married a woman who was not so entwined with her own family?

Heading toward the house, she tried to steady her nerves for what she imagined was the inevitable announcement that Leah had written a letter announcing her betrothal to Freman. Anna's emotions ranged from happiness for Leah, a young woman who deserved a fine husband, to despair over the realization that, at last and without doubt, he loved another.

Stepping into the house, she let her eyes adjust to the dim light and looked toward the sitting area. Salome sat on the sofa, tears streaming down her face as she held the open letter in her hands. Hannah sat beside her, gently rubbing her mother's back as she consoled her.

"*Wie gehts?*"

Salome sobbed and waved the letter in the air.

A wave of relief washed over Anna, quickly followed by guilt. Clearly something awful had happened, something that had nothing to do with a wedding. How could she be so selfish as to secretly hope that the news would not be about Leah and Freman? *For shame*, she scolded herself as she hurried to Salome's side.

"Oh, mercy," she whispered. "What awful thing has happened?"

However, Hannah's next words proved her suspicions wrong.

"Leah is to wed and will be moving away," she said to Anna, tears in her eyes.

"I knew this would happen," Salome wept, dabbing at her eyes with a handkerchief. "How will I survive with her living so far away? And among strangers! What do we know of this man? Of his family?" Another sob escaped her throat. "I never should have permitted that trip to Lancaster!"

The color drained from Anna's face as she sat beside the distraught mother, fighting her own urge to cry.

It is done, she told herself. The decision from eight years ago, the one that she regretted on a daily basis, was now complete. While there had been room for speculation as to where Freman lived or whether he had married, she realized that she had still held out a whisper of hope that, *mayhaps*, circumstances would change and she would have a second chance.

Now, with the announcement of Leah's wedding, that second chance had instantly vanished...both in reality and fantasy.

"*Maem*," Hannah soothed, despite her own tears. She sat on the arm of the sofa and rubbed her mother's back. "You should be happy for Leah."

Salome clutched the letter to her chest. "Oh, I am," she said through tears. "She's a deserving girl. I just wish she didn't have to move."

Ignoring the bad feelings in the pit of her stomach, Anna tried to focus on Salome's words as she rambled on. Apparently Mary and Cris would return without Leah, a surprising but welcomed change of plans. Anna didn't ask what the reasons were for Leah to remain in Lancaster; she could only imagine that Freman wanted to spend some more time with his fiancée before they returned to Sugarcreek. Under the supervision of Jonas and Rebecca, they could make their future plans without facing any gossip from the *g'may*. Once they returned to Leola, they would only get to see each other during brief visits and on private buggy rides until they married.

Fiancée. The word made Anna stop breathing, just for a moment. How was this possible, she wondered? How had life played such an ironic trick on her? She lifted her hand and pressed it against her chest, feeling her heart beating rapidly against her palm. It beat for Freman and would never beat for another. What she had been to Freman, regardless of how briefly, was now reserved for Leah.

From outside Anna heard a shriek which was followed by the sound of a child crying.

"Oh, help!" She stood up and excused herself, not waiting for a response as she ran from the house in order to check on Walter. Thankfully she could tell that his cries were not those of pain or injury. Nonetheless, she hurried anyway, grateful for the excuse to remove herself from the inevitable discussion that would ensue between Salome and Hannah about planning for the wedding. The announcement would certainly take place at church after Communion Sunday, and within two weeks, on a Tuesday or Thursday, the wedding would come to pass, most likely at the Mussers' house.

After the wedding was announced, it would be a busy two weeks, indeed. The house would need a thorough cleaning with all furniture removed, walls scrubbed, and windows washed. Food would need to be planned and prepared, all of the women in the *g'may* contributing to help feed the guests, who most likely would number at three hundred or more. The daylong event would start with a worship service, just like a Sunday. Toward the end of the service, the bishop would stand before the members and beckon for both Leah and Freman to join him.

The vows would be exchanged and they would be wed. No rings. No kisses. Not even handholding. It would be a simple affair, but a binding one. *Till death do us part* was one of the strongest commitments an Amish person could make, second only to committing to a plain life according to the *Ordnung* of their religion.

Just thinking about what would need to be done exhausted Anna. At least, she thought as she entered the barn, the housecleaning chores would keep her mind pre-occupied until the day when she would have to watch Freman wed another.

"Walter? Cris? Where are you two hiding?"

She climbed the ladder to the hayloft and scanned the stacks of hay bales, immediately seeing a few that had toppled over, most likely upon the boys. She hurried over and lifted the bales, restocking them neatly on the side. When she saw Walter and Cris sprawled on the hay underneath, she smiled and pulled Walter into her arms while Cris stood and brushed himself off.

"Are you hurt, then?"

Walter shook his head and wiped at his tears. *"Nee, aendi."*

"Just scared?" She tried not to laugh as she plucked hay from his hair and shirt. "You look like a scarecrow!"

That made him giggle and she hugged him once again.

"Come, boys," she said, standing up and reaching for their hands. "Let's go make some cookies. I reckon that will make us feel better, *ja*?"

Walter stared at her, an apprehensive look in eyes that were still wet from crying. "Chocolate chip?"

This time, she laughed out loud. *"Ja, ja!* Chocolate chip it is."

They climbed down the ladder and, hand in hand, walked through the rest of the barn to head toward the house.

Overhead, a flock of geese flew in a perfect V, heading south for the winter. They honked as they passed over the Mussers' farm, and Anna stopped the boys to watch them. Then, silently, they continued toward the house, a new sense of peace and acceptance falling over Anna. God had plans for her, and *mayhaps* these plans neither included marriage nor having her own *bopplies*. But, rather than feeling disappointed, she said a silent prayer thanking Him for all of the blessings that He gave her. She felt a sense of relief that immediately made her feel better about Leah and Freman.

Later that evening, she managed to take a walk down the lane and onto the road. Salome and Hannah had stopped in, offering to watch the two boys and ready them for bed. Thankful for the break, Anna accepted their invitation. She escaped outside for some fresh air and time to reflect. While she walked, she prayed to God, thanking Him for lifting the veil from her eyes and allowing her to feel better. If nothing else, Leah's announcement gave her the closure that she so desperately needed: the emotional roller coaster that she had been riding since Freman's reappearance in Sugarcreek was over, at last.

The sound of an approaching horse and buggy interrupted her thoughts and she stepped off the road so that it could safely pass. Instead, she heard the beat of the hooves and gentle hum of the wheels slow down until, eventually, the buggy stopped by her side.

"What a pleasant surprise!"

Anna smiled at Willis, a slight flush covering her cheeks at his overly cheerful greeting.

"Out for a walk then?" he asked, although the answer was obvious.

She nodded. "A few moments of peace after watching my nephews all day."

"I heard," he said. When he saw her puzzled expression, he quickly explained. "I had promised to stop into the Mussers' house. I saw Salome and her daughter. They told me you were walking."

Anna wondered why he stopped at the Mussers' house and, even more curious, why he would inquire after her at all. They had just met the other day at the store, and being cousins of a more distant nature, there was little reason to develop a friendship. She didn't voice this question, however, not wanting to be construed as prying.

"Here! Let me give you a ride, Anna," he said, dropping the reins and jumping down from the open buggy door. Before she could decline, he reached for her hand and led her to the buggy step. Unless she made a scene, one that would certainly embarrass him as well as her, she had no choice but to lift her foot and climb into the buggy.

The buggy jiggled as the horse began trotting again, carrying them farther away from the Mussers' farm. She knew that she had to return soon in order to relieve Salome and Hannah. After all, once it was nightfall, Hannah would most likely meet up with Caleb. Almost every night at eight o'clock, Anna heard a buggy roll down the lane toward the other house. Moments later, it would leave again. Because Anna sat by the window, reading her daily devotional or the Bible, she couldn't help but notice Caleb driving with a passenger to his left as he departed the Mussers' farm. Anna had no doubt that he had come calling on Hannah. With Leah's impending marriage and Caleb's intentions more than clear, Anna did not doubt that a double wedding might be in the plans.

"I stopped by your *daed*'s farm today," he said as a way to break into conversation with her. "What a charming property!"

She glanced at him, wondering how she should respond. Again, she chose to not say anything, since her first thought was wondering why he would stop there at all. Obviously he knew that her father was in Pinecraft, Florida, and the house had been let out to another. However, since she had always been taught inquisitiveness was a sign of not minding one's business, she remained silent.

"Such a shame that it's not larger," he added, more to himself than to her. "Another twenty acres and a man could make a right *gut* living there."

"I imagine my *daed* did all right," she finally said, feeling slightly defensive for her father. Despite his flaws, she knew that he was a good man who had worked hard to provide for his daughters. While his erratic spending habits raised eyebrows, that didn't take away the good qualities that he had demonstrated.

"*Ja vell*, he supplemented with selling those minerals, ain't so?" He held the horse's reins with one hand and leaned back against the green velvet seat.

Anna nodded. She had never taken much interest in her *daed*'s mineral business. She knew that he had regular customers and that paid the bulk of the bills. Of course, he mostly saved money, but only because his wife was much more frugal than he. Since the house was paid for and there were few expenses, the bank account had grown until she became ill. After paying medical bills, what was left began to dwindle away under William's management, or lack thereof.

Anna knew that Willis was more than aware of the circumstances. She wondered why he would bring up such an unpleasant memory. After all, it was after their mother died that William began suggesting that Elizabeth would marry Willis. When the opportunity came for a family reunion, he was most insistent in insuring that Elizabeth spent time with Willis, hoping that such a match would salvage his financial situation. After all, Willis's family owned a larger farm only five miles away. Since he had numerous brothers, Willis would need to acquire his own home when he married.

And so, at first, it had seemed as if William's scheme would work. Several nights after the reunion, Elizabeth disappeared after supper. Anna suspected that she went riding with Willis, a theory that was proven true when Elizabeth confided in her that she would soon wed Willis Eicher.

Anna hadn't paid much attention to Willis at the reunion, choosing to spend her time with a group of younger women who sat on folding chairs near the older ones, just in case their help was needed. With over two hundred people at the gathering, it had been easy to miss meeting her distant cousin. But she had certainly heard enough spoken about him, especially when he married another woman without any regard for Elizabeth's feelings or the family's expectations.

Now, as Anna rode next to him, she wondered about why he had misled Elizabeth in the first place. Even more concerning was why, after seven years, he suddenly reappeared and seemed intent on making amends with the family. Had years of remorse and guilt finally gotten to his conscience? Or had he simply matured and realized the mistake that he had made?

"Do you farm, then?" she finally asked, feeling compelled to break the silence.

He nodded. "I did, *ja*, with my *daed*."

She tilted her head. "But you were..."

When she didn't complete the sentence, he finished it for her, "Married. *Ja*, I was. At the time, we lived at her *daed*'s for a few years. When she went home to Jesus, I stayed with her parents for a short while then went to visit my parents in Pinecraft." He paused. "Now I'm pondering

205

my future. Even the best laid plans can change so quickly, I reckon."

"I'm terribly sorry for your loss," Anna said in response. "How very tragic!"

Willis nodded, remaining silent for a long moment. While Anna didn't know the circumstances surrounding his wife's death, she felt certain that he had suffered at the loss. If they had invested heavily in trying natural cures, traveling to Mexico as Salome had heard, they must have fought hard to win the battle of her illness. Like most Amish people, however, he did not speak about the emotions regarding his loss. And Anna knew only too well the pain of death to someone far too young. Still, she also knew that losing a parent must feel different than losing a fiancée or a wife. It was expected for a parent to precede their children to heaven, even if that parent died at a young age. God called His people home when He wanted them to come, not necessarily when they wanted to go. It dawned on her that both Benjamin and Willis had suffered very similar losses, yet the former still visibly grieved while the latter seemed ready to move on.

Willis directed the horse and buggy to trot down another side road that Anna knew looped back toward the Mussers' home. As they approached the farm, he seemed to deliberately slow down the horse and glanced at her as he spoke. "Sunday worship is at the Troyers, *ja*?"

Slowly, she nodded her head. "*Ja*, it is."

It just so happened that the worship service was to be held at the bishop's home this week. It was the last worship service before new members of the church would accept their baptism, an event that triggered a busy season for the *g'may*. First there would be the autumn communion, a members-only service, and then the weddings would begin. Most of the weddings would be held on Tuesdays and Thursdays in the homes of the brides. Some wedding seasons, Anna would attend five or six weddings, most of them in her own church district or a neighboring one. While always happy for the newlyweds, Anna couldn't help but feel a touch of bittersweet regret for having given up her own chance at happiness.

"Will you be attending the fellowship meal afterward, then?"

His question surprised her and Anna couldn't help but laugh. "Of course! Surely you remember that I am watching my *schwester*'s *kinner*. It will do them good to see their friends and have time to play outside while the adults eat."

"The *kinner* must keep you busy all day!" He shook his head as he regarded her situation. "Certainly you are too young to be so burdened with their care!"

Not wanting to point out that most women her age already had two, three, or even four of their own *kinner*, Anna shrugged off his comment. "They are no trouble. Well, at least not when they are with Salome or . . . sleeping!"

This time Willis laughed with her.

It was almost quarter to eight when he dropped her off at the house. She thanked him for the ride, although she still wondered why he had taken the long way back to the farm. With a wave of her hand, she watched him leave, the blinking lights on the back of the buggy slowly fading as he drove down the road. Despite her unasked questions it had been pleasant to spend some time with Willis, especially since she suspected that he might, after all, have intentions of becoming her brother-in-law.

❦ *Chapter Sixteen* ❦

THE FOLLOWING DAY Anna avoided Salome and Hannah, claiming she wanted to thoroughly clean the house before Cris and Mary returned home. She kept the two boys busy by challenging them to see which one could help scrub a section of the floor first. Their reward was a batch of freshly baked sugar cookies. During the early evening, she let the boys play outside while she cleaned out the flower beds, making certain to look up each time Cris Junior or Walter cried out for her to "look at me" as they climbed a tree branch or threw a rock into the fields. By the time that the sun began to set, she hustled the boys inside to bathe and dress for bed. Having been a long day, one that gave her enough distractions that she had little time to reflect on her own concerns, she was thankful to hear the boys' evening prayers and tuck them into their beds. An hour or two of quiet and solitude might be just enough to restore her strength for her sister's upcoming return and the ultimate announcement that she would eagerly share without regard to Anna's feelings. After all, Mary observed little of Anna's emotions and certainly never gave one inkling that such an announcement would all but break her sister's spirit.

At eight o'clock Anna was surprised when not one but two buggies pulled into the driveway. Sitting in the rocking chair by the side window, she peered outside and saw that one of the buggies pulled into the small gravel spot behind Cris and Mary's house while the second buggy, likely Caleb's, continued down the lane to the other house.

Shutting her devotional, Anna set it beside her on a small table and quickly stood up. She could hear the sound of footsteps on the gravel and a low voice speaking to the horse. A man, she realized. After straightening the bottom of her dress, she hurried to the door, wondering if someone had come with news. She knew it couldn't have been a message from Lydia, for she had visited earlier that morning and stayed for the noon meal. And she could not think of anyone else who might come visiting, especially at such an hour.

She stood on the porch, rubbing her arms to keep warm. The night air was cool at this time of the year, and she almost retreated into the house to grab a sweater from the mudroom. Her curiosity, however, kept her poised on the porch, waiting to see who had arrived.

"Anna," a voice called out.

Still standing in the open doorway, she frowned. Willis? Why on earth was he stopping at the house so late in the evening? It was very late for visiting with the Mussers. Besides, didn't he know that Cris and Mary had yet to return? Then it dawned on her that Willis hadn't come to see the Mussers. Instead, he had come calling on her!

Before she could comprehend that thought, Willis walked up the steps to the porch and stood before her. "You must be freezing!" he said.

Her teeth almost chattered. "I am!" She gave a soft laugh. "I didn't know who was here. I must not have been thinking when I opened the door."

In the darkness she could sense a smile on his face. "I won't stay long, but *mayhaps* you should get a shawl?"

Without being asked twice, Anna left him on the porch and hurried back into the house. Alone, she stood there for a moment and tried to make sense of this unexpected visit. Nevertheless, he was a relative, so she owed him the courtesy of her attention. Quickly she put on a black sweater and grabbed a shawl as an extra measure of precaution. On the way back outside, she paused and reached into the cabinet for a battery-operated lantern. No sense in sitting in the cold and the dark, she reasoned.

"Better?" he asked when she emerged from the house, shutting the door behind her and leaning against it. He kept a respectful distance from her, just in case anyone drove by and saw them.

In the soft glow from the lantern she nodded, feeling shy in his presence. The idea of being called on by her sister's former suitor made her feel self-conscious. She didn't want to read too much into his visit, yet the idea of getting to know him better was not entirely dissatisfying to her. After all, the only man she had ever considered marrying would soon wed another, and that lingering fear of being a burden seemed far too real. *It is time to be more open-minded*, she told herself.

"I wanted to check on you," he said, breaking the silence. "I hear tell that your sister and her husband shall return by the weekend."

Again, Anna nodded, wondering where he would have heard that news but knowing that it was not her business to ask, even if she was curious. "That's what I'm told." A letter had arrived that morning, and Raymond had told her the news when she saw him earlier in the day.

He leaned against the porch railing, fiddling with his hat in his hands. He seemed a bit nervous, and that made Anna even more curious, for he had always seemed overly confident in the stories that her father told. Of course, her father hadn't been particularly fond of Willis, either... at least back then. "They've been gone for almost two weeks, ain't so? A long time for others to care for your *kinner* and work."

When he said it that way, she realized how long it truly had been. Not only had Anna been burdened with tending to the children for the last week, Jonas been left to tend to all of the farm chores without Cris's help since their trip to Lancaster. The decision for both Mary and Cris to stay in Pennsylvania had impacted more people than Anna originally realized. "*Ja*, it has been nearly two weeks," she said. "It'll be good to have them back."

In that moment, as she spoke those words, Anna realized that she hadn't really spoken the truth. After all, when Cris and Mary did return, everything in the house would go back to the way it was before the Lancaster trip.

To Anna's surprise, despite the extra work and constant demands for her attention, she had enjoyed her time at the house without her sister. The boys' behavior had improved tremendously, something that Salome pointed out on more than one occasion. There were fewer tantrums, arguments, and spells of crying, that was for sure and certain. The stronger sense of peace, calm, and love that filled the house made her long for her own home and family.

Anna feared that the peace and calm would dissipate immediately upon her sister's return. Mary surrounded herself with noise, conflict, and controversy. In fact, her younger sister seemed to thrive upon it. And, upon their return, Anna knew that she would lose her authoritative role in the house, relegated to, once again, serving Mary during *her* tantrums, arguments, and spells of illness.

The idea did not seem pleasant to Anna and she felt a sense of dread fill her chest.

"You're quite remarkable," Willis said, a slight hesitation in his voice, "to have taken on such responsibility during their absence."

She was thankful for the darkness so that he couldn't see the color flood to her cheeks. Compliments were far and few between among the Amish, and in her case, almost nonexistent, at least from her own family. "It's no more than anyone else would do, I'm sure," she finally offered, a gentle way of deflecting the compliment so that she didn't seem prideful in having received it.

They talked for a few more minutes, Willis telling her about a horse auction that he had attended recently. She listened, appreciating the detail with which he described a horse that he had bid on but lost. Then, after the conversation dwindled down, he made his excuses and bade her good night. Since no one else was home, it was only proper that the visit be kept brief. Anna, however, was left pondering whether the visit had been a good idea at all. It was a question that remained unanswered when she finally retired to her bedroom for the night.

The following day, Friday, she was washing the breakfast dishes while little Cris and Walter were helping their grandfather, when Hannah waltzed into the kitchen. The glow on her face and the way she practically danced across the floor told Anna all that she needed to know.

"Why, *gut mariye*, Hannah," she said as she set down the dish towel. She tried not to smile, wanting to let the young woman tell her own news before she congratulated her.

"Oh, Anna! You'll never guess!"

At this, she smiled but still waited.

"Caleb and I..." Hannah hesitated, lowering her eyes modestly for just a moment as she sought the right words. "Well, I know it's supposed to be announced at worship and all, but you are like a *schwester* to me, and..." She laughed and grabbed Anna's hands. "Leah is not the only one to marry this season!" Another laugh and a quick embrace followed her announcement.

"What a blessing!" Anna said. And she meant it.

When Hannah pulled away, she still held Anna's hands. "I should like for you to be one of my attendants, Anna. And I know *Maem* will be asking for help with the cleaning and all."

"Of course!"

She gasped as she gushed, "*Mayhaps* Leah and I might have a double wedding!" Then she shook her head. "*Nee*, Caleb wouldn't like that at all, I reckon."

Anna smiled. "It's to be your special day, Hannah."

"Oh, you're right, I know you're right!" Laughing, she released Anna's hands and hugged herself, giddy with happiness. "Oh, to think! I'll be Caleb's Hannah forever!"

Caleb's Hannah. While the young woman gushed on about Caleb's farm and his wonderful family, Anna was haunted by those two words. She had given up being Freman's Anna; that spot was now reserved for Leah.

Would anyone ever claim her, or would she simply remain "Just Anna" or, even worse, "The Old *Maedel* Anna"? The thought sent a wave of anxiety through her and she had to turn her back to Hannah, just for a moment, to compose herself.

For the rest of the day, she tried to focus on anything but the upcoming wedding season. Now that the Mussers would host not one but two weddings, Anna knew that the upcoming weeks would be chaotic and busy. For that, she would be thankful. After seeing Hannah's joy, Anna knew that she dreaded seeing Leah's reaction. To watch Leah laugh and blush over Freman was more than Anna could bear.

Instead of thinking about it, she catered to the boys' every whim, making them cookies and coloring pictures with them. In the afternoon, she kept herself busy by cleaning the house. There was something satisfying about scrubbing the kitchen floor and washing the woodwork. It kept her mind from wandering and her heart from breaking.

With Cris and Mary scheduled to return by noon the next day, Anna knew that, undoubtedly, Mary would be exhausted from the journey and want to rest with her feet raised. And then, of course, she'd want to share every minute detail of what had transpired since Anna had returned to Ohio. Mary would have an opinion about the upcoming wedding announcements, the rash decision of Leah's choice of a husband garnering more attention than Hannah's since Freman was in a better situation than Caleb. Anna could only imagine her sister's reaction to that realization; it was one thing for her sisters-in-law to marry, but to marry into a situation that afforded them a more comfortable lifestyle was something that would cause Mary a great deal of distress.

Invited to Salome's for supper, Anna listened patiently to Hannah talk about her upcoming wedding. Caleb had already gone to the bishop, she informed everyone, her eyes sparkling and her smile bright. "We're to be one of the first announced!" The delight in Hannah's expression helped Anna realize that, even if she personally was never to marry, she could share the joy of others.

With a deep breath and stronger commitment to overcome her feelings of guilt and regret, she vowed to not let her past cast any shadows on either Hannah or Leah's future. She leaned forward, forcing herself to eagerly listen to and participate in the discussions regarding the required preparations for the two weddings.

By the time she returned to Mary's house, the boys were tired, Walter especially, since he had played outside for the majority of the afternoon with his brother in the hayloft. Unlike most nights, both boys were fast asleep before she extinguished the lantern and, with the upmost of care to not make any noise, shut their bedroom door behind her.

In the darkness of the evening light she made her way back downstairs. To her surprise, she heard a soft knock at the door. As she was tucking the boys into their beds, she had heard a buggy drive down the driveway, but assuming it was Caleb for Hannah, she hadn't paid much attention to it. The knock at the door, however, startled her. She looked out the window and saw that there was a buggy parked behind the house. When she recognized the horse, a pretty black mare with one white sock on her hind leg, she didn't need to guess who stood at the door.

"Good evening, Anna," Willis said, just as pleasant and formal as he had been Wednesday evening. "Just wanted to check on you."

She gave a soft laugh, uncertain how to respond to such attention from a man. If she had wondered about his intentions the other evening, she was fairly certain now that his visits were not just a distant relation rekindling a long-lost family tie. "That's kind of you, Willis. I can assure you that I'm fine. Tired, but fine."

He leaned against the doorframe and smiled. In the glow from the lantern, she noticed that he never once took his eyes from her face. "You have undertaken quite a bit and succeeded quite well." Another compliment. This time, she knew that he saw her blush.

The sound of an approaching buggy caused them both to look toward the entrance of the driveway. When the horse turned, Anna knew that it was Caleb. His visits were regular and prompt; she could almost set the clock to them. He would make a fine husband for Hannah, she thought. And, with his farm located nearby, Salome would not lose both of her daughters.

"I had forgotten how nice this area is," Willis said after Caleb passed, pausing just momentarily to wave.

"Oh, *ja?*"

"I'm staying at my *aendi*'s, you know."

She had heard that and she said as much.

"Still contemplating whether I should go back to Florida or not." He crossed his arms over his chest and glanced upward, as if searching his memory. "The community is small and caters more to the elderly, I reckon."

Anna wanted to point out that Elizabeth was there. She didn't.

"And the summers are rather hot." He returned his gaze to hers. "*Nee*, I suspect I shall stay here, instead."

"Oh?" It was all that she could think to say when she realized that he waited for a response.

"I suspect that you will be busy tomorrow, what with your sister and her husband returning. I did, however, want to inquire whether or not you might be attending the singing after worship service on Sunday."

"Oh." It came out like a little gasp. While it wasn't unusual for people of all ages to attend singings, she hadn't gone in quite a while. With all of her girlfriends married, she had started to feel out of place, more a chaperone than a participant. "I had not planned on it," she admitted.

He nodded his head just once, his tone suddenly somber. "*Ja vell, mayhaps* you might consider it? I understand that another group of youth will be visiting from Bishop Kauffman's *g'may*." She remembered Bishop Kauffman from the van ride both to and from Lancaster.

"I…I reckon I could go." She didn't want to go, didn't want to feel like an old, unmarried woman. But she also knew that it would keep her mind occupied.

He grinned. "*Wunderbarr*! I shall look for you, then!"

That night, as she lay in bed, she tried to imagine herself married to someone like Willis. What little she knew of him conflicted tremendously with what she had heard about him from her father and Lydia. Elizabeth, being far too proud, was never one to discuss what had transpired. He seemed pleasant enough, Anna thought, full of energy and good humor. Still, she did not hold him in the same regard as she held Freman.

While she knew that it was not fair to compare the two men, the unfairness leaning more toward Willis than

Freman, she couldn't help but do so. It wasn't the difference in their appearances, Freman having a more striking presence than her cousin. No. The truth was that Anna much preferred Freman's thoughtful conversations that often touched on God and faith to Willis's more pointed and trivial dialogue. And, of course, that eight-year-old emotional tie still bound her heart to Freman. That was something Willis would never have.

While Anna was aware that autumn courtships often happened quickly, Leah's wedding to Freman being a perfect example, she had no desire for such a speedy courtship for herself, no matter her age. However, Willis's interest seemed genuine and she needed the diversion. *Mayhaps* attending a singing wouldn't be such a bad idea after all, she thought. She rolled over and shut her eyes, hoping for sleep to take her quickly so that she could forget the dull sense of loss that still lingered in her heart.

❧ *Chapter Seventeen* ❧

MY WORD!" MARY laughed as she exited the van, clutching her oversized purse in her hands in front of her as if creating a barrier between herself and her two excited children. Anna immediately noticed that her sister did not greet the boys with anything more than a smile. While Anna suspected that they were both disappointed, as was she, for both boys would have benefited from some affection, perhaps even a hug, from their mother, she knew that such affection was not typical for Mary. Or many other Amish mothers, she thought. Her mother, however, had always spared the three girls a kind word or gentle touch, something that had clearly not rubbed off onto Mary.

Making her way toward the porch, Mary glanced toward the garden and inspected her flower bed. "I see that someone must have been busy working!" There was an edge to her voice as she looked at Anna. "Such productivity! Why, I'd barely recognize the place, we've been gone so long."

"It's been only two weeks," Cris said, a weariness to his voice that Anna had never before heard. She could only imagine that, while living in close quarters in someone else's home, his wife's fussiness had taxed his nerves.

While Mary's observation was clearly exaggerated, Anna's examination of her sister was not. In just two weeks Mary's stomach had bulged. And so had the rest of her extremities. Anna immediately knew what she suspected would never be said: Mary's weight gain was not just from a pregnancy but from not helping as she had promised while staying at the Eshes' house. Her sister relished being pampered and waited on. In the past, during her last pregnancy in particular, Mary often remained in bed, forcing others to bring her meals and claiming illness when it was time for chores.

While Anna looked forward to another baby to love, she knew that Mary would be even more impossible to deal with over the next few months. And, because she was the one living at Mary's house, the weight of her care would fall upon her shoulders and no one else's. It wasn't a particularly encouraging thought to make her rejoice in Mary's return.

The driver pulled two suitcases from the trunk and set them on the driveway. After Cris paid the man for his services, he turned his attention to his sons. To Anna's satisfaction, he spent a few moments asking them how they were and commenting about how much they had grown. Walter beamed at the comment, which caused little Cris Junior to nudge him with his elbow.

"Now, now," Anna said softly.

Cris forced a tired smile and turned his attention to her. "We would have returned earlier but..." He didn't finish the sentence, leaving it dangling for Anna to figure out on her own. "Things have been well here, then?"

She nodded her head. "Oh, *ja*, just fine." She smiled at the boys. "Right as rain, wouldn't you say?" Both boys nodded eagerly.

Mary huffed under her breath.

"And the boys have been remarkable," Anna added with a glance toward her sister. "Quite helpful and very mindful during your absence."

At this compliment, both boys glowed and their father leaned over to tousle little Cris's mop of curls.

"I'm surprised you haven't asked after Leah," Mary said sharply, deliberately changing the subject so the attention fell back to her and not her two children.

"There have been several letters," Anna responded, trying to keep her tone even and kind. "From Rebecca Esh, anyway. She was quite consistent with her writing. Why, I do believe Salome received at least three letters from her."

"She doesn't have much to do, I reckon."

Mary's sharp remark did not go unnoticed by both Anna and Cris. Both looked at Mary, but only Anna managed to reply. "I suppose a farmer's wife always has something to do," she said. "Even more impressive that she thought to use her spare time to write to Salome."

Ignoring her sister's comment, or perhaps not even hearing it, Mary headed toward the house, leaving Cris to deal with the luggage and his sons. "*Ja vell*, in case you are curious about Leah," she said over her shoulder before climbing the steps to the porch, "she's recovered quite nicely, if I do say so myself."

Reluctantly, Anna followed. "I'm sure your care was greatly appreciated."

Mary smiled at the compliment. "I must say that I was surprised at how attentive the Esh family was," she added, lowering her voice. "She certainly was not lacking in companionship!"

Anna knew what her sister meant. "So I heard."

Stepping inside the house, Mary looked around as if seeing it for the first time with fresh eyes. The air smelled like lavender due to Anna using vinegar and water with a dash of lavender oil to clean. And the floor shone, the result of a good scrubbing on her hands and knees. With everything put away and no papers strewn about, it was as pristine and orderly as anyone could hope for.

"Everything seems so..." Mary paused as if looking for the word. Anna raised an eyebrow, wondering at the serious look on her sister's face. "Small!"

If Anna was wounded by the lack of appreciation for her efforts, she did not show it. She had not spent her time cleaning the house in the hopes of receiving compliments from her sister. Praise and appreciation were two things that did not slip through Mary's lips too often.

"After spending so much time at the Eshes, with that grand room of theirs, it makes this place feel as if I'm returning to an old, dilapidated *grossdawdihaus*!" The look of disgust on Mary's face said more than her words. It was true that the farms in Lancaster seemed to have a different layout than the ones in Holmes County. But Anna would be hard-pressed to call Cris and Mary's house dilapidated.

Fortunately, she didn't have to respond. No sooner had Mary started complaining than the door opened and Cris stumbled through it, a large suitcase in his hands. He set the bag to the side and looked around the kitchen. Contrary to Mary, he seemed well pleased with his sister-in-law's efforts. "Well done, Anna," he said. "You've definitely been working hard during our absence. It certainly shows!"

"*Danke*," she replied, too aware that a scowl had crossed Mary's face when she heard Cris's compliment.

"I reckon we'll all be working hard over the next few weeks," Mary added. She made no move to assist Cris with the bag. Instead, she headed toward the sofa and sank into it. Lifting her feet, she leaned back and stretched out, one arm tossed over her forehead. "Oh my, how travel makes me tired. I can't even imagine taking that drive to Pinecraft. Sheer torture!"

Once again, the door opened, and the two boys raced inside.

"Take off your shoes!" Mary scolded, her loud voice and angry tone surprising Anna as well as Cris and Walter.

"We don't have no shoes on!"

Mary lifted her head, her dark eyes looking in their direction. Indeed, neither boy had shoes upon their feet, for they had left them at the door as Anna had taught them to do during their mother's absence. Rather than praise them, Mary sank back into the pillows and groaned. "My head is throbbing. Cris, be a good boy and fetch your *maem* a cool cloth."

Gesturing that she would do it, Anna hurried to the sink. As she ran the water, letting it run so that it was cold before she soaked a washcloth beneath it, she waited for Mary to begin updating her on the events from Lancaster. The two boys took advantage of their mother's indisposed nature and slipped back through the door. Within seconds Anna caught sight of them running past the window toward their grandparents' house.

"Those Lancaster Amish," Mary sighed. "Quite different in nature."

"How so?" Anna handed her the washcloth and sat in the chair beside her sister.

Mary waved the washcloth in the air, its purpose forgotten. "So much commercialism out there. Even at this time of the year, the tourists are everywhere and quite brazen with their cameras and questions."

Not wanting to get into a debate with Mary, Anna remained silent. She did, however, feel differently about Lancaster County. Granted that they had only stayed a short while, she had enjoyed the different scenery and felt that the people she met were warm and welcoming. She hadn't noticed an excess of tourists, although they hadn't ventured into the main town.

"I simply cannot believe that Leah would move there!" The washcloth slipped from Mary's fingers, but Mary made no moved to collect it from the floor.

Anna frowned. "You mean she's moving to Indiana, *ja*?"

A harsh laugh escaped Mary's throat and she sat up, just enough to lean on one elbow so that she could stare at her sister. "Indiana? Whatever for?" She reached down for the washcloth and handed it, absentmindedly, to Anna, indicating that she wanted it refreshed. "Although I do envy that house, I do not envy the work she will have ahead of her." Glancing at her sister, who took the washcloth, a confused look upon her face, Mary quickly added, "Envy with a small 'e,' of course."

But Anna wasn't focused on Mary's admission of jealousy. She was, instead, focused on the fact that Leah was to move to Pennsylvania, not Indiana. "Is Freman to move his business there, then?"

Snatching the washcloth back, Mary lowered her head once again and dropped the cloth on her forehead. "Freman? Why do you bring him up?"

None of this was making any sense. "I thought that he..." She paused. Dare she state what she had presumed? "That he and Leah..."

"Oh, heavens, no!" This time, when Mary laughed, there was great mirth in the sound. "Freman Whittmore?"

Time seemed to stand still as Anna processed this information. Wasn't it just a few days ago when the letter arrived that so upset Salome? Hadn't Salome told her that Leah was to wed? "I'm afraid that I don't understand any of this," Anna confided. "Salome said that Leah wrote of an upcoming wedding. I presumed that she meant with Freman, especially since he left right away to return to Pennsylvania."

Still laughing, Mary finally sat up. She shook her head, smiling at her sister as if she were completely daft. "Freman didn't return to Pennsylvania. He was called back to Indiana, Anna," she said. "And Leah is to marry Benjamin." A slight pause helped Anna comprehend what she had just learned. "Benjamin Esh," she added, as if that might help clarify.

"Oh, my!" The two words slipped out in a whispery tone. She lifted her hand to her mouth as she turned away from Mary, not wanting her to see the shocked expression upon her face. How could she have gotten this so wrong? The sleepless nights, the tear-stained pillows, and the heaviness that clung to her like a weight around her neck had been for naught.

"We were all shocked, frankly," Mary continued. "But he was so attentive to her care, I rarely had to sit with her.

227

I don't think he left her side more than an hour at a time." A sigh escaped her lips as if the memory was a dear one. But, just as suddenly, her wistful look changed to a frown. "Although I'm not certain I approve of such a short courtship. They just met, after all—not to mention that he was still in mourning."

Anna remained speechless.

As usual, Mary did not seem to notice. She continued talking, oblivious that her sister had not responded to anything she said. "And both Cris and I did wonder, though, at how Freman would take the news. We were all so certain that Freman was going to ask Leah to marry him! Poor man, to have been jilted not once, but twice."

Anna spun around. Mary's words seemed to echo in Anna's head. She could scarcely believe that she had heard her sister properly. "What did you say?"

"Apparently, this is not the first time that his attention to a woman has been rebuffed."

Horrified, Anna stood there, her mouth agape and the color draining from her cheeks. Had people known? Was it possible that she had not heard other members of the Amish community whispering about his rapid departure from Charm eight years ago? How could she have been oblivious to the Amish grapevine? And, with Mary having most likely learned this in Pennsylvania, was it possible that such gossip had spread throughout the different Amish communities? The only saving grace was Mary's casual discussion of the matter. Clearly, the object of Freman's professed affection (and cause of his emotional devastation!) had been kept secret. For that Anna would be eternally grateful.

And, just as quickly as she said a prayer of gratitude, another thought struck Anna. Perhaps it was humiliation, and not rejection, that had driven Freman away from Holmes County so many years ago. If that was truly the case, the only reasonable question to ask next was what could possibly have brought him back?

Stunned, Anna felt as if the room spun around her, and she reached for the back of a chair to steady herself.

"As for Leah," Mary continued, oblivious to her sister's racing thoughts, "certainly you noticed that Freman had developed an attachment to her. Why, he practically visited here every day since his arrival! And arranging for her to travel to Lancaster. It's any wonder that Raymond agreed to it! It could have been quite the scandal if the bishop hadn't traveled with us. Of course, with Cris and me chaperoning, no one would have reason to speculate either, I suppose." She said this last part in a condescending tone. "And surely you saw how Freman was so concerned for Leah's well-being..." As if disapproving, Mary shook her head and clicked her tongue: *tsk, tsk, tsk.* "I was convinced that his warm feelings toward her were returned in kind. Makes me wonder at how fickle the young love of a woman can be."

In a moment of rare courage, Anna lifted her chin and stared at Mary, a look of defiance in her eyes. "Or that of a man," Anna retorted, surprised at the force with which she spoke. "Why, only six months ago, Benjamin was committed to another."

Mary shooed away Anna's comment by waving her hand.

"I will not be dismissed so easily," Anna said. "I'm not certain which is worse: Leah's apparent fondness for Freman, or Benjamin's acclaimed tenderness for his beloved. If both could find a replacement so easily, perhaps they never loved at all! A woman who truly loves a man cannot simply turn off her feelings, replacing the one with another! As for a man, Benjamin's mourning, while admittedly drawn out, ended quick enough and demonstrated that, given even a short amount of time, even a man can recover from the wounds of emotional loss...unless he too was not truly in love!"

Mary was not impressed. "What would you know, anyway, of love?"

Her comment cut through Anna and she felt a tightness in her chest. "I know that once found it would not be easily replaced!" She paused before adding, "At least for a woman."

"But not so for a man?" With a smug look upon her face, Mary lifted an eyebrow as she asked, "And what of *Daed*? He has remained true to our *maem*'s memory."

"I'm not certain if he is the exception to the rule...or if he simply could not afford a replacement!"

"Anna!"

Anna herself was dismayed at her comment about her father, but in her confusion over Freman, some of her deepest thoughts had spilled out. In these weeks apart from her father, older sister, and then her younger sister, she had had the leisure to reflect on their characters and to realize, to her growing dismay, that she could never truly love and deeply respect her own family. She could do right by them and feel some small affection to them as those she was tied to by blood and circumstance, but as for the deeper emotions of earnest trust, open and friendly compatibility, and a most loyal love—those emotions would remain locked away, perhaps never to be experienced again.

"I think I'll excuse myself," Anna said, a strained tone to her voice. "Get some fresh air and check on the boys while you rest." She took a step toward the door and paused, her back facing her sister. "And Mary?"

Her sister made a noise, indicating that she was listening.

Anna looked over her shoulder at her sister, stretched out on the sofa with the cloth draped over her forehead. "I know plenty about love, a love that never wavers and is always strong. The love of our heavenly Father for His children." Without saying another word, Anna pushed open the kitchen door and stepped outside, grateful that, finally, she had found the resolve to stand up to Mary—and to teach her a much-needed lesson too.

❧ *Chapter Eighteen* ❧

THE SHOCK FROM learning that Leah was not engaged to Freman as she had thought—a thought that had occupied her every waking moment since she had first suspected their mutual attraction—gave way to a new emotion: despair. Her heart ached for Freman, knowing that he must truly be distraught over the turn of events. However, she also realized that, once again, Freman had removed himself from Holmes County, the humiliation of rejection chasing him back to Indiana.

When she resigned herself to the fact that, most likely, she would never see him again, her heart felt heavy and her throat constricted with grief.

Would she ever again have a night's sleep without tears staining her pillow?

In the morning she went through the motions of dressing for church and helping to prepare breakfast. Mary fussed over the two boys, always insistent that they be dressed before breakfast in their white shirts with black bow ties already fastened at their necks. As for their shoes, she inspected them closely, mindful that there was not one speck of dirt upon them. When Walter's shoes appeared scuffed, Mary hastily removed them and insisted that Cris polish them one more time.

Anna paid no attention. Seemingly overnight, she built a wall around herself and retreated inside her own fortress. It was not the first time that she had done such a thing, taking comfort in her own distress and blocking out the world around her. Had she insisted on staying in Lancaster, had she forced Mary to behave like a proper mother, Anna might have been able to save Freman from a second round of heartbreak. Once again she realized with a perfect blend of remorse and shame, her inability to stand firm and her tendency to permit family members to persuade her had impacted the future of the man she loved. She remained pensive and withdrawn as she placed the sliced bread and cup of butter onto the table, her own appetite vanished and her eyes dull with sorrow.

No one seemed to notice, anyway.

It was a dreary day, with gray clouds hiding the sun, and a moistness in the air. The two buggies departed together, Cris with his family in one and Raymond with his in another. Anna sat in the back seat, holding little Cris and Walter as the buggy headed down the road toward the bishop's house. Had it been a sunny day, they might have walked, even though the distance was a bit far, since Bishop Troyer's residence was at the edge of the church district.

Between the overcast skies and her own dark mood, Anna remained lost in her thoughts, paying little attention to the conversation in the buggy. She was only vaguely aware that Mary was speaking, most likely complaining about a headache or morning nausea. Sitting in the back of the buggy, holding the boys on her lap, Anna stared out the back opening, watching the road behind them. It was long and winding, empty of traffic and lined with trees that were shedding their leaves. The bleak gray mirrored her mood and she shut her eyes, leaning her cheek against the back of Walter's head.

When they pulled up to the Troyers' farm, Anna barely saw the line of black buggies that had arrived before them. Young boys ran toward their horse, one grabbing the horse's bridle while another pointed toward an empty spot on the grass, indicating that the buggy should be parked in that spot. After the Musser family and Anna climbed through the door and stood in the driveway, the boys led the horse away. Absentmindedly, Anna watched as they backed the buggy into the indicated spot and, with expert precision, unharnessed the horse.

"Anna? Are you coming, then?"

Her empty thoughts interrupted, Anna looked at her sister, so anxious and impatient, and nodded her head, willing her feet to move in the direction of the Troyers' house.

The usual line of other women stood waiting to greet the newcomers, each newly arrived woman expected to pass through the line to shake hands and exchange a quick kiss on the lips from each one, until she assumed her role at the end of the line. The practice had been passed down for generations, a way of following the apostle Paul's command to greet each other with a holy kiss.

Mary often offered her cheek, claiming that she was sickly or not feeling well. The older women found her actions snobbish, but no one ever complained to the bishop.

Today, with downcast eyes, Anna obediently shook hands with everyone and greeted them as expected, but as she received Lydia's kiss, she remained silent. She couldn't look up from the floor, her eyes avoiding the older woman's as they shook hands.

Unaccustomed to such a response from Anna, Lydia did not release the young woman's hand and leaned forward. "Are you unwell?"

"In spirit only," was her simple response.

She felt a hand on her elbow and looked up as Lydia gently guided her away from the other women so that they might talk in private.

Standing to the side of the kitchen, partially inside a large food pantry that was stocked with rows of canned food, Lydia forced Anna to meet her gaze. "What's wrong, Anna? I haven't seen you so forlorn in years."

"Eight years," she replied softly. "To be exact."

This statement startled Lydia. "Eight years?" She frowned as she looked at Anna. "How curious that you should say such a thing! Whatever do you mean?"

Anna shut her eyes and exhaled, the effort a telling sign of the distress that she felt. Was it possible that Lydia didn't remember? How could something of such importance that altered the entire course of Anna's life be so insignificant and easily forgotten by another who professed to care so much for her well-being? "Oh, Lydia," she whispered. "I'm so terribly confused."

The older woman patted her arm. "Let me assure you that your father and sister will come to see reason." She smiled softly. "Willis Eicher is a right *gut* man, even given his past history with your *daed* and Elizabeth." She glanced up as if to ensure that no one could overhear her next words. "The fact that he is more partial to you does not surprise me. You always were the most godly and righteous of the three *dochders*. A man like Willis would certainly find you a *wunderbarr* partner."

For the second time in less than two days, Anna remained speechless. Was it possible that Lydia thought Anna was referencing feeling forlorn over Willis Eicher's past desertion of Elizabeth? That Anna might possibly be contemplating marriage to him and worried about Elizabeth's feelings? Such an idea seemed preposterous to Anna. While he seemed pleasant enough and the thought of restoring her family to their home was appealing, a marriage to Willis was not. And while it was one thing to have Lydia caution her from marrying someone, she bristled at the idea of Lydia pushing her into marrying a man she did not even love. So she said, stiffly but firmly, "I think most highly of Willis Eicher; we are, after all, family. But I can assure you that we would not suit as husband and wife."

Lydia ignored her words. "You are so like your *maem*," she said, a wistful expression on her face. "She would be so pleased to see you assume her place at the farm. She did so love that garden and house."

Anna gasped at what Lydia insinuated. "Oh *ja*, I do so love our house and garden, but I would not marry a man I do not love simply to secure maintaining them."

"True love comes after marriage," Lydia reassured her.

Oh! Anna wished with all of her being that could respond, that she had the courage to speak her mind in regard to that common cliché that the older Amish women told the younger ones. Anna wanted to voice her thoughts, to admit that her heart could be held by no man, save one. That she knew she could not be like Benjamin Esh and, after professing such deep feelings of love, suddenly turn to another for comfort. While Benjamin suffered for only six months, Anna was content to suffer for sixty years if that was what it took to prove the injustice of her decision to listen to others when she, and she alone, knew that Freman's place in her heart could never be replaced.

Furthermore, Anna couldn't help wonder how Lydia had learned of any interest held for her on Willis's part. After all, Elizabeth's letters to Salome indicated that Willis's intentions were elsewhere: with Elizabeth! If he had been deceiving her yet again, that alone spoke volumes of his character. "He has only returned to my *daed*'s good graces just recently. What do we truly know of him, beyond the pain that he caused both *Daed* and Elizabeth so long ago?"

Lydia laughed softly. "Ah, that is in the distant past. And Willis assures me their cordial relationship has been restored."

So Willis himself had gone to Lydia, hoping to secure her tacit approval of his plan to court Anna. How Anna recoiled at the thought! But thankfully, a stirring at the doorway interrupted their talk, and Anna could turn away without saying anything she might have regretted.

The church leaders entered the room, evidence of rain on the brims of their black hats. Still bristling at what she had just learned from Lydia, Anna quietly reassumed her place in line, once again between the stern Kate Schwartzentruber and the love-struck Hannah Musser. The bishop and preachers greeted the women with strong handshakes before they took their places in the middle of the room. Only when they sat did the women begin to file to their places on the far side of the room.

Hannah seemed antsy, barely able to stop herself from glancing in the direction where the men were gathered, just outside of the side door to the house. "Oh," she gasped softly, tugging at Anna's sleeve. "I think I just saw him."

In front of Anna, Kate gave a quick glance of disapproval toward Hannah. The room was supposed to be quiet while everyone found their places on the benches.

Hannah's comment, however, had reminded Anna that somewhere outside in the crowd of men, all dressed in black with their hats properly positioned upon their heads, stood Willis Eicher. With a tightness forming in her chest, Anna remembered that he had asked her about attending the singing. Surely he meant to escort her home, and that would signal to the others his intentions. She knew that she could not—must not—attend that singing.

The women had just been seated when the men began to file into the room. Anna stared at the ground, refusing to look up for fear of catching Willis's eyes upon her. She had a decision to make: to court Willis in order to marry or to risk remaining alone, left only with a fading memory of her dreams of what might have been. If only she could speak to Freman just one more time and with the freedom to apologize for the hurt, both old and new.

Her thoughts were so deep that, when Hannah nudged her, Anna startled.

"My word!" Hannah whispered. "I didn't know Freman had returned."

Immediately, Anna lifted her head, her eyes scanning the sea of black hats crowding into the room as the men assumed their positions against the back wall in the section of the room opposite the women. The indiscretion of her desperation to find him was not unnoticed, and she ignored the scowl that Kate cast in her direction. Instead Anna continued blatantly searching for the tall, broad-shouldered figure of Freman Whittmore.

She caught her breath when she finally saw him, seated on the farthest row with his back against the wall. For a moment, she heard nothing, a sense of peaceful stillness silencing the soft noises surrounding her: people fidgeting as they tried to get comfortable or the whisper of thin pages being turned in the chunky black hymn book. Her mouth opened, just enough that her surprise upon seeing him was visibly noticeable to anyone who might have observed her.

But Anna did not look elsewhere.

Her eyes remained upon Freman, stunned to see him at worship, and even more astounded to see him returning the look, his eyes meeting hers with a fierceness and intensity that confounded her. She could barely turn away.

"Why, I had heard he returned to Indiana!" Hannah risked whispering once again. "I wonder what brings him back…"

At this last statement, Kate reached over, her arm brushing against Anna's back, and poked at Hannah's arm. "Shh!"

With a slight rolling of her eyes, Hannah returned her attention to the middle of the room where the bishop and deacons sat, waiting for the singing of the first hymn to begin.

While the rest of the congregation sang, Anna merely moved her lips, no sound coming from her mouth. Indeed, she wondered, why would Freman return? Was it possible that he had not heard of Leah's engagement to his cousin, Benjamin? She doubted that was likely. Certainly Sara or even George Coblentz would have notified him, if not his aunt in Lancaster. And, numerous times during the hymn singing, she glanced in his direction only to find that he too was often looking in her direction.

For the first time, the worship service that Anna usually enjoyed so much seemed to drag on for days, not hours.

Immediately after the final prayer, she lost sight of him. The men hurried to convert the benches into tables, fitting the legs of each handmade bench into a truss so that the members could eat. Meanwhile, the young boys made a game of collecting the *Ausbunds*, their arms laden with the hymnals as they tried not to run back and forth to the empty crates used to transport them.

Anna barely had time to search for Freman. Immediately the bishop's wife put her to work slicing bread in the kitchen. With her back to the eating area, she couldn't look for him without the risk of embarrassing herself further.

"Can you believe it?" Hannah whispered into her ear, bumping up against her as she took two plates of bread from the counter. "I wonder that he's returned so soon!"

Anna bit her lower lip and acted as if she wasn't following Hannah's train of thought.

"Freman, you goose!" Hannah clarified. "He was sweet on Leah, you know!" Then, as if in afterthought, Hannah gasped and stared at Anna. "Oh, help! You don't think that..." She paused and looked around, making certain no one could overhear her. "I saw him staring during the service. *Mayhaps* it wasn't Leah after all..."

From Hannah's expression, Anna read her mind.

"Oh, help!" Hannah whispered as she took the plates of bread and started to walk away. Hesitating, she looked back at Anna. "You'll tend to the men, *ja*? I don't want Freman thinking... I mean, I am engaged to Caleb now..."

During the fellowship meal, Anna made certain to position herself so that she was responsible for refilling water cups for the men. She lingered behind Freman, the pitcher of water heavy in her hands, as she waited. Her heart beat and she felt weak in the knees. She needed to speak to him, but she was uncertain how to approach him.

When she finally noticed that he lifted the cup to his lips, she took a step forward and ever so softly touched his shoulder. When he glanced up, she saw a different look upon his face. Gone was the harsh looks from his initial days in Sugarcreek. In its place was one of warmth and—dare she breathe the word—hope.

"More water?" she said softly, averting her eyes.

"*Danke*, Anna."

With a trembling hand, she reached for his cup at the same moment that he too stretched out his arm to retrieve it. For a split second, their hands brushed against each other, and when he glanced at her, she blushed.

Holding the cup, she tilted the pitcher so that it was filled once again and handed it back to him. And then, she hesitated, just long enough to realize that she might not have such an opportunity again. "*Mayhaps* we shall see you at the singing tonight." Her words were uttered so softly that she wondered if he had heard her, for he had turned his attention back to the man seated to his left. She could only hope that he had and pray that he did.

"Anna?" someone called out from the other side of the table. She looked up and saw Willis staring at her. He cleared his throat and glanced down at his own glass, indicating that he too needed a refill. Then, with a smile, he lifted his wide eyes back to meet hers. Several men seated around him noticed and she saw them nudge each other as if they shared a newly found secret. Willis continued to smile at her, not seeming to care if others were paying attention. She wondered if he had overheard her words to Freman; it wasn't like Willis to call attention to himself, or others, like that. With a heaviness filling her chest, Anna returned to her duties and tried not to cast sideways glances in Freman's direction while she attended to the demands of the other men.

With so many people to feed and only so much space at the tables, the *g'may* always had at least two seatings. At some worship services, when guests came visiting or a special preacher stopped by, they might have even more attendees so they had to serve three meals. The unmarried men and women always ate last while the older men, visitors, or the men with smaller children usually congregated outside, or in the case of inclement weather, in the barn. Freman had eaten with the first seating, so she suspected that he now stood outside, perhaps talking with the other men or eager to harness his horse and leave, for she saw no sign of him when she sat at the table.

Almost an hour passed before the second seating finished their meal. Anna barely ate anything, just picking at some pretzels and cup of cheese. Only Lydia noticed Anna's lack of appetite.

"Not nourishing your body won't nourish your soul," Lydia said softly to Anna as she carried her plate and cup to the waiting wash tub in the kitchen.

Anna tried to smile but couldn't. "I'm just feeling..." She couldn't finish her sentence. She wasn't certain what she felt.

Lydia nodded her head and took a deep breath. "I understand, Anna. There's a lot weighing heavily on your mind." Gesturing toward the kitchen door, open to let in fresh air for the room had grown warm with so many people crowded inside, Lydia added, "*Mayhaps* you might walk on home before Mary finds you and has you watching her *kinner* again."

The scowl on Lydia's face almost made Anna smile, knowing full well that the comment was not out of line. Despite having been away for so long, Mary would undoubtedly seek out her sister so that she could sit and visit without having her sons tugging at her apron. "That's a *gut* idea, Lydia," Anna said quietly. "*Danke.*"

Once outside, she glanced at the sky. The heaviest of the rain seemed to have passed by, leaving puddles in the road and a sheen of glistening raindrops on the grass. Anna walked alone, grateful to have the quiet and solitude to sort through her thoughts.

Between Willis's unwanted determination and Freman's unexpected appearance, she felt torn: How could she thwart the one's attention while trying to attract the other? She knew that to achieve the former, she'd hurt someone's feelings, while in order to attain the latter, she risked embarrassing herself and possibly others.

Oh! she thought. *What to do!*

No sooner had she paused at the stop sign, looking both ways to ensure that neither car nor buggy approached before crossing, than Anna heard someone calling her name. At first she thought she had heard incorrectly, but when she heard a male voice shout, "Anna!" a second time, she turned around and squinted as she looked down the road from the direction she had just walked. Barely could she make out the tall, dark figure walking toward her from the bishop's driveway. But as soon as she did, she inhaled sharply: it was Freman, and he had called her name. To her further surprise, he beckoned for her to pause so that he might catch up.

Standing beside him, she felt small in his shadow. She had forgotten how tall he was, especially as he stood before her, his hands behind his back. He looked so proper in his black suit and hat. Unlike some of the younger men, he chose to wear a black vest under his coat, which added to both the austerity and the attractiveness of his person.

She could scarcely meet his gaze, and she wondered if he would reproach her for having commented about the singing, a gathering intended for the youth, not someone of his age.

"You are walking?"

His question, asking something that required no answer because of its obvious nature, caused her a moment of pause. *That* was not like Freman.

"I am," she admitted and glanced up at his face.

"But it's raining."

Looking upward, she gave her head just a slight shake. "*Nee*, I think it has passed. It's just a drizzle and I wanted the exercise."

While the air felt damp, the clouds were not as dark as before the church service had started. After realizing that she was correct, which made him not quite certain how to respond, Freman hesitated and stumbled over his words. "*Ja, vell*... then *mayhaps* I shall walk with you?" He

245

brought forth his hand and lifted it, just slightly, so that she could see what he held. "I've brought an umbrella," he said. "I've come prepared today."

The sincerity with which he spoke those words caused Anna to smile as she remembered Mary's fuss over not having an umbrella on a walk prior to their Lancaster adventure.

Silently, they fell into step, walking side by side down the road.

"I have just yesterday returned from Indiana," he said, opening up the conversation as they rounded a bend near a small farm. He seemed quick to add, "When we returned from Lancaster, there was a letter waiting for me at Sara's *haus*...your *daed*'s *haus*, I reckon...I needed to return to sort through a business issue."

Uncertain how to respond, she settled with a simple "Oh?" Anna knew it would appear too inquisitive if she questioned him further.

"*Ja*...and I received a phone call at my shop from Benjamin while I was there," he added. "He wanted to tell me the news."

At this statement, she remained quiet.

"He inquired after everyone, you in particular." Freman cleared his throat. "He wanted to know if the news had reached you and if you would be altered by it."

"Me?"

Freman quickly added, "I told him that I was not certain regarding your knowledge, but I was convinced that nothing could alter you, at least not in my eyes."

Anne hid a smile at his last statement, remembering how it contradicted his first observation of her when he returned to Sugarcreek, when Mary reported that he had found her greatly altered. She was, however, curious why anyone would have worried about her. For the moment she chose not to think about it, enjoying this light side of Freman, so reminiscent of the man she had known eight years prior.

"And...and what brings you back to Sugarcreek?" she dared to ask.

He lifted his head and stared straight ahead, a blank expression on his face. "Unfinished business" was his simple reply.

"Anna!"

They both turned to look in the direction of her name being called. A buggy drove up alongside them, and to Anna's mortification, she saw Willis slowing down on the side of the road. He smiled at her, sparing only a quick but polite nod in Freman's direction. "Your *schwester* asked me to find you. They're going to visit with the Troyers, and the boys wanted to return home."

Anna's eyes flickered to the back of the buggy, and to her surprise, little Cris and Walter grinned at her. "Oh..."

Willis gestured to the seat beside him. "Come now," he said cheerfully. "*Mayhaps* we might take them for a walk down that lane behind your *haus*."

Unable to speak, she felt Freman take a step away from her, his hands behind his back and his chin jutting forward. She thought for a moment of arguing, of telling Willis that she was not able to watch the two boys. Immediately she knew that she couldn't do that. Not to the boys.

"Enjoy your afternoon," Freman said as a parting remark, an edge of curtness the only clue that he might be resentful or (dare she hope?) jealous of Willis's attention. Anna climbed into the buggy beside Willis, prepared to send Freman a look of regret, but he had turned away, headed toward the Troyers' farm, and did not look back. To her dismay, he had disappeared once again, and along with him any hopes that she had of reconciliation or even reunion.

❧ *Chapter Nineteen* ❧

B Y THE TIME that Mary and Cris returned, Anna had fed the two boys an early supper. After cleaning up the few dishes, she sat with them on the sofa, looking through a book about Daniel in the lion's den, another favorite book that kept them entertained. She took her time reading it, pausing on each page to ask them questions and awaiting their response with the utmost of patience.

The afternoon hadn't progressed quickly, despite the energy level of both boys. After sitting for three hours at the Troyers' house for the worship service, one that they barely understood, for both the hymns and sermons were conducted in High German, they wanted to run outside, even though the damp grass made the hems of their pants wet.

Willis hadn't left right away. True to his suggestion, he walked alongside her as little Cris and Walter chased each other down the lane. When they came to a puddle, he was quick to offer his arm so that she could step over it without muddying her Sunday shoes. They walked in silence for a while, Willis occasionally commenting about the changing seasons or laughing at the antics of the boys.

Anna would smile in response, but her silence indicated just how distracted she truly was. To her relief, Willis did not seem bothered in the slightest by her lack of contribution to the discussion. If anything, he appeared to feel encouraged, rather than repelled, by it.

When they returned to the house, he lingered by the door as if anticipating an invitation to stay longer. Of course, without anyone else home, Anna couldn't invite him inside, but he seemed surprised when she didn't even offer him a refreshment.

"I best go see what the *kinner* are doing," she said, her hand on the doorknob as she anxiously waited for him to leave. She needed to be alone, just for a few minutes, to try to understand what Freman's appearance at worship, coupled with his gesture of walking her home, might mean.

His disappointment was more than apparent. To his credit, he hid it behind a smile. "*Ja*, best rest up too," he said as he headed down the porch steps. "We've a big night ahead of us."

She wondered at his choice of words, for she certainly would not consider a singing to be a big night. But as soon as the sound of his buggy disappeared in the distance, she leaned against the door and shut her eyes, thankful for just a moment of peace.

Freman's eyes, she thought. There was something in his eyes when he had looked at her, his solemn expression masking the true nature of his remark about the umbrella. He had thought ahead and intended to seek out her company, a premeditated action that suggested more than she dared to hope.

Is it possible, she wondered again, that his unfinished business had something to do with her?

"Oh, heavens!" Mary exclaimed when she entered the kitchen, pausing to set her basket on the counter. "Where did you have the boys this afternoon? Their shoes are covered in mud, Anna!"

"They'll clean up fine."

"True enough, I reckon." To Anna's surprise, Mary didn't argue. Instead, she crossed the room and sat in the rocking chair beside the sofa. With a loud sigh, she leaned her head back as she watched the boys beside her sister, pointing at the pictures in the book. Pushing against the floor with her feet, she rocked back and forth, the gentle motion seeming to relax her. "What a long day, *ja*?" She didn't wait for Anna to answer. "Hannah disappeared after the meal, I expect with Caleb. Why, I'm surprised at how open they are! In my day, everything was kept so hush-hush until the bishop made the announcement!"

"In your day was not that long ago, Mary. You talk as if you are an old woman," Anna chided gently.

"Oh, you know what I mean! Can you imagine if one of them changed their mind?" Just the thought caused Mary to shake her head. "The scandal it would cause!"

"They'd hardly be the first, I'm sure," Anna responded just as Cris walked in from having unharnessed the horse.

"Scandal? What scandal?" he asked, having overheard the tail end of his wife's statement. He set his hat on the counter and joined them in the sitting area.

Mary waved her hand in the air, as if he should already know what she was referencing. "Your *schwester* and Caleb. They're so *ferhoodled* that everyone already knows about their engagement. I was just saying to

Anna, just imagine how scandalous it would be if one of them changed their minds!"

"Back in our day, we kept it secret," he said, causing a laugh to escape Mary's lips. It was a genuine laugh, one that Anna hadn't heard from her sister in a long time. At the sound of it, Cris smiled at her, patiently waiting to be let in on the joke.

"Oh, Cris," Mary said lightly. "That's exactly what I said! And Anna teased me for saying it!" For a moment neither one of them spoke, and for the first time since she had been staying there, Anna observed a tender look pass between them. It dawned on her that Cris's boundless patience balanced Mary's never-ending grievances. Underneath their differences was one commonality: love.

"Best to save the reputation of them both, I suppose," he finally stated.

"I'm sure Freman wishes he wasn't so open about his affection for your other *schwester*," Mary added, too casually for Anna's care. "And he just shows up at our worship? Just out of the blue?"

Snapping his fingers, Cris abruptly turned toward Anna. "Speaking of Freman," he said as he reached into his pocket. When he withdrew his hand, he held a white envelope between his fingers. "I'm not certain why, but he asked that I give this to you." Before he handed it to her, he glanced at the front of it, quickly assessing the neat, cursive handwriting that spelled out Anna's name. "Must be from Sara, I reckon."

The surprise of his words coupled with the envelope forced her to stare at him, unable to reach out and take it. He waved it, just twice, as if to awaken her from a trance, and laughed when, with trembling fingers, she finally removed it from his possession. Mary, however, had lost interest in the conversation and leaned forward, reaching for the book that rested in Anna's lap.

"Where are you in the story?" she asked, looking from one of her sons to the other. "*Mayhaps* your *aendi* wouldn't mind if I finished reading it with you." The suggestion, a rare moment of attention bestowed upon them, caused the boys to nod their heads eagerly. She patted the stool next to the rocking chair, indicated little Cris should sit there, and opened her arms for Walter to sit upon her lap.

Despite her burning curiosity over the contents of the letter, when Anna stood to excuse herself, she couldn't help but notice the satisfied smile upon her brother-in-law's face as he listened to his wife reading to their children. Mary's voice became animated when she read the lines of King Darius calling for Daniel. Setting aside her prejudices about their individual flaws, she suddenly saw them for what they truly were: a family. The realization caused her a moment's pause as she watched them, the boys enjoying their mother's undivided attention on a dreary and lazy Sunday evening.

Quietly Anna excused herself, the envelope clutched in her hands. She had recognized the handwriting on the envelope as Freman's. Needing to read the letter alone, she sought the solace of her small bedroom upstairs.

Anna,

With a firm resolve to remain silent no longer, I have decided that the written word must suffice to carry my voice to your eyes.

Eight years have passed since my hopes were dashed and my heart broken upon learning that the disapproval of certain members of your family would keep us apart.

I made clear my intentions for finding a bride when I returned to Holmes County just a few weeks past. Yet, I fear that my intention may have been misunderstood, perhaps even by myself.

Do you not see, Anna? Even after all these years, it is you that drives my every waking moment!

You, and you alone, brought me back to Holmes County—something I realized almost immediately upon setting my eyes on you once again and hearing your sweet voice.

How is it possible that, when a creature so giving and godly pierces a man's soul, his affections could fail to be deciphered by the intended recipient?

Tell me that I am not too late and that your feelings are not gone. Once again I offer myself to you with a heart even more hopeful than when I first presented my intentions.

A word, a look...that is all that I need from you this evening. Into your hands I entrust my heart. I pray that you grant me the honor of proving my worth, both to you and to those who have, in the past, persuaded you otherwise.

With God's blessing, I shall remain very truly yours,
Freman Whittmore

❧ *Chapter Twenty* ❧

ANNA?"

At first, so lost in her thoughts, Anna did not hear Willis behind her, saying her name.

She was standing in the back of the gathering room at the Troyers' house, feeling awkward among so many young people. Earlier that afternoon, she had decided to go to the singing that evening, hoping to ward off Willis's attention in the optimistic hope that she might find Freman there. Having just arrived, her eyes scanned the gathering, seeking him out. After a few long minutes she finally spotted him on the other side of the room, detained by Bishop Troyer. She lingered nearby, hoping to catch his eye, but Freman seemed focused on whatever the bishop was saying. It didn't surprise her; Freman loved to talk about Scripture and how to live out his faith. It was one of the traits she favored in him.

After her initial reading of the letter, she had spent a good hour in her bedroom. It took her that long to compose herself, knowing that she dare not return downstairs until she could conduct herself in a manner so as not to draw attention to the change in her demeanor. Without doubt, Mary would recognize how unnerved

Anna had become, and in all likelihood, she would inquire as to the cause.

Anna knew it was better to remain isolated in her room than to expose her emotions.

While she sat on her bed, that precious single sheet of paper held between her two hands, her eyes reread each line. She savored everything about it: the words, the handwriting, the crisp white paper. Most importantly she felt the power of the heartfelt message intended to convince her, at last, that she had been mistaken, oh so very mistaken, in presuming the object of his affection.

Freman loved her and no other.

The world dissolving around her, she replayed the events of the past few weeks. Freman had returned so unexpectedly and made it clear that he sought a wife. Perhaps, in the beginning, he thought to find another, to repay the pain she had inflicted upon him in their youth. But soon he must have realized that her past rejection of him had been innocent in nature and true to a character that sought only to please. Torn between the wishes of her father and Freman's desire to marry her, she had defaulted to what she had always done, pleasing her family even at the expense of her own—and Freman's—happiness.

The events from the past weeks began to replay in her mind, her recollection of what she perceived as happening colliding with what she now understood so clearly. Contrary to what she and perhaps so many others believed, Freman's frequent visits to the Mussers' house had not been to court either Leah or Hannah; they had been a disguise for catching a glimpse of another: Anna.

While his presence at the farm had caused her endless grief and regret, his hope of seeing her had motivated him to make those trips from Charm to Sugarcreek.

Memories initially perceived as trivial suddenly took on a new meaning. It hadn't been a strange coincidence when Freman entered Mary's house, claiming to seek the Mussers' daughters when he rescued her from a rambunctious Walter. Nor had it been mere chivalry when he insisted upon her riding home in the carriage with the Coblentzes after that walk up the hill. She even began to second-guess the true reason behind the invitation to Lancaster, for according to his words, his interest lay not in courting Leah but in finding a way to reach Anna.

He loved *her*.

That thought, and that thought alone, had changed her.

"Anna?"

Now, it was only when she heard her name being called a second time and felt a hand upon her arm that she turned and found herself staring directly into the face of the only person she had not wanted to see: Willis Eicher.

"Oh, I..." She started to turn, to look in Freman's direction, but Willis's persistence forced her to pay attention to him.

"A moment, Anna," he said, a soft smile on his lips. "Please..."

Unable to say no without causing people to notice, Anna nodded her head, and with one last glance toward where Freman stood, relented to follow Willis onto the porch of the Troyers' house.

Outside, the cool air chilled her. Unlike the first time that he had stopped by Cris and Mary's house, his appearance unexpected and disarming, he didn't seem to notice that she shivered. Instead, he took a deep breath and lifted his chin as he prepared what she quickly realized was a speech that he had practiced, most likely more than once, before speaking the rehearsed words to her in person.

"I have made my decision," he proclaimed in earnest. "I shall not return to Florida."

"Oh?" She wanted to glance over her shoulder and through the door window, but resisted the urge.

"It is my intention to reside here, Anna, and in due time assist in recollecting your family to your rightful home in Charm."

A light dawned within her and she suspected that she knew what would soon follow. She knew she had to extract herself and return inside, the friendly atmosphere perhaps offering her the only hope she might ever have of approaching Freman.

"I'm sure that it would be painful to return to Barbie's family," she said. "It has only been but a few months."

Her mention of his deceased wife caused him a moment's pause. Her words clearly impeded his planned speech and he needed that time to recollect his thoughts.

"A few months gone," he admitted, "but a man needs to move on and live his life, wouldn't you agree?"

"Ah," she quipped lightly, grabbing the opportunity to alter the tone of the conversation. "Like Benjamin Esh and his engagement to Leah Musser."

"I..."

"You aren't familiar with Benjamin, of course, being that he's from Lancaster. Surely, however, you must have learned of the circumstances surrounding Leah's engagement." She sighed and added, "Although I did not know

Benjamin's fiancée, I am certain that she would not have easily, nor so suddenly, forgotten her intended."

"It's true that I do not know the Esh family, but I'm sure that his fiancée doted on him."

Anna nodded. "It is not in any woman's nature who dotes on her beloved to abandon the memory so quickly, not if she truly loved him." She sensed a presence behind her but resisted the urge to see who it was.

"Do you claim that women have stronger emotions than men, then?" Willis asked.

"Oh, I wouldn't go so far as to presume that," she countered. "But I do believe that we cling to memories much longer than you do. And is it any wonder? From the moment of our birth, our fates are so very different."

He seemed genuinely interested in her opinion. "Do explain, Anna."

"Certainly." She paused for good measure. "What is an Amish woman's role but to think of her future home? We are taught to manage the house, our chores focused on supporting our husband and raising godly *kinner*. Our worth is measured by those near and dear to our hearts. Men, on the other hand, are responsible for a profession that, in most cases, entails interactions with others, a chance to see worldliness for what it is, and, as such, protect his family from its grip. Even more important, his righteousness and reputation improve with the outward exertion."

He laughed, clearly amused by her statement. "And a woman's reputation?"

As she started to respond, she heard the door slowly open behind her. "Why, hers would decrease in similar conditions, for it is expected that only inward efforts, namely those within the walls of her home, extol her true virtue."

Someone cleared his throat, and without turning around, Anna knew who it was.

Willis glanced over her shoulder and greeted Freman with a smile of recognition from earlier in the day, giving her the opportunity to step aside to make way for the newcomer. The two men introduced each other with a simple, but firm, handshake. When Freman made no move to excuse his interruption upon their discussion, Willis easily shifted the conversation to a less intimate topic: their occupations. The irony of this subject matter, in light of what she had just stated, was not lost on Anna. In silence she stood between the two men, positioning herself so that she faced Freman more than Willis. While subtle in nature, she hoped the gesture would be recognized by the one while overlooked by the other.

"Oh, dear," she said when there was a lull in the conversation. She lifted a hand to her throat and forced a slight cough. "I think I shall go for a lemonade."

"Permit me!" Willis offered, all too eager to demonstrate his care for her needs.

He was gone but for a moment when Anna turned to Freman, knowing her limited chance to freely speak her mind, to share her thoughts, after reading his profound declarations of endearment.

Under the steady gaze of his eyes, cleverness escaped her. She opened her mouth, expecting words to flood out, wanting to respond in kind to the sentiment that he clearly crafted with intense consideration.

"Freman…" Her voice broke and it was all that she could do to contain the burning feeling that tightened her throat and threatened her eyes.

He delivered her from more suffering by lowering his voice as he said, "That is a word, Anna."

She nodded her head, emboldened by his gaze. "It is a word," she said softly. "The one and only word that I wish to say first thing in the morning and last thing at night." A single tear clouded her vision, and as it fell down her cheek, she gave a soft, embarrassed laugh and quickly wiped it away.

A look of relief replaced his pensive expression. Had he truly doubted her response? She could scarcely believe he had not known, all along, that she had never stopped loving him. With his confidence restored, he reached for her hand. Lifting it so that it brushed against his chest, the very spot where his heart beat, he sighed and smiled at her.

"We should leave here, Anna," he said, quickly glancing over his shoulder. She understood what he meant. Courting couples simply slipped away during the singing in order to spend time alone in the buggy, their disappearance an indicator that they were, indeed, courting someone, even if the companion was unknown. Some made a game of it, the woman leaving the group after the man had left. Leaving together would be the kindest way to signal to Willis that any sentiment he held for Anna would best be saved for another young woman.

In the privacy of the buggy, under the shadows of darkness, Freman shared the details of the past eight years. She listened without interrupting, her heart aching once again for having caused him such distress. To think that he had moved to Lancaster in hopes of bettering his prospects with the sole intention of returning to gain her favor! Tears filled her eyes once again, especially when he added how, after several years passed, his pride took precedence over his passion and he decided not to return. Despite hoping otherwise, he simply presumed she had wed another and tried to forget.

"Indiana is where I decided to live," he told her. "*Mayhaps* in the back of my mind I thought I would hear word of you and learn of your fate. Who had you married? How many *kinner* were you raising? Never did I imagine that my *schwester* would rent the very house where we said good night... and eventually good-bye!"

She lifted her hand and touched his arm. "I should never have yielded to the wishes of others!"

"And so I regained hope, Anna, when you said as much today!" He slowed down the horse and the buggy came to a standstill. Shifting in the seat, he turned toward her. "I knew that I had only one choice and that was to bare my feelings to you before another stepped forward."

Without saying his name, Freman's reference to Willis was understood.

She had not been dreaming when she suspected his jealousy earlier that day. That had fueled both the intimacy and urgency of his prose.

"No other could step forward," she said in response. "Did my behavior not indicate so much?"

"It did, Anna. But I was blind to see it." He laughed and pressed his lips to the back of her hand. "*Mayhaps* I feared that you could still be persuaded against me, especially when I suspected that my devotion to you was misconceived by others."

"I am afraid I could not discern your feelings," Anna said softly.

"Nor could I read yours. You kept them well hidden!" he laughed.

Then he spoke with regret of his unintentional misleading of Leah. Only when Benjamin told him of his engagement to Leah, seeming fearful of his reaction, did Freman realize how everyone had misinterpreted his attentions to Leah. He assured Anna he had been quick to congratulate Benjamin and assure him of his unwavering support. And Anna could rest in the knowledge that, indeed, Freman had never intended to mislead Leah, play on her emotions, or deceive her. Rather, he had relied on his friendship with the Musser family to enable him to be near Anna in order to ascertain whether she might yet have some feelings for him.

"And what of your father... and Lydia?" Freman spoke with some hesitance, revealing the old wound that lay beneath the surface.

She allowed herself a moment to think before she responded. What would they say when they learned the news? Would Lydia realize that her previous advice had been faulty? Would her father, having faced the very financial hardships that had caused him to scorn the Whittmore family eight years ago, be softer and more accepting?

"I am of the opinion," she began slowly and thoughtfully, "that my love and respect for my *daed*, Lydia, and even my *schwesters* is enough to persuade them of the sensibilities of my decision in such a way that we will receive their favor, if not also their blessing." She paused, her resolve strengthened as she realized that submitting her life to God meant that His will should take precedence over the wishes of her family. If she had not succumbed to the pressure of others' opinions, God would have led her to make wiser decisions.

For a moment she was sobered by the thought, but then another followed, which she shared with Freman. "And we will put the past behind us and show mercy to my family as God has shown mercy to us. After all, He sent His Son, Jesus, to take on the burden of our sins. I have learned, Freman, that God's mercy is about second chances. God needed to teach me to rely more on Him than on the desires and opinions of others. Then He graciously gave me a second chance to make right the wrong I did to you—to us."

Freman seemed to digest her words, nodding his head as he silently mulled over her acceptance of culpability in the decisions that had so impacted their lives. Then, with a deep and satisfied sigh, he reached for her hand and lifted it to his lips, gently pressing them to her skin. "There is my sweet Anna. I've waited so long for her to return to me."

Anna leaned her head against his shoulder, shutting her eyes as she savored the feeling of her hand still being held by his. "And your sweet Anna will never leave your side again," she whispered.

For the next hour Freman directed the horse down the dark roads surrounding the Mussers' farm. They talked of the future, having both readily agreed the past had been a time of chastening and maturing, an interlude that fulfilled God's plans for them rather than their own. Who were they to question the path chosen for them, especially since the destination was exactly to their liking? He had led them apart, knowing that their time would be well spent. Now, in the way only God could do, after so many years apart their paths converged once again, and they knew they would never stray onto any other road.

Neither could be persuaded otherwise.

⚜ *Epilogue* ⚜

ITH THE BASKET of food tucked over her arm, Anna headed out the side door of the house and walked, barefoot, across the dry, dusty yard toward the large cluster of outbuildings on the other side of the stable. Two horses peered out from the opened Dutch stall doors, one chewing some hay while watching her walk past.

In the small patch of grass between the stable and the driveway leading to the buildings, a small flock of brown chickens scratched and pecked at the dirt. Their big yellow feet kicked up the soil, looking for bugs or worms to eat. As Anna walked through them, a large rooster, his red comb dangling to one side of his head, came charging at her. She had anticipated the move and swung the basket in his direction to scare him away.

The noise of saws cutting wood and hammers smashing nails came from the open doors of the larger of the two buildings. Even though it was the last week of March, an early spring had blessed them with cool breezes and warm sunshine, while other sections of the northeast still battled a cold front from Canada. Anna suspected her sister Mary still wore a black shawl to ward off a chill while her father and Elizabeth were enjoying the Florida sunshine.

"Hullo there!"

She smiled shyly at the young man who greeted her.

He sat atop the roof of a shed just outside the building, nailing shingles to the naked wood. He pushed his hat back and pointed toward the basket which he undoubtedly knew was filled with her good home-cooked food.

"That's for me, *ja*?" the man teased.

"*Nee*, Luke, not today." She smiled back at him. "You know I bring food for all of you on Fridays!"

Laughing, Luke pointed toward the doorway. "He's in there, Anna. In the back."

She nodded and hurried through the opening, letting her eyes adjust to the darkness as she scanned the building, hoping to spot her husband.

Only four months had passed since she had moved to Indiana. If she had feared that she'd miss Ohio, she soon realized that she barely gave thought to Sugarcreek or those that she had left behind. Oh, she prayed for them, each and every one of them, each night when she asked God to bless her family. But to say that she missed Ohio and tending to her sister? Not at all.

From the first week she arrived in Indiana with Freman, she felt that she had finally arrived home. A few years ago he had purchased a small white house with a lot of potential. When he lived there alone, he had only furnished it with the bare essentials. Now that Anna had arrived, she had transformed it from a cold bachelor house into a warm and inviting home.

The people in Freman's *g'may* welcomed her with open arms. Within days of her arrival, a steady stream of women arrived, their arms laden with boxes of canned goods to donate to her pantry. Since they had married in Sugarcreek without the benefit of Freman's community in attendance, the gifts of food were their way of helping her prepare for the winter until she could start her own garden in the spring.

From that moment onward, Anna knew the true meaning of feeling blessed.

He spotted her before she saw him. She could feel the intensity of him staring at her and turned, not expecting to see him leaning against the office door, a clipboard in his hand and the hint of a smile on his face.

"You scared me!" But she smiled anyway.

"How so, Anna? You were looking for me, *ja*? Now that you've found me, why should you be startled?"

She laughed at his gentle teasing, loving the little word games that he played with her. "I think you enjoy surprising me!"

He set down the clipboard on the file cabinet outside of his office and strode toward her, his eyes quickly scanning the building to see if anyone was nearby. Most of the men were out back, sitting at a picnic table and eating the food that their wives had packed for them, while a few men still worked out front on the shingling. With the building being empty of inquisitive eyes, Freman stretched out his hand for her to take and pulled her toward him, his tall frame overshadowing her small, petite one.

"I enjoy many things about you," he said, his voice soft and his eyes staring into hers. "But nothing more than this…just having you here, with me, in my arms."

She felt the color rise to her cheeks.

He leaned down and placed a gentle kiss upon her forehead. "And a basket of your *wunderbarr* good food helps too."

Still holding her hand, he gestured toward the door that led outside and toward the area where the men sat at the picnic table. He didn't have to speak for she could read his mind. With his full and open affection upon her, she did not need to hear words from his mouth to understand his language of love.

Overhead a hawk soared high in the sky, its wings spread open as it floated so elegantly through the higher altitudes. Its proximity to heaven seemed to be nature's way of praising God. Each gentle swoop was a silent reminder that glory remained to the One who created such magnificence... from the gentle ability of the hawk to glide through the air to the powerful capacity of the human to love over the years. It was a lesson not lost on Anna as she walked alongside her husband. Never again would she succumb to the persuasive forces of others. Instead she would rely on and rest in the good and gracious providence of her heavenly Father. For she knew God had the power to ensure His plan was followed, regardless, and no matter what man might say or do, His will would always prevail.

❧ *Glossary* ❧

ach vell—an expression similar to "Oh well"
aendi—aunt
Ausbund—Amish hymnal
boppli—baby
bruder—brother
daed—father
danke—thank you
dochder—daughter
Englische—non-Amish people
Englischer—a non-Amish person
ferhoodled—confused and mixed up, often describes a
    young adults who realize they like someone
fraa—wife
g'may—church district
grossdawdi—grandfather
grossdawdihaus—small house attached to the main dwelling
grossmammi—grandmother
gut—good
gut mariye—good morning
haus—house
ja—yes
kapp—prayer covering or cap
kinner—children
kum—come
maedel—older, unmarried woman

maem—mother

mayhaps—maybe

nee—no

Ordnung—unwritten rules that govern the *g'may*

Rumschpringe—period of "fun" time for youths

schwester—sister

verrickt—crazy

wie gehts—what's going on?

wilkum—welcome

wunderbarr—wonderful

vorsinger—the lead singer at worship services, youth gatherings, and school

❧ *Other Books by Sarah Price* ❧

THE AMISH CLASSIC SERIES
First Impressions
The Matchmaker

THE AMISH OF LANCASTER SERIES
Fields of Corn
Hills of Wheat
Pastures of Faith
Valley of Hope

PRISCILLA'S STORY
Contains four novellas: *The Tomato Patch, The Quilting Bee, The Hope Chest, The Clothes Line*

THE PLAIN FAME TRILOGY
Plain Fame
Plain Change
Plain Again

OTHER AMISH FICTION BOOKS
Amish Circle Letters
Amish Circle Letters II
A Gift of Faith: An Amish Christmas Story
An Amish Christmas Carol: Amish Christian Classic Series
A Christmas Gift for Rebecca: An Amish Christian Romance

A complete listing of Sarah Price's books can be found on her Amazon author page at www.amazon.com/Sarah-Price/e/B00734HBQM.

❧ *About Sarah Price* ❧

THE PREISS FAMILY emigrated from Europe in 1705, settling in Pennsylvania as the area's first wave of Mennonite families. Sarah Price has always respected and honored her ancestors through exploration and research about her family's history and their religion. At nineteen, she befriended an Amish family and lived on their farm throughout the years.

Twenty-five years later Sarah Price splits her time between her home outside of New York City and Lancaster County, Pennsylvania, where she retreats to reflect, write, and reconnect with her Amish friends and Mennonite family.

Contact the author at sarah@sarahpriceauthor.com. Visit her blog at www.sarahpriceauthor.com or on Facebook at www.facebook.com/fansofsarahprice.

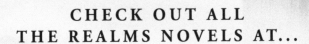

MORE AMISH CLASSICS FROM SARAH PRICE...

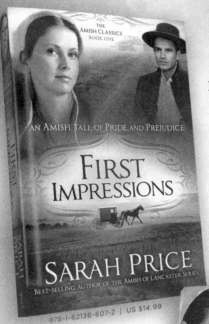

WILL PRIDE AND PREJUDICE KEEP THE BLANK SISTERS FROM FINDING LOVE?

THIS AMISH RETELLING OF THE POPULAR JANE AUSTEN CLASSIC *PRIDE AND PREJUDICE* IS A BEAUTIFUL TAKE ON THE POWER OF LOVE TO OVERCOME CLASS BOUNDARIES AND PREJUDICES.

WILL EMMA FIND A LOVE OF HER OWN?

THE MATCHMAKER, AN AMISH RETELLING OF JANE AUSTEN'S *EMMA*, PULLS AT THE HEARTSTRINGS AND GIVES YOU RENEWED FAITH IN LOVE AND FRIENDSHIP, SHOWING US ALL THE HAND GOD HAS IN OUR LIVES.

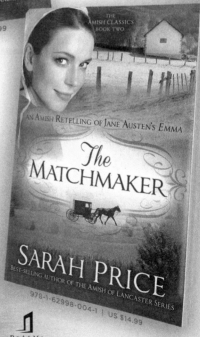

REALMS

AVAILABLE IN BOOKSTORES AND IN E-BOOK